LEARNING TO DANCE

ALSO BY ELIZABETH JOLLEY

Stories
Five Acre Virgin
The Travelling Entertainer
Woman in a Lampshade
Fellow Passengers

Novels
Palomino
The Newspaper of Claremont Street
Mr Scobie's Riddle
Miss Peabody's Inheritance
Foxybaby
Milk and Honey
The Well
The Sugar Mother
My Father's Moon
Cabin Fever
The Georges' Wife
The Orchard Thieves
Lovesong
An Accommodating Spouse
An Innocent Gentleman

Non-fiction
Central Mischief
Off the Air
Diary of a Weekend Farmer

LEARNING TO DANCE
ELIZABETH JOLLEY
HER LIFE
AND WORK

Selected and introduced
by Caroline Lurie

VIKING
an imprint of
PENGUIN BOOKS

VIKING

Published by the Penguin Group
Penguin Group (Australia)
250 Camberwell Road, Camberwell, Victoria 3124, Australia
(a division of Pearson Australia Group Pty Ltd)
Penguin Group (USA) Inc.
375 Hudson Street, New York, New York 10014, USA
Penguin Group (Canada)
90 Eglinton Avenue East, Suite 700, Toronto ON M4P 2Y3, Canada
(a division of Pearson Penguin Canada Inc.)
Penguin Books Ltd
80 Strand, London WC2R 0RL, England
Penguin Ireland
25 St Stephen's Green, Dublin 2, Ireland
(a division of Penguin Books Ltd)
Penguin Books India Pvt Ltd
11 Community Centre, Panchsheel Park, New Delhi – 110 017, India
Penguin Group (NZ)
Cnr Airborne and Rosedale Roads, Albany, Auckland, New Zealand
(a division of Pearson New Zealand Ltd)
Penguin Books (South Africa) (Pty) Ltd
24 Sturdee Avenue, Rosebank, Johannesburg 2196, South Africa

Penguin Books Ltd, Registered Offices: 80 Strand, London WC2R 0RL, England

First published by Penguin Group (Australia), a division of Pearson Australia Group Pty Ltd, 2006

1 3 5 7 9 10 8 6 4 2

Stories, essays and poems copyright © Elizabeth Jolley 2006
Introduction copyright © Caroline Lurie 2006

The moral right of the author has been asserted

Cover and text design by John Canty © Penguin Group (Australia)
Typeset in 10.75/15 pt Stempel Garamond by Post Pre-press Group, Brisbane, Queensland
Printed and bound in Australia by McPherson's Printing Group, Maryborough, Victoria

National Library of Australia
Cataloguing-in-Publication data:

Jolley, Elizabeth, 1923– .
Learning to dance : Elizabeth Jolley : her life and work.

Bibliography.
ISBN 0 670 02974 2.

I. Lurie, Caroline. II. Title.

A828.307

www.penguin.com.au

True ease in writing comes from art, not chance,
As those move easiest who have learned to dance.

Alexander Pope, 1688–1744, *An Essay on Criticism*

CONTENTS

INTRODUCTION

Elizabeth Jolley celebrated her eightieth birthday in 2003. *Learning to Dance* is designed to look back over her life, to appreciate her achievements, to see the various ways in which her personal story informed her writing and the variety of ways in which she used her imagination and art to create something more revealing, more artistically truthful than a conventional autobiography. Although originally planned as a book of non-fiction, some of Elizabeth's stories and novels draw so directly on her life that it seemed illuminating to include a small selection of her fiction. And then there were a few rarely seen poems, which show yet another facet of Elizabeth's creativity. It seemed wasteful not to include them.

This volume opens with a particularly autobiographical essay. In 1990, when Elizabeth was at the height of her fame, both internationally and within Australia, the Gail Research Institute in America asked her to contribute to a series on writers and their work. At this time she had completed the first two books of her autobiographically based trilogy, *My Father's Moon* and *Cabin Fever*. She had won most of Australia's important literary prizes, her radio plays had been broadcast in Australia and England, her fiction had been published by the *New Yorker* and in other American periodicals, and her early novels had found enthusiastic American publishers and were being translated into various European languages. Her novel *The Well* had been filmed, as had one of her stories, 'The Last Crop'.

Because recognition came to her late, she was able to embrace it to the full, and not be unbalanced by it as sometimes happens to younger people. No matter how well known she became, she was always careful to make sure that no one should feel she was ignoring them, playing the *grande dame*. She never did ignore people, and in fact it was her acute observation of everything around her – people, places, feelings – which gave her writing its uniquely compassionate quality. That, and her unflinching honesty in bearing witness to the perversity of the human heart.

Many of the themes and incidents which surface in Elizabeth's fiction are laid out in 'A Scattered Catalogue of Consolation' and in places she tells us precisely how and where she has used real people, actual events or fleeting but powerful impressions in her work. With characteristic generosity and gentle humour, she lays bare the processes by which her fiction is brought to life.

The intense and complicated relationships within families are a recurrent theme in Elizabeth's work, so a request to contribute to an anthology on the subject of sisters gave her an opportunity to write the three-part 'meditation' reproduced in *Learning to Dance*. The games and stories of childhood shared by Elizabeth and her sister Madelaine make their appearance here, and are a motif throughout. This is reminiscent of the endless stories which the Brontë sisters wrote together during their Yorkshire childhood a century earlier. The warmth and security of having a sister close in age is evoked in 'My Sister Dancing', prevented from falling into cloying sweetness by the equally strong recollection of anger, jealousy and hair pulling. 'My Father's Sister' is painfully sad, telling of the estrangement between Elizabeth's father and his own sister, the little girl for whom he'd been responsible during their childhood. Looking back with the wisdom of maturity, Elizabeth realises how her own situation as a young woman – her 'disgrace', as her aunt saw it – led to a rupture between the siblings. While Elizabeth's father remained doggedly faithful and kind to his sister, whom he recognised as unfortunate, her criticism of his daughter was a step too far.

The examination of motherhood in this collection is another example of Elizabeth's ability to look all around a familiar topic, refusing to confine it to biological motherhood. Her story 'Paper Children' deals with this subject, as well as that of exile, in an extraordinarily rich and complex way.

Elizabeth's memories of her childhood were continuing sources of inspiration for her writing. Summer holidays, Christmases and the painful experience of being sent away to boarding school informed much of her non-fiction, and the story 'One Christmas Knitting' shows how real-life events can be transformed into fiction. In this story the eccentric Anti Mote's peculiar habits are seen as a source of both amusement and distress. Indeed, it is the mingling of sorrowful tears with a child's puzzlement and an adult's wisdom which gives the story its power. 'In every place, however desolate, there will be some saving quality.' This is the mature writer looking back over a confusing, sometimes alarming childhood. But every childhood has its comforts and here Elizabeth recounts with great poignancy her homesickness at boarding school, together with the bizarre lie about her parents which she invented on the spur of the moment, perhaps to make herself seem more interesting, perhaps to diminish her misery at being sent away. Her astonished pleasure in this invented story of her parents presages her future imaginative development.

Homesickness and exile combined to inform much of Elizabeth's writing. What is striking is how the early experience of homesickness at boarding school affected the older woman. Even as she relished her invitations to literary festivals and international readings, taking great pleasure in the company of other eminent writers and in the admiration of her readers, she longed to return home almost before she had left it. *Milk and Honey*, the most 'European' of all Elizabeth's novels, deals directly with themes of exile and displacement.

As soon as school was finished Elizabeth started her training as a nurse. It was 1940, and on her very first night as a probationer she was thrust onto a ward full of seriously crippled children, and men who had been wounded in a nearby attack on an aircraft factory. The shock made the seventeen-year-old want to flee immediately, but she couldn't, and her nursing experiences have enriched much of her fiction. Some of her most mordant humour was constructed as a protection against the acute distress of caring for the sick and wounded and dying. The pressurised situation of a hospital in wartime led to intense friendships amongst the nurses, and these powerful female relationships are also a feature of Elizabeth's work.

She first met her future husband, Leonard Jolley, while nursing in 1941. He was more than ten years her senior, a conscientious objector like her father, and married. Over the next few years Elizabeth, Leonard and his wife became close friends; Elizabeth was always in awe of what she felt to be their sophistication and she spent increasing amounts of time with them. While Dr Metcalf in *My Father's Moon* is given some of Leonard's attributes, as Oliver George in *Cabin Fever* is given others, it is important never to forget that fiction writers are spinners of tales, not reporters of facts. 'Even when a fiction is based on "real life" a transformation takes place.' Perhaps inevitably, Elizabeth fell deeply in love with Leonard, and endured all the pangs of conscience and despair which afflict a serious, sensitive young girl fatally attracted to an older, married man. She bore his child, which shocked and disappointed her mother. Furthermore, with no social security, Elizabeth was forced to work in demeaning domestic situations which would accommodate her daughter. 'Fairfields' gives us a glimpse into the kind of positions available to unmarried mothers at the time. It is hard to imagine now the bleakness of life in exhausted, post-war England, let alone the difficulties of a woman who had rendered herself a social outcast. It took Elizabeth most of her life to be able to use these experiences in her novels, but the sympathy for outsiders so noticeable in her work was rooted in the experiences of her childhood and youth.

In 1950 she and Leonard were finally married and in 1959 they sailed to Western Australia, where Leonard had been offered a job as librarian at the University of Western Australia. Although Elizabeth had always kept a diary and, since 1944, had been writing stories and radio plays, I believe it was the experience of moving across the world, leaving behind one life and embracing another, completely different, which stimulated her creativity. The new landscape was such a contrast in every way from the Black Country of her childhood and the grim British cities of her youth. 'A Small Fragment of the Earth' gives some indication of her early impressions.

Elizabeth and Leonard now had three children, but Elizabeth was determined to earn her own living. She always wrote with a fountain pen, so had to pay to have her work typed; in addition, postage from Australia to England, where the publishers were, was expensive. In later years she would often present her potted autobiography as 'door-to-door salesman (failed), real estate salesman (failed) and flying domestic'. Certainly selling was not Elizabeth's forte and the experience of trying to sell household items in remote areas was one which gave her 'a sinking feeling, a sense of failure which descended as soon as I woke up'.

Cleaning peoples' houses was more to her taste; the working hours could be fitted round the family and she revelled in discovering the small, secret details of other people's lives. She had always harboured an admiration for cleaning ladies; her image of them was of strong, successful types whose children got on well in the world. Both the travelling salesman and cleaning experiences are recalled in 'Only Connect!'. She also taught creative writing in remote prisons; this involved driving long distances through West Australia's wheat belt, which provided her imagination with a vehicle for the setting of one of her novels, *Foxybaby*, of which a small extract is reproduced here.

Elizabeth's first published story was 'A Hedge of Rosemary' in 1967, but I was fortunate enough to discover two previously unpublished ones amongst her papers. These early stories are much simpler, more straightforward than her later work. They accurately reflect the uneasiness of adapting to a new life, attempting to put down new roots while encumbered with – though also sustained by – a family.

The small literary magazines, especially *Westerly*, began to discover and appreciate Elizabeth's particular voice, and between 1976 and 1980 the Fremantle Arts Centre Press published her first two collections of stories, *Five Acre Virgin* and *The Travelling Entertainer*. The title of *Five Acre Virgin* comes from a story in which a hard-working cleaning lady yearns to own a piece of bushland for herself and her children. Her wit and cunning in obtaining something she cannot afford, and the variations on this theme, feature in many of Elizabeth's early stories, including 'Pear Tree Dance', and in her second novel, *The Newspaper of Claremont Street*.

In 1970 Elizabeth and Leonard bought their own five acres in the hills outside Perth at Wooroloo, and this property, which they turned into an orchard, held a central position in Elizabeth's life. Owning a small piece of the land in which she now lived was a way of establishing herself psychologically within a new life and country. They populated Wooroloo with hens, ducks and geese, and planted roses, fruit trees and vegetables. The whole family worked together on the cottage and the incipient orchard, and Elizabeth and Leonard appear to have had some particularly happy, harmonious times together there. 'Being on this piece of land makes me feel very much aware of the shortness of life, I mean our human life in comparison with the land and the big old trees,' wrote Elizabeth in her farm diary, which later formed the basis for *Diary of a Weekend Farmer*. And elsewhere, 'To walk barefoot on the fragrant sun-dried grass and eucalyptus leaves is a remarkable experience. Suddenly the soles of the feet become important. In the extreme dry heat in summer, in the bush, all life seems withdrawn. To sit with closed eyes on the warm earth, to breathe in the fragrance and to listen to the magpies and to the strange cries of parrots and cockatoos and the wild mad laughter of the kookaburra is to realise that this is indeed a foreign country where human life can be of very little account.'

Wooroloo meant a great deal to Elizabeth. All the poems in this volume were written in response to that place. During unbearably hot summer days she would make the two-hour drive from Perth simply to water her orchard and a few struggling bushes and flowers. The decimation of her goose flock one Saturday in October 1988 caused her enormous grief and it was perhaps this shock which brought forth the lyrical prose and reflections of 'The Goosepath'. 'I discovered all the geese, except one shocked gander, slain, horribly bitten, by a fox. Probably a vixen. Such a shock. I had to gather the corpses, they looked like ballet dancers in attitudes of penitence – everlasting acts of contrition – they did not smell, being freshly attacked, probably the Friday night. I made an enormous heap of them and burned them using up a year's kindling wood. I have arranged for 4 ladies "in egg" to keep the gander company, but geese, you see, remember their wives/husbands. The gander looks very perplexed. Sad.'

Elizabeth's first novel, *Palomino*, had been accepted by a new

Melbourne publisher, Outback Press, in 1976 and in 1980 it was published. It is the story of a loving relationship between Laura, an older woman, and Andrea, a younger one, set in the harsh but sternly beautiful landscape of West Australia. The place is reminiscent of Wooroloo, and Laura's feeling for it is reminiscent of Jolley's for her five acres. 'I have land,' Laura wants to explain to Andrea in *Palomino*. 'For me it is a homecoming. My voyage for the healing of my spirit is over.' Laura is an Australian doctor with disgrace in her past. Andrea, the object of her love, also has a shameful secret. Their backgrounds, ages and attitudes are painfully incongruent and the reader knows from the beginning that their affair cannot flourish for long. With hindsight several typical Jolley themes can be identified: intense love between women; the healing power of land; the importance of music; the inevitability of loneliness.

In 1983 Elizabeth had two novels and a further collection of stories published. *Mr Scobie's Riddle* is set in the dubious precincts of the St Christopher and St Jude nursing home, a place of chaos and controlled anarchy, both horrifying and hilarious at the same time. The novel was a great critical success and won *The Age* Book of the Year Award, thus alerting the general public to Elizabeth Jolley as a writer to watch.

Her next novel, *Miss Peabody's Inheritance*, sets up the device of two parallel fictions which, starting from widely different viewpoints, gradually converge, raising questions about competing realities and the capacity of humans to creatively transform themselves and their lives. The story of the eccentric headmistress of an Australian boarding school who longs to show the world of European culture to her schoolgirl protégée is contrasted with that of the sad spinster Miss Peabody, living with her widowed mother in a dreary London suburb, her only pleasure an intense correspondence with an Australian novelist who opens up to her another, more spacious world. With saving humour, the novel explores human loneliness and the various ways in which it can be overcome.

Shortly after *Mr Scobie's Riddle* won *The Age* Book of the Year Award, Elizabeth was invited to participate in Canada's prestigious Harbourfront Festival. She hadn't left Australia since her arrival more than twenty years ago, and she enjoyed herself thoroughly, though found the relentless all-night parties a bit exhausting. She also had the extraordinary experience of meeting a woman whose children had been at the English boarding school where Elizabeth had been briefly employed in 1950, a place which had an enormous influence on her fiction. The woman was writer Elizabeth Smart, whose best-known novel, *By Grand Central Station I Sat Down and Wept*, is a passionate lament for a doomed love affair, an incredibly power-ful outpouring of emotion. The two Elizabeths had no idea that each had become a writer. Nor had they known anything of each other's circumstances when they'd met, unequally, in their youth. Elizabeth Jolley later wrote of this meeting most movingly in her story 'By the Waters of Babylon' (reproduced in *Central Mischief*).

On her return to Australia she found that the Literature Board had awarded her a two-year writing fellowship, an endorsement which greatly encouraged her. The years of being rejected by publishers had battered her confidence, though she always claimed that she would have continued to write even had she been rejected for ever. And in fact she had many stories and novels in various states of completion by the time publishers began to show an interest in her work, which meant that she appeared to be extraordinarily prolific. *Mr Scobie's Riddle* was followed by *Milk and Honey* in 1984, *Foxybaby* in 1985 and *The Well* in 1986.

Milk and Honey won the New South Wales Premier's Award and the awards dinner that year went down in the annals of Australian literary history as an exceptionally rowdy event, which Elizabeth found highly entertaining. 'The meat was nice but the pudding awful and on the platform I dropped my big medal. Someone shouted Middle Class Novelist – someone booed a poet when he thanked his mother and father, Grace Perry was assisted on to the platform where she recited at great length until she was eased off and back to her seat. 2 Feminists gave me several pieces of their little mind.' Elizabeth's letters were always a delight to receive.

The Bicentennial Authority was charged with devising different ways of celebrating two hundred years of white settlement in Australia in 1988. One of their more creative projects was to invite fiction writers to submit outlines of novels which, if they could possibly be considered to reflect some aspect of Australian life, might be commissioned by the Authority which would then offer financial support to both the writer and the publisher. Elizabeth sent in part of a novel she had been working on for some time, *The Sugar Mother* (sugar being a play on the word 'surrogate', which is too fancy for some of the novel's characters to manage). There is both absurdity and great pathos in this novel, in which an elderly, unworldly university professor, Edwin Page, is trapped into believing a number of improbabilities. While his wife is away on a year's study leave, he is inveigled by a manipulative neighbour woman into imagining it would be a good idea if he fathered a child with her daughter. The prospect of an affair with an 'innocent' young girl naturally excites the lonely professor, and he allows himself to believe that the resultant baby will delight his wife when she returns. The reader is taken empathically inside Edwin's heart, so that for whole pages it is possible to share in his impossible fantasy, to feel his excitement and joy at the prospect of fathering new life. Of all Elizabeth's open-ended novels, this wins the cliff-hanger prize, closing with Edwin about to collect his wife from the airport after her year away, still undecided as to how to break his news.

In 1986 Elizabeth had her first story published in the *New Yorker*. Entitled 'Frederick the Great at Fairfields', it became the opening episode of her next novel, *My Father's Moon*, published in 1989. This work, together with *Cabin Fever* (1990) and *The Georges' Wife* (1993), form a trilogy, a *roman à clef*, and arguably the finest of all Elizabeth's work. The occasional archness of her earlier novels falls completely away in this extraordinarily musical rendering of the episodes in her own life which had been most significant, transformed into fiction by a writer at the height of her powers.

The story of Vera Wright's life is not that of Elizabeth Jolley, but Elizabeth gives to Vera everything which matters to her. Her portrait of her beloved father is masterful: the faithful, serious man who is always meeting trains or seeing people off on them; who endures the sorrow of knowing he is unable to make his wife happy and humbly accepts her need for a more 'cultivated' companion; who takes his children for country bicycle rides to introduce them to the pleasure of 'a splendid view'; who comforts his unhappy daughter by assuring her that she is 'doing God's work' – this is the father Elizabeth gives to Vera. Edwin Page from *The Sugar Mother*, the Professor in *An Accommodating Spouse* and Henry in *An Innocent Gentleman*, all seem to have some of the qualities of Elizabeth's own father. They are all somewhat ineffectual, occasionally infuriating but well-intentioned men drawn with enormous affection and understanding.

Similarly, the ambiguity in the relationship between Vera and her mother sounds very close to the uneasy relationship Elizabeth has written about with her own mother. The homesickness of boarding school tempered by its peculiar camaraderie; the exhaustion and difficulty of hospital nursing under wartime conditions; the small jokes and secret betrayals which accompany institutional life; the shame of bearing an illegitimate child; the struggle to find a place in a hostile world; falling under the sway of people who appear more sophisticated, intellectual or artistic; the longing for the warmth and safety of a stable, loving relationship – all these were an integral part of Elizabeth's own experience in the world and, in this trilogy, are rendered into carefully crafted and wonderfully lucid fiction.

But to see these novels as pure autobiography would be to miss the point. As with any worthwhile fiction, there is much reworking of raw life into something which we call art. There are some extraordinary characters here who may or may not have been part of the author's life, but more likely are amalgams of a number of people. The artist takes one person's way of speaking, another's way of dressing, some episodes and conversation which may or may not have occurred, and from these ingredients a fictional character is born. Sometimes the reader may feel closer to a fictional character than to anyone she knows in the flesh.

Although the three novels do have a narrative progression – Vera is a young girl in *My Father's Moon* and by the opening of *The Georges' Wife* she is wheeling her elderly, forgetful husband along Australian streets in a wheelchair – the narrative is far from straightforward. One of Elizabeth's interests is in rendering the erratic way in which the mind actually works. 'Memories are not always in sequence, not in chronological sequence,' Vera muses early in *Cabin Fever*. By this time she is no longer a nurse and downtrodden single mother, but a respected doctor attending a conference in New York. 'Sometimes an incident is revived in the memory. Sometimes incidents and places and people occupying hours, days, weeks and years are experienced in less than a quarter of a second in this miraculous possession, the memory.' And so, unexpectedly, oppressed by the overheated hotel bedroom, incidents from her earlier life crowd Vera's mind. Once again she relives the painful relationship with Dr Metcalf and Magda. In *The Georges' Wife* a similar but different relationship is formed between Vera and the 'arty crafty' pair, Noël and Felicity. Again the theme of exploitation arises, for Vera is naïve and vulnerable to entrapment by more worldly people. Her mother sees this clearly, but Vera cannot listen to her mother, who endlessly reproaches her daughter for her unmarried pregnancy.

Repetition is another of Elizabeth's themes. 'The strange thing about living, I often nearly speak of this during a consultation, is the repetition. It is as though the individual enters the same experience again and again. The same kind of people make the same demands, the giver, blessed with giving, gives yet again in what turns out to be the wrong direction.' There are repetitions in her writing too, never more skilfully used than in this trilogy. Just as the mind returns over and over again to a hurt or a joy, sometimes an image from decades ago, so Vera remembers and re-remembers her mother's strictures, her father at the train station, her despairing love for a sophisticated, slightly older nurse.

In recognising Elizabeth's literary achievement in this trilogy, we must not discount her later works. A delightful novella, *The Orchard Thieves*, came out in 1995, in which Elizabeth was able to express many of her subtle, complex feelings about children and grand-children. The grandmother in the novella suffers acutely from anxiety and a highly active, catastrophist imagination. It may be significant that Leonard Jolley had died in 1994 after many years of illness and Elizabeth, unsurprisingly, found the adjustment extremely hard. She was lonely for the companionship of earlier years and she gives to the grandmother fears of ageing and death and what will happen to the family after she is gone. In *The Orchard Thieves*, too, there is the expression of the tremulous tenderness of a grandmother towards her grandchildren, her wish for them to retain their innocence, coupled with the knowledge that this is an impossible wish.

As Elizabeth became a respected figure in Australian literature, she was increasingly asked to write short articles for newspapers and magazines on a variety of topics. The later pieces in this collection are a selection of such pieces. At the time of publication, 'The Little Dance in Writing', written with the help of her friend Barbara Millich, is Elizabeth's last piece of published work.

Elizabeth frequently dealt with unconventional love relationships, and it is one of these which dominates her last novel, *An Innocent Gentleman*. Elsewhere she has written about Mr Berrington, an educated man, a barrister, who came to the house every week for Sunday lunch after church during her childhood and youth. He and her father would discuss the sermon and at times he would speak German with her mother. He would give elegant presents to the children and once took Elizabeth and her mother on holiday in Europe. Mr Berrington never married, but it was clear to the adult Elizabeth that he loved her mother very much, and that her father was aware of this, and grateful that he brought some culture into her life, just a hint of old European graciousness and courtesy. Similar relationships form the framework of *An Innocent Gentleman*, though the literary imagination takes flight and weaves another story around the remembered reality. The novel is a fitting close to Elizabeth's career as a writer, ending with the birth of a much-cherished baby who, it is clear, will heal the ruptures within the little family into which he has been born.

Although she started writing very young, Elizabeth suffered many years of rejection and misunderstanding. Like many artists, she had to wait for the society around her to arrive at a point where her work was acceptable. She fully enjoyed her success, even though the enjoyment sometimes came at a price.

But it isn't just because she's a fine writer that virtually everyone who encounters Elizabeth has found her irresistible. Rather, it's because her warmth and humanity inform both her writing and her way of being in the world. She connects with people through the heart, whether it's via the page or more directly in person. Readers of Elizabeth's fiction feel they actually *know* her. And in a sense it is true – the kind of meta-truth which all writers aim for, which goes beyond mere fact. Elizabeth's work welcomes the reader into her world, a world which is sometimes playful, sometimes absurd, sometimes touching or tragic, but never dull. It has been one of the pleasures of my life to have been able to share so much of Elizabeth's, and I hope this volume of her writings will reward her faithful readers as well as some new ones.

Caroline Lurie

A Scattered Catalogue
of Consolation

All this goes on inside me, in the vast cloisters of my memory.
In it are the sky, the earth, and the sea, ready at my summons,
together with everything that I have ever perceived in them by
my senses . . . In it I meet myself as well. I remember myself . . .

St Augustine

*You must have come to terms with your own sexuality to write
about sex the way you do. Can you tell us something about this
please?*

*How can someone who looks like you, I mean that lilac shawl,
the spectacles and your hair going grey – how can you, at your age,
write about sex?*

How could you *have written the filthy scene on page 139?*

Have you had lesbian relationships? but the question was in the
eyes only and came out as *How many grandchildren do you have?*

Sometimes other people in an audience or at a book club answer questions for me.

The washing up basin in our house, when I was a child, was sacred. One afternoon when my mother was out Françoise, our French governess who had a white mackintosh, took the mackintosh and a nail brush and the washing up basin full of hot soapy water into the garden. Until Françoise came to our house I had no idea that there were white mackintoshes. I watched Françoise kneel on the lawn beside the washing up basin. It seemed then that I had never seen anything quite like this before. The white enamel gleamed on the bed of green. Françoise then spread out the white mackintosh on the grass and began, at once, to dip the little brush in the hot water and, with a slight swaying movement, she set about her scrubbing. She scrubbed in deliciously neat little circles on the mackintosh, a bit at a time, replenishing her tiny brush frequently with quick little dippings into the basin. As I watched I longed to take the delicate brush and have a turn at the scrubbing. It seemed then to be such a nice thing to be doing. I forgot, for a time, about the basin and how it was suddenly in the wrong place, *outside the house and on the lawn*.

My mother would be coming home quite soon. The scrubbing was taking a long time and I became anxious. I ran out to the front gate to look up the street. I did this a few times, darting back and forth, absorbed in the little spreading circles of soap but watching the street.

I did not say anything because what could I say? And then, all at once, I saw my mother coming, walking home from the bus. I ran to and fro several times, from the washing up bowl to the street and back to the washing up bowl, not knowing whether to tell Françoise to take the bowl back to the sink as quickly as possible or whether to rush up the road to beg my mother not to be cross with Françoise. I was nine then. Ambivalence has pursued me. Indecision, the time waster and the consumer of energy – whether a child should stay in bed or be sent off to school, which dish to use to serve the boiled peas, whether to buy brown onions or white, butternut pumpkin or ironbark – the list is endless.

'Please do not be cross with Françoise . . .' I ran, breathless, up to my mother. I even carried her shopping bag for her. The result was, of course, terrible. Françoise, weeping and leaning on my father's arm, left for the boat train that evening.

Often something prevents me from writing. There are things I would write but when I start on one of them clear images come to mind for something else. My pen then becomes half-hearted, as if unsure, not quite certain. It is impossible to write with an uncertain or an unwilling pen. Perhaps it is because of the lace curtains that I put up to hide the walls of the new house next door. Because of this new house it is no longer possible to see my own hands reflected in the green leaves. Sometimes, when I dipped my pen in the ink, it seemed as if my own hand was reaching towards me from the thick foliage immediately outside my window. For many years, until now, I looked through this tall narrow window into the deepest green. Sometimes I caught sight of the corner of a white sheet, pegged and billowing lazily on a clothes line, fresh and damp, against this green background. I have used this image to create the character of Edwin Page in the novel *The Sugar Mother*. He is an elderly academic given to romantic thought and quotation. He is enchanted by the image of this sheet and likes to imagine that green and white were the chosen colours of the Elizabethan court. His area of study being, together with desultory wanderings, the Renaissance.

Vera in the novel *Cabin Fever*, looking from the upstairs window in the nursing home during the first stage of labour, is amazed that a woman in a nearby garden can, in apparent tranquillity, in spite of the drama in Vera's own body, hang out her washing. Vera notices the gentle rhythm of movement between the clothes basket, the pegs and the clothes line, a contrast to her own movements and feelings. She notices too that a white sheet folded and pegged to the line is beginning to billow slightly but it is in a leafy green place that is too damp for drying. The same image but used differently and showing different things about the characters. When using an image for a second or a third time I do not, as a rule, remember using it before. It is only after the works are finished that I see this repetition. A repetition with changes.

Perhaps the lace curtains, in spite of their pure clean whiteness and a delicate pattern, both of which are attractive in themselves, make me feel shut in.

The new walls of the new building do not offer me the imaginative possibilities of a magic place close to where I am sitting. And, I have lost forever the rising sun which, for years, decorated the wallpaper on the opposite wall of my room, a moving changing pattern of light and shade every morning as the new day came up through the tremulous leaves.

It is New Year's Eve and people are at parties. Once at a party, years ago, all the husbands except mine, at midnight, kissed their wives. I felt really clumsy, not being kissed. Later I thought that these party kisses in public, after lots of wine, were rather superficial. My husband has never done the conventional thing, like putting his hand at my elbow to let me go first through a door or introducing me to people. I think this is a kind of shyness. I made up my mind to go through doors by myself and to tell people what my name was and so on. I have been nursing my husband at home now for many years. He has rheumatoid arthritis and is frail and helpless. I do not mention this in interviews or autobiographical pieces because it would be an invasion of his privacy but I will just say one or two things here because a long illness in a household affects everyone. It affects the attitudes of other people to the household. The illness has affected my whole life. Recently I was offered respite care in a nursing home for him and I was forced to understand something about myself. Apart from his not wanting to be in a nursing home, even for a short time, I realised that, unless I had some specific travelling to do, because of my work, I was absolutely unable to face the idea of having a holiday. A great big empty space seemed to lie before me. I even had dreams in which I was incredibly lonely or lost. I probably need counselling. Awful though it is, I expect it is useful for me to have had this realisation. This reflection may be of use to other people. Another thing that might be of help to someone else is that often, it seems to me, it is difficult to divorce the long illness from the person who has it so that other people, oneself included, blame the person rather than understanding it is the illness that is such a nuisance. And a nuisance most of all to the person who has it. People outside the household, not understanding, might be critical, for example, at a buffet dinner where guests are expected to help themselves. Some women, with feminist leanings, voice their disapproval at the sight of a wife carrying a plate and a glass to a husband.

There are times when I feel I lack grace. Perhaps, because of having a bit extra to do, I have lost the art of the gentle pre-dinner drink or sitting over a meal in a leisurely way. When people ask me how my husband is, I tell them, which is nearly as bad as telling people how you are yourself when they say, 'How are you!' I also have a regrettable tendency to tell other women's husbands where and how to park their cars. In addition, as if that is not enough, I read in bed and at meal times and often sit with one or both elbows on the table. Most days I have champagne at breakfast, alone – and flat because of it being uncorked days before, and usually in a small glass jar of the kind used for the more precious kinds of jam. I have the idea that this is beneficial.

I have always thought of myself as immortal and at the same time I am surprised to find that, up to the present, I have lived as long as I have. It seems to me that pleasure in living must come from within. There are certain thoughts and feelings and experiences that are consoling. Over the years I have tried to put these things in particular and known places in my fiction. By giving them to certain characters these consolations are kept as if in a storehouse where they can be found at any time. A sort of scattered catalogue of consolation. This does not mean that the fiction is autobiographical. It simply means that certain truths and moments of awareness are saved for recollection at some time in the future. Memory has an odd way of giving things back to us, not in any chronological sequence and often most unexpectedly.

In my novel *Foxybaby* Miss Porch goes back to her house during a time when she is resident at the school where she works. The way in which 'she comes upon' her house is written from an experience I had myself once when, thinking I had forgotten to turn off the water main, I went back to the cottage where our orchard is. I did not drive back but approached from a place where the road curves back near the foot of the property. I walked across an old railway line and down into a gully, across the creek and up the slope of a neighbouring property – as if in a dream, as if in a strange country and then suddenly coming upon my own place from an unaccustomed direction. The cottage looked quite different. It seemed to sink in the grass (which comes up to the walls and the door) as if nestling there. It seemed to be closed up (which it was) but closed up in a secretive way like an unopened flower. It seemed in its secretiveness to not want anyone to come, and it looked as if no one had been there for years. By giving something of this to Miss Porch, in creating her character I hope I was able to show her in such a way that a reader could see all round her, make a picture of her without any judgement offered from me as the writer. (I had, of course, turned off the water.)

It is only now after many years of writing that I begin to understand something of the healing power of certain times and people and places remembered. This power goes in the opposite direction too, and moments of abrasive conflict presenting the destructive side of human life are often the material for the creation of characters, situations and dramatic incidents. Time spent in experience is never a waste of time.

Some years ago the image of a glass door covered by a lace curtain manifested itself several times together with the idea of the possibility of peering through the edges of the curtain at the lodger in the room beyond; only his back, as he sat at the table, being visible. When I was a child we played with a little girl who lived across the road. Her father was a stoker in the steam laundry and her mother was a dressmaker. They kept chickens and a lodger. My father was a teacher and we had no lodger and no chickens. The lodger, picking his teeth and reading his newspaper, sitting with something called a cruet at his elbow, was fascinating. At home we did not have a cruet either. For years I wished we had this little collection, the cruet, so neatly held in a special stand, the salt, the pepper and the sauce bottle. I wished too for a lodger.

An early editor removed the recurring glass door and the lace curtain so that the image would not be repeated after its first appearance. I know now that an image can be repeated often as a phrase of music can be repeated, perhaps with slight changes of rhythm or key, or it can be written again in its original form. An example being the freshly washed white sheet moving lazily in a damp wind against a dark green background. In this repetition the style of the musician or the writer is formed.

Once, when I was almost the last person to leave the beach at Bunbury in the south-west of Western Australia, I saw the sun go down leaving only a long red line of sky far out over the water, which was rolling up as if boiling over, dark, along the deserted sands. In this turmoil of waves, where the sea was meeting the shore, some thin white fingers reached up out of the water as it ran pouring up and out over the sand before swirling back into itself. The thin white fingers grasping the froth of the wave offered me a character that evening. I did not see the person they belonged to – only the animation expressed in the hands reaching up out of the sea at dusk. The thin white fingers, gleaming in the dark waters as the evening rapidly moved towards night, gave me more than a character; they presented a family and, in addition, this family's place in society and its efforts towards survival.

It has often seemed to me that the fiction writer needs to examine his own place in society before attempting to place his characters. In fiction the writer is able to present reflections from his surroundings. An example of this is Ibsen's character Gina in *The Wild Duck*. She is shown to be a character knowing her own place satisfactorily in a group of emotionally bankrupt people who have lost their way.

To add to the catalogue of consolation is to overcome certain weariness or a sense of futility in a world that contains so much human suffering in the face of which we seem to be utterly powerless. The Mozart piano concerto that has a certain significance (perhaps mistakenly) for me can always be found now.

'It's number eight,' Daphne said, 'number eight in C major, C Dur, the third movement, but it's not as you said. It's not the coming to the mistake and going back and playing over again to correct the mistake. It's not a putting right, not a fresh start – only something going on in the way it has been going. It is the actual music; in the actual music, I should say; it is the way it was written – it's even more inevitable that way.'

The picture I have when I listen to this music is of the pianist flipping up his coat-tails and then leaning forward, with more energy, in order to go back a bit in the music before playing it over again. I gave this idea of correction, being able to correct by replaying, to Edwin Page in the novel *The Sugar Mother*. The music, the phrase from the piano concerto, becomes a metaphor for the mistake Edwin might be making in his life and the possibility of going over a part of his life again to put right the mistake. Daphne, however, corrects him, telling him that the music is not in fact repeating itself in this way. The music and the imagined correction (the metaphor) offer a parallel to events in Edwin's life.

Similarly a game of horses and carts parallels the displacement of the boy's ageing father in the story 'Two Men Running'. This game of horses and carts was described to me over sixty years ago. I cannot explain why, at the moment when it was useful, the memory of my father telling me about the game came to me so vividly. It was as if all those years later I could hear his voice telling how he and his sister, when they were children, had a screw-top jar full of screws and nails and nuts and bolts. They put these out on the kitchen table which was, for their game, the street. They played, moving the screws and things up and down the table dot-dot-dotty-dot up and down and to and fro on the table. The horses and carts (as they became) passed each other and turned round in the street. I gave the game to the man in the story, a flashback to *his* childhood. Some things in the story are shown through the progress of the child's game.

When my father told about this I must have been about five or six. He was making cocoa for me and for my sister. My sister, who is fourteen months younger than I am, has no recollection of his telling about the game.

The above is an indication that though writing is an act of the will for me, once I have written something, the act of writing unlocks more writing, the next idea is set free. But *having* an idea is not the same as *developing* it in detail on the page. This is where persistence, the will to write, comes in.

Music can be used to show a great deal about a character. Some phrases of music belong so much to some of my characters that when I hear them it is as if I am still writing about the specific character concerned and all kinds of detail, finished with years ago, comes back to me all over again.

When a certain kind of person listens to music a change takes place in their demeanour. Hester, in the novel *The Well*, is one of my characters shown in part through music:

On the day of the Bordens' party Hester, straight after their early breakfast, listened to Mozart. She knew from listening alone that while she listened her mouth took on a different shape, the lips drawn together and pursed. Once, seeing her music-listening mouth in the rear mirror, while she was driving home with a string quartet in the cassette player she understood the possibility that her whole body was, during the music, different. Without meaning to she knew that it was not only her lips; it was all the seriousness and tenderness which entered and set the bones of her jaw and changed the movement of her eyebrows and the tilt of her head. The first time, the first time while driving home, she had been taken by surprise and mostly now she did not think of it.

Hester then remembers going to a quartet from school and she recalls the players and 'the deep concentration which was evident in the sensitive movement of the muscles of their faces, particularly round the mouth'. To me equally important as the forward-going action of the novel is the *dwelling* in the novel, the passages that enable a reader to look about the landscape, to study the situation and above all to see all round a character. Hester is not a particularly pleasant person. By showing her in some detail of music it is possible that a sympathetic attitude will be developed towards her. In my fiction I do not want to offer judgement. Though I want and hope to avoid plodding prose, I do not consciously, at the outset, seek to write in a particular way. On second or third or fourth rewritings I may see what I have done and perhaps will heighten the effect in some way. Fiction is usually a reflection from ordinary human life but a part of the art of writing is this heightening. On the whole I do not stop and consider these things except on an occasion like this when I am actually writing about writing. Apart from trying to avoid plodding, I do record in my fiction some things that have special meaning for me so that they will be in known places for future reference when I might need the consolation of memories. These include things like the little roundabout of painted horses which used to be on the foreshore of the Swan River at Crawley here in Western Australia; and a shop in Claremont, quite near where I live, where it used to be possible to sit on a broken chair up against the varnished wood of the counter and keep in touch with countless neighbours:

> The shop was still an emporium, it belonged to a time which had gone by. Bolts of cloth were on a wide shelf next to cups and dishes and a glass case of faded haberdashery . . . Sacks of wheat and laying pellets stood on the floor next to a modern biscuit

stand. It was possible to buy an incinerator and a birthday card and a pair of stockings without moving an inch. You could buy kerosene and candles and icing sugar and a box of chocolates all in the same breath, though chocolates were not a wise choice in the hot weather . . .

These things are in, for ever, the short story 'A Hedge of Rosemary' and the little novel *The Newspaper of Claremont Street* respectively. Both were written during that strange time of impact a short time after coming to a new country.

Having only recently written the novel *Cabin Fever* I am unable to explain my reason for keeping the character of Oliver George deliberately, it seems, vague. I made him from details of his age, expressed with some horror by Vera's mother, from his white hair, his russet pullover, his innocent pleasure at sending flowers to Vera, a certain understood devotion to his elder sister Eleanor, fifteen years his senior, his narrow single bed which, he explains, he has always had – and then once more the use of music. He explains to Vera, before they really know each other, that he is susceptible to music which seems to contain an everlasting youth. He says too that he responds to music and feels he should not simply pass on this response to her. He says to her that she can escape from his room if she wants to. But Vera does not want to escape. She shamelessly asks him to make love to her a second time and then a little later considers her own response:

> Somehow it is, just then, as if the remembered reddish colour of his pullover is blending with the glowing floor boards and the cherry wood furniture of the attic bedroom, and I wonder why I should, during the wild sweet moments, consider this woollen garment and the attic chair, the woodwork of the wash stand and the floor boards.

Before this Vera has worked swiftly in sensing Mr George's susceptibility and talks about her own feelings over the cello in connection with a staff nurse, Ramsden, an object of her admiration earlier.

> Mr George is so nice, without meaning to, I go on talking and tell him about Ramsden, staff nurse Ramsden, and how I wanted once to tell her about the downward thrust of the cello and about the perfection in the way the other instruments come up to meet the cello. I tell him that I did not feel able to tell her that I thought someone had measured the movements of the notes controlling carefully the going down and the coming up in order to produce this exquisite mixture.

727 CHESTER ROAD

I don't, as a rule, write an autobiographical note but for some reason I remember some things which, in reality, came to my mind some time ago and I gave the two remembered things to two of my characters. I did not try then to write out the actual memory as I am about to do now.

Perhaps my mother was in hospital, or something, but I remember staying with an Aunt and Uncle who were not really Aunt and Uncle, they were just called that. I was about six. 727 Chester Road was a tall narrow house in a terrace. On the wall by the front door was a brass plate bearing my Aunt's name and the qualification, which I read as *Must Be Singing*. I realise now it was an abbreviation for a degree in music with singing attached.

Aunty Mary played something called 'Gopak' by Mussorgsky for me on the piano. It seemed to me then, as it does now, to be very special – this having the piano played especially for me. I mean, my being the only person in the room and the piano player turning to me and smiling while she played. Not smiling only with her lips, smiling and smiling with her eyes and with her shoulders and with her hands. She said the music was a sort of little dance.

Later, in the upstairs attic room where the piano was, we sat together high up in the window and played a game. Trams did not go along Chester Road but they must have crossed the end of the street because I remember I liked hearing the grind and screech of the nearby trams and the sound of clocks chiming somewhere through the subdued steady roar of the city. The game we played was invented by Aunty Mary. She took one direction along the road and I took the other, and with pencil and paper (I was very fond of pencils) we counted the cars and lorries and bicycles each from our chosen direction. After a certain time the one with the most traffic on their side won the game. I liked this very much.

I have given the piano playing to staff nurse Ramsden in the novel *My Father's Moon* and the game to Emily Vales and Little Lewis in the radio play and story *Little Lewis has had a Lovely Sleep*. I hope that by doing this I have been able to show more things about the characters.

Here is the little passage as it is in *My Father's Moon*. The main character is nursing during the war. She has not been at the hospital very long. (She is uneasy, it being her first night as Night Runner. She has to prepare the meal for the night staff in the hospital.)

This first night it takes me a long time to clear up in the little pantry. When at last I am finished Night Sister Bean sends me to relieve on Bottom Ward. There is a spinal operation in the theatre recovery room just now, she says, and a spare nurse will be needed when the patient comes back to the ward.

On my way to Bottom Ward I wish I could be working with staff nurse Ramsden.

'I will play something for you,' she said to me once when I was alone and filled with tears in the bleak, unused room which is the nurses' sitting room.

She ran her fingers up and down the piano keys. 'This is Mussorgsky,' she said, 'it's called Gopak, a kind of little dance,' she explained. She played and turned her head towards me nodding and smiling, 'do you like this?' she asked, her eyes smiling. It is not everyone who has had Mussorgsky played for them; the thought gives me courage as I hurry along the unlit passage to the ward.

There is a circle of light from the uncurtained windows of the office in the middle of the ward. I can see a devout head bent over the desk in the office. I feel I am looking at an Angel of mercy who is sitting quietly there ready to minister to the helpless patients . . .

The game, Aunty Mary's game, comes into the story of Little Lewis first as a game between Little Lewis and the babysitter and later on as a sinister game of chance between the babysitter and a kidnapper.

My early childhood was contained in my mother's hats. I waited once for my mother to come to fetch me from hospital. I sat high up pressed close to a tall window looking down to the street below. In all the movement down there I could not see my mother's white hat. My head was wrapped in bandages. She said she would wear the white hat.

'What are these stalks of dry grass here for?' I asked the nurse. She said there wasn't any grass. What I thought was grass, she said, was only the frayed edges of the bandage. I was bandaged because of a mastoid operation. The white hat had a wide soft brim. There was another one, a navy blue velour trimmed with black grosgrain deepening the shadows round her eyes. It made her face fragile and increased her paleness. I thought she was sad when she wore this hat. There was too a small round hat – light-coloured, a colour as of peaches, and the colour was wrapped in silk softly round the hat. A small veil of dark, spotted gauze went with this hat. My mother's eyes shone in the spider web of the veil as if they were pleased to be caught there.

When she came that day to fetch me from the hospital she had a new hat. It was a circle of fur all round her head low just above her eyes. Her eyes were bright with laughter and tenderness and I tried to melt into her perfume. I was five then.

My mother was an exile because of her marriage. Her homesickness lasted throughout her life. It was a longing for Vienna as it was, not for the Vienna it had become. Her father had been a general in the Imperial Army and he belonged to the great number of people whose reason for existence disappeared with the Emperor.

My father's exile came about because of his beliefs and his ideals. He was a pacifist, and suffered brutal imprisonment in World War I because he refused to fight. He was disowned by his father because of this (in public, in front of shocked neighbours). He did not help matters by going to Vienna with the Quaker Famine Relief and then bringing back a wife with aristocratic pretensions from the enemy country.

I experienced the migrant's sense of exile in a vicarious way before having the experience myself. I have always been on the edge, in a sense – growing up in a German-speaking household in a neighbourhood where, and at a time when, foreigners were regarded with a mixture of curiosity and hostility; being sent to a Quaker boarding school and not being a Quaker by birthright. Then there was the nursing training alongside girls from 'good' families whose mothers kept maids – 'county families' in England where twin-sets and pearls were not just a joke.

Perhaps the adverse, or seemingly adverse, experience can produce an advantage. The person concerned can make for himself the herb of self-heal, as Kenneth Grahame (the author of *The Wind in the Willows*) calls it in his autobiography.

It would seem that all writers draw heavily on their early experience but in different ways. It would be interesting to know to what extent migration causes people to look back to events and customs in childhood. Tolstoy, Wordsworth and Traherne are examples of writers who recall and use childhood experience; Gorky and Dickens too (one might imagine that both Gorky and Dickens would have obliterated all memory of their childhood). None of these writers migrated to another country.

Nymphomaniacs and murderers, perplexed housewives, greedy spoiled children, unfaithful husbands and angry maiden aunts inhabited our dolls' houses. Joan, a cleaning lady with loose pink legs too big to fit in any bed, sat all night on a wooden kitchen chair and later rattled her celluloid flesh and bones as she took to the stairs with a dustpan and brush, her energy mounting as she entered the day with gossip. My sister and I played with dolls' houses for many years, an endless story with characters, dialogues, situations and incidents. When separated from the dolls' houses, that is, when travelling in buses and trains, we drew matchstick people in our drawing books and yelled their conversations across to each other. In crowded buses, being children, we had to stand. We were often at opposite ends of a bus and had then to really raise our voices.

I always thought I came from a family of no consequence and without inheritance. For years I did not understand how things stood with me but looking back now I remember that when I was about eight years old my father invented heat and light. He wrote two textbooks for schoolchildren; the one on heat had a red cover and the one on light was blue. As for inheritance, what fool would claim, ticking the appropriate boxes on the application form for an exclusive school of nursing, a grandpa who died of blood poisoning following severe scalding from the freshly boiled kettle he was carrying when he fell in his last epileptic fit? Then there was the other grandpa who must have owned a disease which, though not acute for himself, destroyed my mother's mother and subsequently three stepmothers. (My mother grew up in a convent.) Aunt Maud and a mysterious cousin called Dorothy were talked about in whispers. Both were said to be mad. Who would acknowledge, with irresponsible ticks, the grandfathers, the aunt, the cousin?

Perhaps I was 'born like it', as people seem to be, from the cradle – swimmers, actresses, excellent cooks, good at sums, able to draw umbrellas, dogs and horses . . . I loved pencils and empty pages and had my wrist slapped in Mixed Infants for covering, in five minutes, all the clean pages of a new exercise book with the dots and curves which I took to be writing, before any of us had been shown how and where to make the first pot hook.

I have always wanted to write things down and I never used the box camera Aunty Daisy gave me one Christmas. My mother said I never used it because Aunty Daisy borrowed it back every summer – but I knew differently.

When I was a child I listened to the concerned voices of my mother and my father and their visitors and especially to the voices of my grandfather, grandmother and aunt (on my father's side). It was a household of two languages, German and English. Two languages are a disadvantage when it comes to starting school.

During the 1920s many people were out of work and were very poor. The coal miners had their strikes and the Hunger March to London stretched, it seemed, the length of Britain. My father, as a teacher, always had work. In 1929 my parents took in a miner's child. It was meant as an act of kindness . . . I remember my mother trying to spoon a boiled egg into the little girl's mouth which was square with crying. My mother tried to push a toffee in with the spoonful of egg but it was no use, the whole lot fell out.

'She's never had an egg before,' my grandmother said. 'Give her a piece.' The little girl was six like me and I could not imagine then how anyone could be six and not know how to eat an egg.

In the late 1930s and later, when Neville Chamberlain's Britain was at war with Hitler, all kinds of people had work, in food offices, in munitions and in replacing conscripts and those who enlisted.

I was born in 1923 at Gravelly Hill near Birmingham, England. My parents moved house several times but always we lived within bicycling distance (about four miles) of the Central School for Boys in Bilston where my father felt he should teach.

In my life with my husband I have had wider moves. He was Librarian at Selly Oak Colleges, Birmingham and then at the Royal College of Physicians in Edinburgh, Deputy Librarian at the University of Glasgow and, finally, Librarian at the University of Western Australia.

I have worked at several things besides nursing. I failed in real estate and door-to-door selling (cosmetics and bath salts in plastic urns). I was good at being a flying domestic (cleaning houses). And I have been a tutor in the School of Communication and Cultural Studies at Curtin University of Technology (formerly the Western Australian Institute of Technology) for several years. I love my work with the students there. I have been involved too with Arts Access from the Fremantle Arts Centre. This gives me the opportunity to drive into the remote areas of Western Australia, especially the wheat belt, where I conduct drama, literature and creative writing workshops.

MR BERRINGTON

We liked our dresses very much. They were blue with little white spots. They were made by our mother's dressmaker. We called them our spotted frocks.

'What pretty dresses,' a woman at the shops said, 'and matching too. Are you twins?' she asked.

'Our frocks are from Mr Berrington,' I said, 'and yes we are twins,' I told her. 'I'm ten and she's nine.'

It did not seem at all strange then that Mr Berrington provided new dresses for us . . .

In the long summer of 1938 Mr Berrington took me and my mother to Europe. I was supposed to be improving my German and my mother was pretending to be finding a suitable place in which I should study music – an ambition she retained even after the war started and even when she knew I could not sing and, after ten years of laborious piano lessons, had made only the slightest progress.

The following year, on the day war was declared, when we heard Mr Chamberlain's voice on the wireless say, 'Britain is at war with Germany,' my father wept. Knowing the suffering brought about by the Great War, he could not believe that there would be another one.

'Is Mr Berrington coming?' I asked my mother while my father was praying in the front room. 'Yes,' she said, 'of course he's coming to lunch as usual.' A sense of safety and relief came over me. It was the feeling that, in the familiar shape of Mr Berrington, everything was to be 'as usual'. I have never forgotten this. I was sixteen then.

No one would have guessed Mr Berrington's occupation from his quiet and ordinary appearance. He came from a long-established professional family. A barrister and a KC, he was chairman of many legal committees and was on the boards of a number of charities. He played bridge and tennis every week, belonging to exclusive clubs of both. He was my mother's Friend. Both Mr Berrington and my father loved my mother. And both learned and spoke German.

For as long as I can remember, Mr Berrington came for Sunday lunch. My father and Mr Berrington exchanged the texts of the sermons at their respective churches during the first course and discussed the weather forecast while the pudding was served.

Mr Berrington was remarkably generous. I understand now, but did not then, that his generosity enabled my mother to re-establish her own good taste which she had suppressed in order to fit in with the dreary surroundings in which she found herself. She had her own dressmaker and Mr Berrington gave the impression, without actually saying anything, that he liked to see her in good quality clothes. I do not know if my father minded. I never heard him make a critical remark. He often paid my mother compliments, perhaps putting into words the things Mr Berrington did not say. It was some time before I came to the conclusion that Mr Berrington did admire and praise her but, of course, only when other people were not there.

That summer of 1938, in the luxury of expensive hotels and seeing for myself things only heard about before, things like the miracle of the confluence, the apparently inexplicable appearance of the brown water of the river Main meeting and flowing with the blue waters of the Rhine, that unbelievable division actually in the water, seems now to have marked the end of my childhood. I began to understand then that our household, because of having Mr Berrington, was different from other households.

SCHOOL

Our headmaster often said he knew which boys and girls would hand in their *Golden Treasury of the Bible* (two volumes) on leaving school and which boys and girls would keep it as a spiritual guide for the rest of their lives.

When I was eleven I was sent to a Quaker boarding school in a small village on the edge of the Cotswolds. Earlier, because my father, in spite of being a teacher, thought that school spoiled children's innocence, he took us away from school. We spent some partly profitable years listening to Sir Walford Davies – the returning phrase of the rondo; to Commander Stephen King-Hall – parliamentary affairs; and to Professor Winifred Cullis – germs in unwashed vests (singlets) and milk jugs – on the radio. Wireless Lessons, they were called. We had too a succession of governesses from France and Austria. Françoise, Gretel, and Marie. We chased them with spiders and earthworms. And, with my mother, they had *misunderstandings*. They departed in turn, leaning on my father's arm, in tears, to the railway station and the boat train.

The journey to school was always, it seemed, at dusk. My father always came to the station. I remember the afternoons seemed dark before four o'clock. The melancholy railway crawled through waterlogged meadows. Cattle, knee deep in damp grass, raised their heads as the slow train passed. The level crossings were deserted. No one waited to wave and curtains of drab colours were pulled across cottage windows.

My father seemed always to be seeing me off at bus stops or railway stations. He paced up and down pavements or platforms to keep warm. My memory is of his white face, his arm raised in farewell and his body getting smaller and smaller as the distance between us increased.

The quiet autumn-berried hedgerows, the brown ploughed fields sloping in all directions, and the rooks, unconcerned, gathering in the leafless trees, made the landscape surrounding the school very different from the narrow street of small houses at home. At the end of our street was a smouldering pit mound; the coal mine and the brick works were close by and we could always smell the bone and glue factory. I was unaccustomed to being in a class with other children. But after the bitter homesickness of the first year I liked it very much there. I still have the friends I made at school. Until their deaths recently I corresponded regularly with my music mistress, known affectionately as the Hag, and with my English mistress, the Bug – also with affection. I think of their teaching with gratitude. I realise too that they can't have been much older than I was.

My sister came to school later. She ran away three times and was brought back from the outskirts of Banbury, eight miles away, by the Bug in her little car. One of the boys, equally unhappy, sent a piece of meat home in a letter to demonstrate the awfulness of the food. The village postmistress brought the envelope, dripping with gravy, back to school where it was displayed at Morning Meeting. The whole school had to send their sweet allowance to a charitable institution that week. The postmistress also took responsibility for a telegram I tried to send to my father on his fiftieth birthday – but more of this later.

The village was said to be the coldest place, next to Aldershot, in England. It was a point of honour never to wear overcoats except on Sundays to Meeting. (Consequently many of us were obliged to go on wearing school overcoats for many years till they wore out.) There were three springs in the village, water bubbled and flowed cold and clear over pebbles at the side of the street. Villagers fetched their water every day. Later the springs were covered and green painted hand pumps were placed there. Once, during the mobilisation, some soldiers camped by the pump immediately outside our school. Though told not to we could not resist going out after dark into the freezing evening to stand by their fire and to exchange stories and trophies with these handsome men in their new uniforms. We took our supper, slices of dry bread, out to them. They accepted the offering with well-mannered gratefulness though it was clear they had plenty of nice things, like baked beans, which we did not have. They wrote, in their best writing, in our autograph books: *It's a grand life if you don't weaken* and *Fight the good fight but don't fight too hard.* One of them gave me a button off his coat which I still have. I had no idea then, in spite of the ideals of pacifism, just what pain and mutilation I was to witness in the course of my work not much later on. These men were on their way to the devastation of the war.

Because of the strong pacifist attitude, which I shared and still do share, in the school, those of us who had defied authority were subjected to the All Day Punishment the next day, supervised by the music mistress, the Hag. The routine began at 7 a.m. with an icy strip-wash. Our free time before lunch and before tea, usually given to rollerskating, was occupied by two more of these freezing washings. Pent up hilarity was in evidence along the row of unprivate wash basins. We were not allowed to speak. Being *on silence* all day was the chief form of punishment at the school. We developed the ability to use the 'deaf and dumb' alphabet with an efficiency that proved useful in my work later. Other punishments for both boys and girls were cleaning windows with wet newspapers, digging weeds out of the tennis courts and helping the headmaster's wife to make marmalade.

Because it was a small school there was always the chance to be in the school play even if you could not learn by heart or act. And to get into the First Eleven hockey team was not impossible. We played matches at country schools and against Village Ladies. Once, in order to avoid showing gaps, we sewed our brown woollen stockings to our knickers. As we ran about the field the result was disastrous.

There is not space to elaborate on my Golden Greetings telegram to my father. The postmistress hovered with her freshly sharpened pencil and crossed out all my best words – *congratulations*, *venerable*, *half a century*, *jubilee*, *beloved* – reducing the message to *loving birthday wishes* followed by my name.

My first editor? Perhaps.

I still have my *Golden Treasury of the Bible*, two grey nondescript books, Part I a fat book of the Old Testament and Part II, slim, the New Testament. There is a pencil drawing of Shirley Temple, or rather her ringlets, in the back of Part I. Part II has pages *The Good Samaritan* and *The Prodigal Son* marked for one of my children in 1950 so I must have looked at it *fairly* recently . . .

Until now I had forgotten completely Shirley Temple's curls.

When the time came to leave school we all went either to work or to some further study or training. Our headmaster reminded those of us who were leaving that he wanted us to go out into the world with the deepest responsibility for standards and judgements. He wanted us, he said, to believe in the nourishment of the inner life and the loving discipline of personal relationships. He said too that we must always be concerned with the relentless search for truth. After six years of boarding school I left, an idealist, at the end of 1940.

My mother felt that nursing was vulgar in some way and my father said it was God's work. My mother said the striped material for my uniform was pillow ticking. She said she had other things in mind for me – travelling on the Continent, 'Europe,' she said, 'studying art and ancient buildings and music.'

'But there's a war on,' I said.

'Oh well, after the war.' A letter from the matron of the hospital saying that all probationers were required to bring warm underwear comforted my mother. She said the matron must be a very nice person after all.

My school trunk, in my room at the hospital before me, was a kind of betrayal. When I opened it books and shoes and clothes spilled out. Some of my pressed wildflowers had come unstuck and I put them back between the pages of the exercise book, remembering the sweet, wet grass near the school where we searched for flowers. I seemed then to see clearly shining long fingers pulling stalks and holding bunches. Saxifrage, campion, vetch, ragged robin, star of Bethlehem, wild strawberry and sorrel. Quickly I tidied the flowers – violet, buttercup, kingcup, cowslip, coltsfoot, wood anemone, shepherd's purse, lady's slipper, jack in the pulpit and bryony . . .

I had no idea of what could go wrong with the human body either from birth or by illness and accident later. At the age of seventeen I had never seen a badly crippled or a really ill person. At the start – an air raid in London, arriving at the hospital late (the stations not being marked, I missed the one I needed), then to going on a ward for the first time at half-past five in the afternoon, when badly burned men from a nearby aircraft factory were being brought in – I thought I would leave the hospital straight away. But I had no idea how to get my school trunk with all my possessions away from there so I stayed . . .

I have used as landscape and setting my own experiences during and immediately after World War II in the two novels *My Father's Moon* and *Cabin Fever*, though I am not the character, Vera. Without knowing it I suppose I banished those years and it has taken me a long time, about twenty years, to write these two books, while writing other stories and novels. On the whole I prefer to write the imagined rather than the autobiographical. I have to understand that the one cannot be written without the other. Imagination springs from the real experience.

Perhaps there is something invisible which a person is given early in life, a sort of gift, but the giver of it, not expecting any thanks, is never given it.

My father liked what he called a *splendid view*. He would dismount from his high bicycle and, parting the hedge, he would exclaim on the loveliness of what he could see. We would have to lean our bicycles up against a fence or a gate, scramble across the wet ditch and peer through the rain-soaked hedge at a sodden field or a dismal hill hardly visible through the rain mist. But first, something about his bicycle. This may seem irrelevant but perhaps it is necessary to say that the bicycle was enormous; twenty-eight-inch wheels and a correspondingly large frame. He collected the parts and made it himself, and once, when it was stolen, he went round the barrows and stalls in the Bullring marketplace in Birmingham and bought back all the parts as he recognised them and rebuilt it. I mention this because it shows something of the kind of man he was.

We had to ride bicycles too. When I was six I had a twenty-four-inch wheel with hand brakes, left and right, back and front respectively.

'Never use the right hand brake before you use the left,' my father said. Excellent advice of course but my problem then was that I was not sure about my left hand and my right. The back mudguard had small holes in it for strings which were meant to keep a lady's skirt from getting caught in the spokes. I was terribly ashamed of these small holes and wished I could fill them in with thick paint or something . . .

The reason that I mention all this is because I believe that my own love of what my father called *scenery* or a *splendid view* comes in part from the bicycle rides he insisted upon. We had to go with him. The bicycle rides through the rural edges of the Black Country in England were his relaxation and pleasure. We stopped frequently while he studied gravestones in small overgrown cemeteries and explained about lychgates. He told us about turnpike houses and about towing paths and locks – those mysterious sluice gates so powerful in altering the water levels in the canals. My own love of the quality of the air comes too, I realise, from my father, who often simply stood at the roadside enjoying what he declared was fresh air, *unbreathed air*. He marvelled at the beech trees in the fenced parklands of the wealthy. He paused before fields and meadows, explaining about the rotation of crops and about fallow fields. He was inclined to make a lesson out of everything. To him, health and learning were the means to a particular form of freedom and the bicycle was the way in which to achieve these.

I developed the habit in my letters to my father of describing in detail the places where I lived and through which I journeyed. Wherever I went I was always composing, in my head, my next letter to him . . .

My mother, who loved order, cleared up her house as she moved steadily into old age. Before she died she had, in a sense, tidied up, thrown away and burned up her household so that nothing remains of my descriptions posted home every week during all the years.

MIGRATION

In 1959 my husband, who was Deputy Librarian at the University of Glasgow, accepted the post of Librarian at the University of Western Australia. We made this tremendous move by ship with our three children – Sarah, thirteen, Richard, six, and Ruth, four. We brought most of our furniture, the children's bicycles and almost all our books, which I packed in twenty crates.

I came to Western Australia from Britain in the middle of my life. I never thought of myself as a migrant but that is what we were called. Migrants. I realise that the freshness of my observation can distort as well as illuminate. The impact of the new country does not obliterate the previous one but sharpens memory, thought and feeling, thus providing a contrasting theme or setting.

During the initial voyage, while the ship was in the Great Bitter Lake waiting to go through the last part of the Suez Canal, I remembered, quite suddenly, my father's hands. Sorrow lay below the wide colourless expanse of water. The picture I had of his hands was, as they so often were, cupped carrying something to show, to describe, to tell about. It seems now, when I think about it all these years later, that he had come part of the way, part of the long journey as he used to come, when seeing off a train, 'as far as the first stop'.

I thought about my father's hands on the ship that day and thought how, in that way, he was, in fact, accompanying me and it was as if the lake offered from its secretive depths this sudden memory and that pain of homesickness for which there is no remedy.

'A Hedge of Rosemary' is the first story I wrote after arriving in Western Australia. In it there are the two contrasting landscapes, an attempt perhaps to close the enormous space between my two worlds. (The journey by ship having taken just over three weeks.)

When he [the old man] went out in the evening he walked straight down the middle of the road, down towards the river. The evening was oriental, with dark verandahs and curving ornamental roof tops, palm fronds and the long weeping hair of peppermint trailing, a mysterious profile . . . the moon, thinly crescent and frail, hung in the gum leaf lace . . . the magpies caressed him with their cascade of watery music . . .

On my first evening in Western Australia I went out to post a letter, a short way along the road and round a corner. I walked down the middle of the road, the evening was oriental with dark verandahs and curving ornamental roof tops. Back home again, I wrote the few lines of description and followed these immediately with a few words about the stillness and the eerie quietness. And then I wrote of my own longing for the chiming of city clocks through the comforting roar of the blast furnace and the nightly glow across the sky when the furnace was opened. Recalling the house where I had lived as a child in the Black Country (the industrial Midlands of England) I wrote that the noise and glow from the blast furnace were like a night light and a cradle song. I gave these memories to the old man in the story. I doubt that I would ever have written these things down if I had not come to Western Australia. On arrival in a new country, sense of place has to be established by a scrutiny of previous places in comparison with the present one.

I never thought of myself as a migrant. But migration, the travelling, the state of chosen exile, has given me the feeling of inhabiting several worlds. Though the same language is spoken here there are colloquial differences. The climate and the customs and the clothes are different. The bright light and the blue skies in Western Australia made all our clothes seem very shabby. In Scotland (where we lived before changing countries) the doors and windows along the street were kept closed winter and summer. Curtains and blinds covered the windows, these coverings were not intended to keep out the sun in Glasgow! All along Parkway, the little street of houses on campus at the University of Western Australia, there were always women and children moving forever on the grass verges, in and out of each others' gardens and in and out of each others' houses, constant visiting and exchanging of children and dishes and recipes, the doors behind the fly screens always open, winter and summer. There was a greengrocer who came to Parkway with his van, he uttered the famous words: 'Whichever house you go to in this street the same woman always comes to the door.'

People often ask me if moving from one country to another has affected my writing. 'What would you have written if you had stayed in England?' is their question. My reply is that I have no idea. But what I do know is that, without being disloyal to my previous country, there are certain experiences and observations I would have missed if I had remained in England. Until I came to Western Australia I had no real conception of the importance of water and its effects in and on the earth. In a dry country, water, either the lack of it or sudden floods, can be uppermost in a person's mind. My teaching work in the remote townships and farms in the wheat belt gave me fresh insight. A farmer's wife once described the effects water has on the appearance of a paddock. Later I quickly made a note and gave this passage to my character in 'Two Men Running'. He is running in his imagination through the remembered landscape of his childhood.

'The gravel pits, the hills, the catchment and the foxgloves in the catchment. Did you know,' I ask him. 'Did you know that where the water collects and runs off the rocks there are different flowers growing there? Did you know that, because of this water, a paddock can be deep purple like a plum? And then, if you think about plums, the different colours range from deep purple through to the pale pearly green of the translucent satsuma before it ripens.

Because of water that's how a paddock can look from one end to the other. It's the same with people . . .'

In writing the above I was trying to show something of my character's need to recreate for himself the wholesomeness of this remembered landscape. A consolation for him as indeed I have come to understand that the earth is consoled with the gift of water – providing it is not too much water.

The ability to make changes and to accept the differences, to be at home in the new country, depends on the development of the person in the country of origin. Exile, if forced, is intolerable for most people. Chosen exile is not easy.

Some of my fiction is based on my experience of exile during the 1930s when my father and mother were helping refugees to escape from central Europe. My father would go in the night to meet trains and the people stayed in our house till jobs could be found, usually living-in work – housekeeping and gardening – for people who had never, in their lives, done this sort of work. Many of the people were only part of a family. I remember nights filled with the sound of subdued weeping and the deep voice of my father consoling.

My fiction is not autobiographical but, like all fiction, it springs from moments of truth and awareness, from observation and experience. I try to develop the moment of truth with the magic of imagination. I try too to be loyal to this moment of truth and to the landscape of my own region or the specific region in which the novel or story is set. I have always felt that the best fiction is regional. In Western Australia, in the vastness of this one-third of the whole continent, there are a variety of regions from the seacoast through to the deserts that separate us from the rest of Australia (port, city, suburbs, river foreshore, sand plain, escarpment, the partly cleared semirural, the rural, the bush, the wheat belt and the outback. In

Western Australia we even have a few mountains. And we have a rabbit- and emu-proof fence separating the outreaches of the farming land from the beginnings of the desert.)

The landscape of my fiction is not to be found exactly on any map but I am faithful to the landscape and I do not make mistakes. I never have water flowing where it could never flow . . .

★

I never called myself writer till I was called writer from outside. For a long time rejection slips and letters poured in . . . 'I don't think any advice could be offered to the author. This does not appear to be the work of a novelist, or indeed of an imaginative writer of any kind, though it does show a limited talent . . .' (1963)

There is an enormous difference between rejection and acceptance. I would have gone on writing in the face of further rejection. The change in status from being an absolutely hopeless case or entirely unacceptable to being accepted is a strange, unexpected experience.

For me, my character comes before plot and incident. I have always been interested in people. My work, first nursing and now teaching, has been essential. I can never understand why anyone should give up a good job in order to write full-time. As a writer I need people very much. Having enough time for writing is always a problem because writing is time-consuming. A Senior Fellowship from the Literature Board of the Australia Council a few years ago helped me to buy time in all sorts of ways, for example to teach for fewer hours a week, to have some domestic help and domestic appliances which are timesavers.

I have developed the ability to make the quick note while shopping or doing housework. This is very useful as I would not be able to write if simply confronted with sheets of blank paper and no ideas in my head!

I read a great deal. Reading and discussing literature with students has proved over the years to be the best way for me to study the art of writing. It is one thing to write and another to craft the writing to make it acceptable to readers. I think it is wise not to rush into publication too soon. It pays to write a number of stories or novels in order to discover themes and direction. I always rewrite a great deal. Of course the writer wants to be published. Who would want to build a bridge and have no one walk across it? It has always been my hope that ultimately my work would be published and read with understanding and enjoyment. While I am writing I do not think of a possible readership. To start with I am both writer and reader. When I come to the final draft, or what seems to be a final draft, I do craft the work with a reader in mind. I would like my work to reach all kinds of people. The fiction writer can offer people something entertaining but at the same time might be able to change a person's outlook on life or their direction, I hope towards the more positive, the more loving and optimistic.

The literary prizes are highlights in a writer's life. The writer does not write in order to win a prize. But if a book wins a prize it is a kind of measurement of success. People like to buy and read a book which has been selected for a prize. Many people do not understand that a book has to be chosen or selected in order to be published at all.

I have always felt grateful for the people who read and select the books first for publication and then later for the selection of prize winners.

Before being accepted (and I was unacceptable for a very long time) I had no idea of the business of publishing. From the time when a book is accepted for publication till it is on sale in a bookshop a whole lot of people are busy working on the production of that book. The writer, therefore, without actually meaning to be, or realising it, is a sort of primary producer. As a failing orchardist I rather like this idea.

It is thought that I have written a number of books in a short time. This is not the case. Because my work was rejected, and because I went on writing, a bank of material built up. I would have gone on writing in spite of the rejection slips, had they continued.

Characters can sometimes be embarrassing to the author. I do not like to be embarrassed by my characters either by their actions or by the things they say. If there is something which seems awkward in this way I usually change it. Awkwardness suggests a change is needed.

In the first writings of the novel *Palomino* I tried to place Laura and Andrea, during the deepening of their relationships, and the realisation of their sensual passion for each other, in direct confrontation. I tried to create dialogue and action for them in these encounters. The result was very wooden indeed; self-conscious conversations and clichéd actions, with one character sounding like a missionary from a hundred years ago and the other a rebellious schoolgirl in the 1930s. After many attempts to bring the two characters together satisfactorily (over approximately twenty years of writing) I tried internal monologue or thought process, as it is sometimes called. The older woman reflects on the speech and actions of the younger woman in relation to her own feelings and this is followed by the thoughts and feelings of the younger woman. Each fragment carries, as heading, the name of the person whose thoughts are offered. Ultimately this seemed the best way to present the material of the novel.

I had no sooner finished writing this novel than it happened that I was to appear on a platform with another writer; we were both to address a group of postgraduate students. The first speaker got up and started off, 'The novel is *dead* and interior monologue is *out . . .*'

I hardly heard the rest of his talk – which was a nuisance because I was supposed to follow him – all I could do was to think of my dead manuscript with its outdated style lying on the table at home ready to be posted off for submission.

It was the fashion for many years for these deaths, either of the novel or the short story, to be announced from time to time.

Miss Thorne in the novel *Miss Peabody's Inheritance* is a character who could be embarrassing because of her large size, her exuberance, her ability to be completely unselfconscious, her desire to initiate, or simply by her desires and her behaviour and by the use of the idiom of the eternal schoolgirl mixed with the language of an educated well-bred woman. The best way for me to get over the problem of awkwardness in the creation of this large and powerful woman and her entourage and her habit of leaving a trail of broken beds ('It simply is not profitable to spend time wondering why hotels invest in cheap frail furniture') across the more cultured spots in Europe, was to give her entirely to an imagined novelist, Diana Hopewell, who writes about her in a flamboyant, cliché-ridden style and, above all, in the form of letters. Writing in letters allows a great deal of freedom – repetitions, poor but vivid phrases, purple passages of description, these are all excused in this rapid and personal method of communication. I would like to write another novel in this style but the novelist is expected to come up with something fresh every time. The word 'novel', after all, does mean 'of new kind, strange, hitherto unknown – a fictitious prose tale published as a complete book'. A perfect description which must not be betrayed.

My husband once made a profound remark about my father and it was this: that my father was never able to see the consequences of his good intentions. I suppose in many ways that remark fits me too. It is especially true about children and their upbringing. The mother is a tower of good intention and is not able to know before-hand the results of her efforts. I think being a mother is one of the hardest tasks with which we are faced. Being a grandmother is an unexpected blessing. I have four grandchildren, Matthew, Daniel, Samuel and little Alice. A great many things are in existence by some force beyond us. I have only to look on a newly born lamb or a grandchild to feel humble and amazed and filled with a deep sense of reverence.

Sisters

MY SISTER DANCING

'Not asleep yet?' the nurse said.

'No. Not yet.'

My sister's face had never been so close to mine before.

'Keep your eyes open,' I told her, 'or they'll come and get you. Go to sleep and keep your eyes open.'

My sister's eyes were very close to mine. They were wide open.

There was hardly room for us in the hospital cot. The nurse had lifted me from my bed. 'I'm putting you in with your sister,' she said, 'she's crying that much, she'll disturb all the others.'

The cot was made of metal and painted white.

'You want a watter?' the nurse leaned over into my sister's sobbing. 'She wants a watter? Watter? Watterdottshiwatt?' the nurse asked me. The nurse wanted my sister to go to sleep, she said. When she came back later the nurse said she *wanted my sister to be asleep.*

'Go to sleep!' I told my sister. 'Go to sleep and keep your eyes open.'

I was five then and my sister was nearly four. We were in the Cottage Hospital to have our tonsils out.

I spat on my finger and smoothed my sister's long dark eye-lashes against her cheek. The porter picked her up out of the cot and her head rolled and nestled into his neck as he carried her off.

When it was my turn I was still awake. The porter called me 'old lady'. 'Come along old lady,' he said, and he carried me along a pas-sage past flaring rings of blue flames.

'What are those flames?' I asked him.

'Gas,' he said, 'to boil up the watter in them big sterilising kettles.'

The porter fastened me on a narrow table with a rubber strap that felt warm. The last thing I remembered was my foot sinking in a very comfortable way into the soft white-aproned stomach of the nurse who was standing within foot's reach. I have never forgotten, even after so many years, the satisfaction I felt then.

Children are not produced essentially as gifts for each other but since they come like gifts, unasked for, very often as surprises to the existing children, as something special to be kept and not broken and discarded, I suppose it is true to say that there is no gift which quite equals the gift of a sister born when you are fourteen months old and still holding a precious first place in the household. Even the displacement, which is bound to occur, provides a certain inde-pendence and an undisputed status, that of 'the elder sister'.

There came a time in my own life when it became suddenly clear to me that my sister was the one person who had known me for the longest time. With this realisation came a number of thoughts. One was that the only person who has ever wanted to hear me sing is my sister. In all the things we have shared – earache, chickenpox, measles, sweets, toys, books, love, ambition, shame, fear, to name a few, our two voices have been the most consistently shared in our endless games carried out in dialogue between the characters in our dolls' houses and in a game called Singing in Turns. Some of the dolls' house characters live on still. Joan, a cleaning lady in my sister's dolls' house, did not fit in a bed and so sat all night on a chair. She rattled about on her pink celluloid legs cleaning the dolls' house and gossiping and, without my realising it till later, she became the forerunner of Weekly in my little novel *The Newspaper of Claremont Street*.

'Let's play Singing in Turns.' Often at night we would sing in turns or if confined to bed, each in separate rooms with an illness, we would sing. We sang songs like 'Drink to Me Only with Thine Eyes', or 'My Bonnie Lies Over the Ocean', or hymns, 'Lead Kindly Light' or 'All Things Bright and Beautiful'. There was a song called 'The Wild Woodland Cherry Tree' which had in the first line the phrase: *so lissom so tall*. Not knowing what the word *lissom* meant gave the song a magical quality. We did not know the whole song but were content with the first few lines. Often, pitching the first notes too high, the singer would be obliged to stop and start again on a lower note. The audience of one was quite uncritical.

Another shared experience was that of our father reading aloud to us. He, during a childhood illness, would stand out on the landing taking care not to enter the rooms where the infection lurked. He was a teacher and could not go to school carrying our germs. He read then in the deep voice he kept for the boys at school.

A very strong memory among the many cherished memories of *sister* is the shared convalescence, in candlelight very often, with the remaking of old familiar jigsaw puzzles or setting up the shabby magic of a book that contained scenes for plays. These could be performed with little paper characters pushed on the stage with strips of cardboard. Cinderella was one.

During convalescence we were given plates of sliced up oranges. The plates sat on the hearth rug in the middle of all the dolls' clothes. The days were spent at the window watching builders next door. The builders made cement and ran up and down ladders with cement and bricks on little boards balanced on their heads. We called one of the builders Dozing John because we saw him having forty winks in the sun. In imagination we talked to Dozing John and made cement for him. We told him about ourselves and made plans to run away with him. I remember my sister packed a case with dolls' clothes in readiness. Perhaps I did the same but have forgotten.

We shared germs too. At that time a lot of emphasis was given to germs. Professor Winifred Cullis (whose Wireless Lessons I loved – human biology) spoke of the risk of sharing a cup or biting someone else's apple. She said that germs grew if you slept in your vest. Every night we took off all our clothes and standing on the landing at the top of the stairs we shook out all the germs from each article of clothing. The bath was another thing we shared. We took turns quite strictly to have either the rounded end or the end with the plug and the taps.

So many things in turn – housework, for one thing:

'It's your turn to do the wiping up.'

'No it isn't, it's your turn.'

Or, 'You're being called to set the table.'

'No I'm not. It's you being called . . .'

We often, in anger, pulled each other's hair. I have a memory of a handful of my hair being torn out by the roots. But perhaps this was the other way round!

We chose records in turn, taking turns to wind up the gramophone. My mother sometimes had a chance to choose. She chose *Tales from the Vienna Woods*. We had a whole pile of records *Gretchen am Spinnrade, Heidenröslein, Auf dem Wasser zu Singen, Der Erl König*, the third movement of Mozart's Symphony no. 39, the Anvil Chorus and the Soldier's Chorus from *Il Trovatore* and so on. These records were all seventy-eights and it was possible to have one movement from a symphony without the rest of it. So, though we knew the third movement of the Mozart symphony, neither of us would have recognised it if we had heard the beginning.

In the line *'Erl König hat mir ein leid getan'* and during Azucena's aria, in which she discloses, in an ever-deepening contralto, that Manrico is the Count's long-lost brother, I hid my face so that my sister would not see tears spilling down my cheeks.

We had spotted frocks, matching each other, frocks with lines and squares on them, embroidered rosebud frocks with reversible ribbons at the waist, frocks with frills and puffed sleeves, and one summer, our mother had our hair shingled and we each had a pair of shorts. No one else in the street had shorts. An old lady passing our front garden looked through a gap in the hedge. 'Are you two boys or girls?' she wanted to know.

'I'm Monica Elizabeth,' I explained, 'and she's Madelaine Winifred, we're boys.'

Later on, being too old for Shirley Temple frocks, we each had a Deanna Durbin dress.

Following the sophistication of the film-star fashion dresses, Marie Stopes appeared on the brush and comb shelf inside our wardrobe. We read the book secretly and, with a silent sort of agreement, we hid the book so that our mother should not see it. It never occurred to either of us then that she, hoping I suppose to offer enlightenment, had placed the book where we would see it and read it.

Perhaps the conspiracy of jealousy is most powerful when it is between, I should say *shared* between, sisters.

The summer after the summer of the shingled heads and the shorts we were taken, by our father, to visit relatives who lived on farms in Wiltshire. At Coopers Farm we discovered a little girl called Betsy.

Fair-skinned with rosy cheeks and golden curls, she wore sturdy pinafores over her serge dresses, black knee-length stockings and lace-up farm boots, also black. Next to her, in our crêpe de chine summer frocks which had low round necks and dropped waists, and our feet bare in Oxford sandals, we were not at all sure how we stood with her.

'I don't like Betsy,' I told my father.

'Why not?'

I did not know how to answer this. 'Well,' I said, 'she can't read.'

'You read to her,' my father said, 'with your finger under the words to show them to her.' This should have made me feel better.

'Shan't!' I said.

My father took us, all three, to the museum in Salisbury and began as always to make a lesson out of everything. Especially he seemed to be showing Betsy everything.

'Have a look at this, Betsy' and 'Betsy, look! Have you ever seen anything like this?' My sister and I did not want to be alongside this Betsy. We had already had a slow race with her eating a banana each. The idea was to eat slowly and the one who had some banana left when the others had eaten all theirs won.

'We've eaten all our banana,' in silent agreement my sister and I folded our apparently empty banana skins over, flapping them at Betsy.

'Empty banana peels. See?'

So Betsy ate all hers, finished it up, and with horrid triumph we revealed that we both had some left.

'We've won. We've won.'

Our father seemed to be concentrating all his attention on this Betsy from Coopers Farm. Who was she anyway? Who did she think she was? The museum was hideously dull. We began to jump over the glass cases which were low down on the floor. First my sister jumped and then I ran and jumped. Backwards and forwards over these show cases, never mind what they contained, just old rocks. I shouted 'Heads!' Over the glass, jump, back over the glass, jump. This would teach our dad to prefer Betsy to us if anything would. We were quite out of breath with our jumping. I found I could land with quite a heavy thud . . .

A lady dressed in a uniform came over to us. We had not noticed her before. She said we were to stop the noise and that jumping the exhibits was not allowed and would we go outside immediately and wait till our father had finished showing the other little girl the things in the museum.

'That woman,' my sister said, when we waited outside on the steps of the museum, 'that woman, she's a woman and a half and she needs cutting up a bit.'

Together, discovering their particular fears, we tormented our Austrian and French governesses with earthworms and spiders. Rushing through long wet grass we terrified ourselves simultaneously by getting our sandals full of squashed slugs.

It was when I was sent to boarding school at the age of eleven that, as well as having to become accustomed to an entirely different life, I missed my sister dreadfully. I began then to write stories for her which I sent home in my Sunday letter.

It came as something of a shock to me many years later to receive a reproach from my sister for having left her in the way that I did at the time. That *she* suffered from my being sent away to school had not been clear to me. In my own struggle to overcome shyness, loneliness, homesickness (that most bitter and wasteful of all 'sickness') and to contend with a cruel bullying prevalent in boarding schools then, I had thought of her as fortunate in being at home still – in privacy and surrounded by all our treasures. I never thought of her in a pathetic position, that of being *left alone* at home.

My sister (for reasons best known to my mother and father) did not come to the school till the first year of the war. The school was in the country and a number of younger brothers and sisters became boarders because it was considered to be safe from air raids.

When my sister was at school I experienced something I have never forgotten and that was (and is) pride. I was so proud of her, my sister. My little sister, who had remained little in my mind, had grown up to be dainty and pretty. She walked with a springing step. She was loved at once by the friends I had made.

In the folk-dancing class on Thursday evenings (which I never liked) she learned all the dances. She danced with a neatness and a delicate energy making the dances, which previously I'd thought of as silly and meaningless, into something special. I saw for the first time an expression of human emotion and life in the movements of the dance.

In order to watch her, and only her, I volunteered to be in charge of the gramophone, winding it up, turning the records over and changing the needle. I sat every Thursday evening watching the ways in which my sister moved to and fro and round and round. I watched carefully the ways in which she moved her hands, her head and her feet.

My sister dancing was better than any of the others. She was perfect.

'That's my sister dancing,' I wanted to say to the others. 'Watch my sister, look at the way she turns. See, she hardly seems to touch the floor.'

I did not speak of this aloud.

That's my sister, I said somewhere inside myself. I could not take my eyes off my sister dancing.

A QUESTION OF UPBRINGING

Once, years ago, my sister wanted to sell me her bicycle.

'Sisters do not buy and sell with each other,' my mother said, 'sisters share.'

A general observation, perhaps when visiting, perhaps at a dinner party . . .

Sisters close in age, brought up by the same mother, have some things in common which can be observed to persist through-out childhood and into later years even if one, giving herself an androgynous nickname, is an adult tomboy and the other is quite clearly small-boned and delicately built with a penchant for beauty preparations, jewellery and fashionable clothes. For example, both women independently of one another will save and fold a piece of greaseproof paper from the inside of the cereal packet and, with exactly the same speed and exactly the same hand and finger move-ments put it away, allegedly for further use, in a kitchen cupboard overflowing already with similar careful foldings.

More important perhaps is the extent of the shared agitation and dismay when the first course of a dinner party is being cleared in either sister's house (or in someone else's house where both sisters are present) and a fork tips and falls from a partly empty plate which is being removed. The sisters immediately exchange impatient glances of concern tinged with more than a little lack of tolerance over this accidental carelessness. One of two things hap-pens – either both women are on their knees examining the carpet and hastily removing any traces of dropped food or one sister calls frowning to the other, who is also frowning, after retrieving the lost fork quickly, saying that there's no harm done to the table cloth or to the carpet . . .

The folding and the frowning and the momentary simultaneous loss of tolerance have been handed from mother to daughters to be shared by sisters.

To see this kind of thing you have to stare.

Perhaps like many writers I do stare at people. It has been said that writers are born watching and staring. It is something they can't help. A quotation from Morley Callaghan sent to me by the Melbourne poet Fairlie Szacinski goes like this:

> There is only one trait that marks the writer. He is always watching. It's a kind of trick of mind and he is born with it.

MY FATHER'S SISTER

Sister might not necessarily mean one's own sister.

My father had to look after his younger sister, he told me. Elder brothers and elder sisters, he said, must always look after the younger ones. He had to take his sister to the Elementary School every day. He was not fond of going to school himself. On one occasion he returned home telling his mother that the school gates were locked because the school had burned down during the night. This was before his sister was old enough to be taken to school. His mother (later on to be my grandmother) said she would very much like to see a burned-down school. And, putting on her hat and coat she walked him straight back down to the school where the bell was ringing and the children, in their separate playgrounds, were lining up to go in.

My father's sister was called Daisy (she, later, was my Aunt Daisy). In taking Daisy to school, my father explained, he adopted a method of getting her there as quickly as he could. He was always afraid of being late. (L-A-T-E spells late, I told my own sister when

I was hurrying her along to school. I had, it seemed, inherited my father's fear of being late. Perhaps I should explain here that we did have a short time in Mixed Infants before my father arranged for us to have governesses at home.)

But to go back to my father getting his sister to school. He hooked an arm round her neck, he told me, and set off at a steady trot with her held fast in the crook of his arm, their metal-tipped boots sounding like little horses along the pavement. Sometimes, by accident, they kicked and bruised each other's ankles. She wore, he remembered, a round knitted cap with loose woollen tassels which he could feel against his neck. On arrival at the school he used to push her hard, he described it as a shove, through the gate which had an archway marked GIRLS in big iron letters. And then he would run off, as if unrelated to her, head down, his responsibility shed, to a similar gateway, arched in iron, and marked BOYS.

My father felt responsible for his sister all his life in spite of her sometimes uncompromising attitude towards the woman (*a foreigner*) he chose to be his wife. He did not expect her 'to speak up' for him, this sister, when she stood wordless, half hidden in the thick curtains of the cold room they called the drawing room, peering out to the street where the neighbours had gathered to watch when he was being disowned, in public, by his father (later to be my grandfather) and turned out of the house with only a shilling, for being a conscientious objector and for being in prison during the Great War.

My father always, when telling this, explained that it was the disgrace of being in prison that had upset his father so much. It was not so much the reason for it. He used to say too, by way of an alleviation, that a shilling was worth far more in those days. For example, a bundle of candles cost three ha'pence, a large loaf was threepence, milk a penny, and so on.

My father found excuses for his sister for every accusation levelled at her by my mother (her sister-in-law) and he visited her every Saturday for years. She always had worries and work waiting for him. He returned home white-faced and exhausted.

I suppose my father's sister never was able to like her sister-in-law, my mother. Though I do recall conspiratorial closings of the bedroom door, either at my grandmother's house or in our own house, for discussions over the Christmas dolls, the chosen books, dresses and other presents. And I have an indelible memory of my aunt and my mother, the sisters-in-law, sitting together one afternoon, a dark afternoon, and my father's sister cried and cried and my mother, with not enough English for the occasion, tried to comfort her. I must have been about eight then and I can remember wishing my father would come home from taking the boys at school to the swimming baths or down a coal mine or something of that sort. In spite of that afternoon, as time passed, the sisters-in-law did not improve in their feelings towards each other.

In fact, the biggest insult hurled between us (my sister and me) was for one to say that the other was 'getting like Aunt Daisy'. My mother took part in this with her own critical remarks intended for our good:

'Don't eat like your Aunt Daisy' and 'Don't sit like your Aunt Daisy,' 'Don't *do anything* like your Aunt Daisy.' And about clothes, the worst thing that could be said was:

'That's the kind of *thing* Aunt Daisy would choose.'

After the death of my grandmother, my father's sister had a housekeeper companion for many years. She was a true daughter of the canal barges, sharp-tongued, energetic, quick at mental arithmetic and spelling; she was knowledgeable about things medical, geographical, historical, political and personal. She was a small thin woman with a pile of white hair and a voice. Miss Clayton and my father's sister got on satisfactorily together by frequent repetitions of that certain emotional release which follows on the heels of an all-time, all-encompassing row. These two, they had many such rows either when they were alone together or in the presence of company or even when there was simply an audience of one. These rows, violent and at screaming pitch, in an agitation of rocking chairs, came unheralded and ended quickly in low-voiced soothing moans and endearments uttered from these same rocking chairs, which gradually subsided on either side of the hearth.

My mother (the sister-in-law), all her life, could not stand the sight of a rocking chair.

My father stopped visiting his sister quite suddenly. He never explained to anyone why he no longer visited her house.

When my father's sister died she died in her rocking chair with a book in her lap and a cup of tea at her elbow. Quite peaceful, Miss Clayton told my father who, in the event of death, was obliged, as he said, to go over there.

He was required to clear up her things.

His sister having bought an annuity for herself previously with what my mother (her sister-in-law) declared was mostly my father's share of the inheritance after the death of, first, his father and then his mother, there was no money left for anyone.

The sad part about it was, my father said later, there was a houseful of possessions, furniture, books, pictures, clothes, knives and forks and plates and cups and photographs all of which were *treasures* to her but unwanted by anyone else. He gave away what he could and had to have enormous bonfires for the rest. There was, for example, a whole cabinet of babies' dresses carefully embroidered, some with smocking, and trimmed with lace by her girls at school. She had been a sewing teacher. She was always very proud of the collection of what she called 'my girls' work'. The babies' dresses were, by this time, discoloured and marked in places with mildew; some were actually rotten.

Even when all the clearing up was finished my father still did not say what had made him stop his weekly visits after continuing them regularly for all those years in the face of my mother's outbursts of anger and reproach.

Before I go on I must explain that my father's sister, my mother's sister-in-law, was a very kind aunty to me. I understand that now. She was kind and fond in the only ways she knew how to be. She always sent postcards from her holiday travellings and letters, especially letters with promises: 'If you and your sister will come on Saturday you will be able to have the new picture books I have for you both.' That sort of thing. I see now that she was lonely and her letters were often pathetic attempts to entice us to visit. It was she who sent the school-girl stories to me at boarding school: *Treacle of St Mikes* and *The Dimsie Omnibus*. The possession of these and some others ensured my popularity for quite a time.

My father often said that the people who were the hardest to love were the ones who needed loving most. I see now that he was sorry for his sister and saw her as a person all alone, unloved and, what was worse, having no one of her own to love. And that was why he went every Saturday on the early train, returning at night exhausted after digging her garden or mending something in the house, very often something which should have been discarded and replaced. But what tired him most, my mother would argue, were the tirades of complaints and worries. My mother often remarked that her sister-in-law was like a dog with a bone. She would describe the dog worrying the bone, putting the bone down and taking it up again to shake it first one way and then the other way. She said her sister-in-law would even, like a dog, bury her bone in order to dig

it up once more and start worrying it all over again. My father, after
one of his Saturday visits to his sister, once asked me what he could
suggest she should buy for inexpensive presents for her friends at
Christmas because she was worrying about Christmas so much, and
it was then still only June.

It was only much later on, after many years, that I understood why,
without saying anything to anyone, he stopped visiting his sister.
He made this big change in his life and in hers because of me. It was
out of loyalty and love for me that he gave up his sister. A great part
of her weekly tirade, for a number of years, would have been about
me.

It was like this. I had not seen my father's sister, my aunt, for
some years when she called unexpectedly to see me one day. I was
working then as housekeeper in a large house belonging to a wealthy
factory owner. I had my own apartment there and a part of the garden was set aside as mine.

Without touching her tea or the bread and butter I offered
her, she began to explain in very carefully articulated words that,
because of the way in which I was living and must have lived (this
with a sidelong glance at the baby clothes arranged for airing along
the fireguard) she had, in her words, been obliged to cut me out of
her will, completely out of her will.

The surprise of this was not in connection with any possible gift
being withheld, it was more to do with the fact that she had planned
to make a long and awkward journey by train and bus for this particular reason, this special intention. The sudden intensification of my
own feelings of loneliness was a surprise too. I was already alone. I
was accustomed to the idea that I was alone, but her words caused an
extra emptiness, that of being removed from belonging to a family.

Immediately, perhaps with the aid of a cultivated practice of self-protection, consolation and rescue, without really thinking, I told her, 'Please don't worry about me, I have been well provided for.'

'Don't tell Dad,' I said later when visiting my mother (my father's sister's sister-in-law).

My mother said that it could be considered a great comfort for us both that the Georgian silver teaspoons I was meant to inherit from my grandmother via Aunt Daisy would hang like a great weight round her neck ... She paused suitably in her finger-pointing pronouncement to let all the possible horrors contained in this image be continued in the imagination.

'Don't tell Dad,' I said again, not thinking that of course my aunt would tell him herself, rail at him, have him on the mat, worrying the subject – the dog worrying the bone – never giving him any peace, wanting to know who was providing for me, what sort of people did his daughter know and mix with and what dark world of sin was she being paid to inhabit.

Not thinking, I said again to my mother, 'Don't tell Dad.' She said she wouldn't but of course she did because, as I should have known by then, she always told my father everything.

And it was after this that he stopped going to see his sister. And I never saw her again either.

I prefer not to remember my aunt, my father's sister, in this way. I like best to think of them, the two of them, as children, as brother and sister, playing a game my father described once when he was making cocoa one evening for my sister and me. The game, he said, was called horses and carts. They played the game at the kitchen table. They had a preserving jar, with a lid, full of nuts and bolts and nails and screws. They said the kitchen table was the road and they arranged the screws and the nuts and bolts all dotted up and down the table – dot-dot-dotty-dot along the table, they were the horses and carts going along the road, passing each other, turning in the road, stopping and starting – this game, my father explained, he played with his sister.

Years later, long after the deaths of my father and his sister, the memory of his telling about the game came to me during a night when I was trying to write a story. I gave the game to the man in the story, as his childhood memory, and events in the story are paralleled by the events in the boy's game.

It is only now while my mind is on sisters, on my father's sister, that I see that, as in *the lives of the obscure*, being supplied *first with gilt-edged note paper and then with baby linen* and that hiding out in the parklands of the wealthy was not what she had had in mind for me during all the years when I had been, as in the promise of Isaiah, graven on the palms of her hands, cherished there and not forgotten. She came to visit me that day because she was concerned and honest and because she loved me.

I am here now never having said anything more to her after those words which jumped from me in defence and which were not true.

I am sitting here remembering all kinds of things like the times when I was with my sister, warm in our nightdresses by the hearth, playing with new building blocks. Each block had an animal, a goat, a lamb, a cockerel, a cow on it and when a special little string attached to the block was pulled, the sound of the particular animal emerged mysteriously from somewhere inside the block. There was, as well, a tiny stove which had a spirit lamp inside. Real vegetables could be cut up and boiled in proper little saucepans. Real tea could be made for the dolls when the water came to the boil in the tiny kettle . . .

My father's sister making the difficult journey, inarticulate in her inability to reach and protect, became judge and critic.

What remains from all this is my father's love for his sister, complicated of course. And, of course, there was their helplessness.

A Summer to
Remember

With my new spectacles I am suddenly seeing, for the first time, all kinds of things. The spider in the bathroom, earlier this morning, reminds me of my mother, of the graceful way in which she places one foot, toe pointing, before the other. When she walks her heels hardly touch the ground. When I consider my mother's feet I understand that I compare all other feet with hers, unfavourably. I notice women's feet and their ankles more than their faces. I do not like, I tell my mother, the washerwoman's shoes because they turn up at the toes. Mrs Mitcham, my mother says, is a laundress and that is why her shoes are as they are. And, she says, will you hold yourself properly, head up and shoulders back and, for heaven's sake, put a book on your head and walk nicely. Secretly, I envy Mrs Mitcham her shoes, and wish mine were like hers.

My mother's slender feet, encased in fine soft leather, and the well-bred way in which one shapely foot is placed before the other, mark her as being different from other women. When she speaks, her accent and her intonation are clearly foreign to the other people in our street. She, though British because of her marriage, is forever Viennese.

It is summer. My mother is standing, in the evening, on the path in her summer-full garden, weeping. Because of my new spectacles

I am suddenly in a magic world of leaves and petals and twigs, of outlines and edges and shadings, and of the patterns of cloth and the expressions in the eyes of people when they speak to me.

I ask my father why does my mother cry. And my father, white-faced from the Central School for Boys, dismounts from his bicycle and explains that she is homesick. He sends me to have a bath saying that he will comfort her.

The light, delicate movements of the spider, unknowingly trapped on porcelain, remind me of my mother folding clothes, with light, delicate movements, and putting them into her small suitcase.

The following day we go to see my mother off on the bus to Bewdley, a country town on the river Severn and on the edge of the Wyre Forest. She tells me there are little lanes round Bewdley and she will walk in the lovely fresh air. She will be staying, she says, with the Misses Galbraith in their elegant Guest House. She will come home in a week's time.

My father cooks kippers for us over the open fire in the living room. He is pale and restless and walks up and down the hall. My little sister and I wash and dry dishes. We mop the linoleum in the bedrooms and on the stairs.

My father announces that we are going camping. He packs his rucksack with potatoes and bread and fastens the kettle and a small tent on the carrier of his bicycle. He oils all three bicycles. He packs a box of matches.

'What about my rabbit?' my little sister wants to know.

'She can come too,' my father says. He puts the rabbit in a paper carrier bag and ties it to the handlebars of my sister's bicycle.

My father has a map, three miles to one inch. We can follow a choice of roads. The first-class roads are shown in red and the second-class are in blue. But my father has it in mind to follow the uncoloured roads, their relative importance being indicated, as they are drawn, by the width of the parallel lines. Footpaths are shown with dotted lines only. But footpaths thus represented, my father says, are not necessarily evidence of a right of way. A farmer, he says, has every right to turn us off his land if we are trespassing.

Trespassers will be prosecuted. I have often seen the notice.

Forgive us our trespasses as we forgive them that trespass against us. I am fascinated by *trespassing* and want to use the word.

We set off on the Penn Road through Penn Fields and Upper Penn, down the Lloyds Hill and past the Lloyds House, through Baggeridge Woods, where there is a coal mine, past Himley Hall and through the village of Himley and on to Wombourn and then the road to Kinver, which is not coloured and is not very wide. My father knows a farm, he says, where we can get fresh milk and put up our tent in a field.

We have to wait in the summer grass and cow pastures for my little sister whose legs have to work much harder than mine. She is still riding a fairy-cycle. I have a twenty-four-inch wheel.

A bit later we stop to let the rabbit out. We leave the bicycles in the ditch and crawl through the hedge. The rabbit hops and pauses at the edge of the crop which my father thinks might be barley. He lies back in the sun and enjoys the fresh air. We follow the timid rabbit, bringing her back whenever she seems to be going too far away.

When he was a boy, my father kept rabbits. He tells us that he had a great many rabbits. 'But we ett 'em,' he says.

I picture my mother walking in the pretty leafy lanes round Bewdley. These little lanes, I would like them.

'Will it be nice in Bewdley?' I ask my father.

'It's Kinver we're going to,' he says, 'to the farm.'

As we walk back to the bicycles, along the edge of the barley, I see with a small sideways look that there are tears slowly overflowing from my father's eyes.

It is dark and the fire has gone out long ago.

'I want to go home,' my little sister cries. It is cold in the tent. We can't help kicking each other and we seem to be rolling downhill all the time. My father unrolls his blanket and digs about in the ashes and brings us hot potatoes, burned black, but cooked at last.

I want to go home too, I tell my father. He says to eat the potatoes. I never want to go camping again, I tell him.

I can't wait to see the trees and the little lanes round Bewdley. It is a long ride. We stop often for the rabbit. In my impatience I ride on ahead, keeping as close to the tall summer grass as possible.

In the flower-filled polished hall of the Guest House, my tired dishevelled father is trying to arrange accommodation when my mother comes in, laughing, at the front door, her hair loose and her cheeks flushed. My little sister bursts into tears and rushes up to my surprised mother. I see at once that immediately behind my mother is her Friend, immaculate in white flannels and a blue blazer. My father, with his cycle clips still on, turns from the sharpened and reluctant pencils of the Misses Galbraith and steps towards my mother's Friend. The two men shake hands and remark on the fine weather. Extraordinary, they agree, the way it's keeping up. My father touches my mother's arm gently but she turns away, holding my little sister in one arm and quickly sweeping me up with the other into her sweet and familiar, her longed-for scent. 'We don't like Daddy,' my little sister says.

It is only now in hindsight that I understand how my father, in many different circumstances – from railway stations to steamship wharves and landings – will have done this chasing many times before, perhaps causing him to make, often, the same clumsy remarks, half in jest, perhaps even this one which so shocked the

A SUMMER TO REMEMBER 77

Misses Galbraith – that the great saddle of mutton, which they were attempting to carve, was, in fact, fit only to be a saddle.

It was then that my little sister drew, from her pinafore, the rabbit and let her hop between the vegetable dishes, the plates and the gravy boat on the polished table. As the frowns deepened between the Misses Galbraith, I saw the laughter start with the tears in my mother's eyes. This laughter and the tears spread across her face till she seemed to be laughing and crying with her whole body, but silently.

The summer of 1934 moved on towards autumn. And in September, dressed in a new uniform (my school trunk being sent in advance by goods train), I was packed off to boarding school. With my new spectacles it seemed as if I was going to go on seeing all kinds of things.

The Silent Night
of Snowfall

On December the third 1782, in preparation for Christmas, Parson Woodforde[1] held a Frolick for those farmers owing him Tithes. He describes in his diary that he, for this occasion, provided Salt Fish, a Leg of Mutton boiled and Capers, a Knuckle of Veal, a Piggs Face, a fine Surloin of Beef rosted and plenty of plumb Puddings. Wine drank 6 Bottles Rum drank 5 Bottles besides Quantities of Strong Beer and Ale.

The parson dined with the farmers in the great Parlour and Nancy, his niece, dined by herself in the study.

Every year, at Christmas, my mother roasted a goose. A goose is very fat and there was a great deal of goose dripping which was eaten, well salted, on slices of bread, for several days until it was all gone. Alongside the goose there was a boiling fowl from which my mother made a golden broth which was flecked with fine green herbs. At the last minute, before serving, she would throw in a plateful of little squares and triangles of fried bread.

Sometimes the goose was too big for the oven and it had to be carried to a nearby bakery where a place would be made for it in the oven there. Someone had to walk carrying the goose both ways. When I was old enough this great responsibility was mine.

Every Sunday, for some years, my father took a cooked dinner, prepared by my mother, for two destitute old men. He rode to them on his bicycle. The dinner, in an enamel dish, hung in a cloth bag from his crossbar. Christmas day, as on Sundays, my father always took a Christmas dinner to the two old men. One Christmas he returned white-faced and shocked. When my mother asked him what had happened he told her that one of the old men had gone back to bed, in all his clothes, and *he had taken a bottle of beer to bed with him.*

'Eat, my little Duchess, please eat.' Tante Marthe, on her knees beside my chair, implored me to eat the scrambled eggs she had cooked herself. It was just that she had forgotten the plate, she said. The mess of egg splashed on the little silver tray was something I could not bear to look at, let alone eat. Perhaps to take my mind off the eggs, she pointed out the places on the wallpaper in the downstairs rooms where there were marks from the recent flooding of the river Thames. Later we sat together, wrapped in coats and shawls, in the summer house in the narrow back garden. The summerhouse was a little wooden hut with a tilting floor which could be turned round so that any passing sunshine could be caught. We sat at a little round table drawing, with frozen fingers, flowers. Tante Marthe enjoyed an *air bath*[2] she said. Her Viennese accent made everything sound like a treat.

'Now a red flower,' she said, 'and now a blue one. And now you must choose a colour,' she handed me the crayons. We could hear the horses passing in the quiet street in front of the tall house and, at times, the chimes of the city clocks reached us through the noise which was London.

For a Christmas present that year, when I was with Tante Marthe, she gave me a painting box. This painting box, blue-enamelled and beautiful, was made up of little white squares in which the clean new colours reposed. These were all named: orange and yellow, brown and purple and green – the ordinary colours, and then there were the mysterious names, ultramarine, Prussian blue and cobalt blue. Others were burnt sienna, yellow ochre, vermilion, crimson lake, rose and rose madder. The black paint and the white each came in a little fat tube.

In winter, at Christmas, it was not easy to remember the real magic of the summerhouse and the warm smell of summer dust and old wood. In winter there was no lazy spider to watch as it crossed back and forth across the tilted creaking floor.

I have no idea now why I was alone with Tante Marthe that Christmas. But I do recall that I told her I did not like the yellow ochre in the painting box. I told her it looked shabby. She told me to put the wet brush on to the yellow ochre. 'Make it wet,' she said. She told me, 'You will see, *it is very nice colour.*' Her Viennese accent, once again, made everything she said sound as if it would be very, very good.

Perhaps the Toy Theatre is the most memorable Christmas present anyone could receive. One year there was the miraculous perfection of a little theatre unfolding from a box which looked like a book – before it was opened. There was a proscenium arch decorated with folds of crimson and gold paper which looked just like velvet. These folds revealed partly naked ladies. The ladies were made of a glossy paper and they had voluptuous bosoms and shapely thighs entwined with vine leaves and rosebuds. This arch framed a neat little wooden stage that had two trapdoors and several different interchangeable backdrops for scenes: a ship captain's cabin, a kitchen, a ballroom, a hideout for thieves, a cave filled with gold coins and precious jewels, a castle turret for kings and queens, and a magic forest in which trees walked and animals could speak.

It was possible to create with the little paper characters, supported on thin wires, all kinds of stories of human conflict and violence. Ordinary events in our own lives could be heightened and placed then in the little distance of pretend.

Nymphomaniacs and murderers, perplexed housewives and angry maiden aunts (and a cleaning woman called Joan who later became Weekly in my novel *The Newspaper of Claremont Street*) inhabited our dolls' houses. They all came flocking, beautifully dressed, to the theatre and were arranged in the space, in front, on the carpet. The larger dolls sat behind. Sometimes one of these, carried away with emotion, would collapse in the hearth and smash her china head on the fire irons. Her soft body would be folded into a music case and she would be left for a week at the dolls' hospital in town.

My father, who was sometimes a part of the audience, said it was necessary in a story or a play for something pleasant to happen – a character might show kindness towards another character, for example. There should be little incidents of goodness and happiness in the story so that the audience would not be upset all the time. Audiences, he said, like to see people comforted or being successful in some way. Perhaps, he said, the people imprisoned and left to die under the captain's floor and the sailor about to walk the plank could be rescued at the last minute.

Sometimes Christmas, in spite of Christmas-card pictures, was mild and grey and wet. Sometimes there was a frost, very cold and with bright sunshine. The iron tips on the fast-running heels and toes of boots and shoes struck sparks on the pavements. There were frost-flowers on the bedroom windowpanes, and a robin, perched on a winter-bare twig in the garden, would sing and sing as if its little heart was bursting with joy.

And then there would be the silent night of snowfall, that strange stillness the next morning and the bedroom ceiling lighter than usual with reflections from the snow-covered world outside.

We had a sledge with heavy iron runners. We sledged down the street where we lived, using wooden pegs, one in each hand, to push down first one side and then the other in order to steer the clumsy *conveyance*. (I am unable to find a better word for it.) Then, of course, there was the dreadful long haul on the rope to drag the heavy thing up the hill so that there could be another ride down. Christmas then was a time of wet coats and gloves and socks and boots arranged at the kitchen fire in the evening to be baked dry ready for the next morning.

I was not very old when I had to understand that there was no Father Christmas and that some people did not believe in the story of the baby Jesus being born in a stable watched over by shepherds and visited by the wise men, the kings, who came bringing rare and symbolic presents. It seems, in retrospect, that I was able to think of Father Christmas as someone merely talked about and even *promised* to us but easily absorbed in make-believe. And the story of the Nativity could be regarded as an existing story which might be an attempt to explain the mysteries of our own existence, our birth and our death and our destiny. We are all made manifest at birth, perhaps not to shepherds and kings from afar, but to relatives, friends and neighbours and even to strangers, many of whom do bring kind and wise words and presents at Christmas and at the celebrations of birthdays as they come in that inevitable way, one after the other;

> Like as the waves make towards the pebbled shore,
> So do our minutes hasten to their end;
> Each changing place with that which goes before,
> In sequent toil all forwards do contend . . .

I was not very old when a visitor to the house explained that the robin singing in the garden, so fresh and happy, on Christmas day was not singing with joy as I imagined. If they sing like this, the visitor explained, persisting with his doctrine of disillusionment, they are singing in distress, usually because they are bereaved or, like now in the snow, starving. Robins, he went on, are territorial and their song reaches Orphean excellence, in our hearing, when their territory is threatened – invaded by another robin, an intruder.

In a family, my mother said then, there is always something the matter. There is always something wrong for someone. And it simply is not possible to close a door on trouble or unhappiness. The same is probably true with animals, she said, and that goes for fishes and birds as well – especially, she said, robins.

Christmas was not all new books and games and dolls and dresses from the ready-made racks in the department store. It was not all food either. One Christmas an aunt came and cried for the whole day. We were given some things on a tray to eat upstairs in the bedroom with Françoise, our governess. And she, because of our bad manners and teasing, cried too. The next day my father, carrying her case, walked with her to the railway station. He travelled with her to London and took her to the boat train so that she could go home to Lausanne. Our governesses never stayed long and Françoise was the only one who attempted Christmas.

A person is never unhappy for ever, my mother said, and everyone has some unhappiness or grief to bear, and this shows more at Christmas because it is then that we are supposed to be happy. In a family it is often hard, in spite of or because of family love, to be happy, or to *know* that you are happy. People in families, she said, will not be each other's students and this is particularly the case during the season of goodwill.

'Just look,' my mother said, 'how the violinist does not part with a glance or with any small movement of her body and yet she lifts us up with her music. She lifts the listener clear of any weight which might be on the mind.' She said the trio, the *Archduke Trio*, was classical and it was remarkable that this music should be played in the restaurant of the department store where Father Christmas had foolishly released a hundred toy balloons filled with hydrogen, and there they were right up on the ceiling and all the little children were howling their heads off for these inaccessible balloons, the red, the yellow, the blue and the green. The pole the assistant brought was not nearly long enough. 'Never mind the balloons,' my mother said, 'listen to the music instead.' And sitting down at one of the little tables, she ordered tea and toasted teacakes and asked what time the fashion show would start.

To end, here is Parson Woodforde, just before Christmas, paying some of his bills:

> To Cobb the Rat Catcher, his annual stipend pd. one guinea
> To my Butcher, Henry Baker, his Bill for the year pd. forty one
>   pounds five shillings.
> To my Butchers Man, Billy Stouton Xmas Gift one shilling
> To Neighbour Howes's Wife for 5 chickens pd. two shillings and
>   six pence
> To Weston Ringers gave this morning two shillings and six pence
> To my Butchers Boy, Billy Stouton gave one shilling
> To my Blacksmiths Boy, Charles Spaule gave one shilling
> To my Malsters Man Js Barrett gave one shilling

Parson Woodforde and his niece Nancy after their enormous meals frequently dosed themselves with rhubarb and were obliged to sit up all night.

1   Parson Woodforde (1740–1803) was a country parson for most of his life in Somerset, England.

2   Some readers might be unfamiliar with the concept of the air bath. An air bath could safely be taken at any time, winter or summer. It was usually approached after deliberation but sometimes was spontaneous. A part of the body was exposed to the air. Quite simply, the clothing would be either drawn back or aside or rolled up or down. The popular choice for exposure would be the part of the limb between the knee and the ankle or from the elbow down. The foot would never be exposed. The air bath could be anything from one minute to fifteen minutes. It was considered to be beneficial. From memory, it was a custom brought to England by relatives from Vienna. In the Black Country (the industrial Midlands) a reaction on witnessing a 'group air bath in the park' was: 'Look you! Them forrin or what?'

One Christmas
Knitting

'Just you mind how you go on the horseway!'

Missis Robbins

Lately I've been thinking about my Anti Daisy and her peaceful death. She simply fell asleep in her chair by the fire and never woke up. My mother always said it was not right and that Anti Daisy should have drowned slowly with all her sins floating in front of her and herself weighted down with Grannie's silver spoons which were meant for me but which she, Anti Daisy, had refused to let me have as I was living through 'the shaded side of a well-known catastrophe' at the time and, because of this, she had as she said, cut me out of her will and would have nothing more to do with me, ever. My mother often said too that by rights the annuity which Anti Daisy bought herself with my father's share of some money should have contributed some pain to her death.

As far as we know Anti Daisy died a painless death.

But why wish pain on anyone.

The other day I received a letter from my mother in England. She had written,

I wish I could find words to tell you how much your father enjoyed your letters, how he looked forward to them and how he spent his time thinking about his replies, making little notes and asking me to remind him to tell you things.

At eighty-seven I wish he could have died in his sleep instead of that terrible road accident. They tell me he died at once but one of the policemen said he died in the ambulance. I hope he didn't see the tanker coming. He was coming home, there's half a letter he'd started to write to you, he'd chosen,

'Die mit Tränen säen, werden mit Freuden ernten —'

I'll send it later —

I can remember the place where he must have been crossing the road, it's the place where he always said to us, 'look both ways'.

Now it's where heaven will have come down to earth to gather him up. Because of his belief in something beyond this life that's how he will have seen it. For myself, I am not sure.

My mother is from Vienna. My father, after being in prison for refusing to fight in the Great War of 1914–18 went to Vienna with the Quaker Ambulance and Famine Relief. He brought his Viennese bride into the household from which his own father had earlier turned him out, in front of all the neighbours, because of the disgrace of being in prison.

'Your mother has such pretty arms,' my father often said. Without him now she has no one to defend her from the world and from herself. She gives everything away. I understand this thing about her because I am defenceless in the same way.

My correspondence with my father started when I was three months old. He did most of the writing then. I suppose I always felt somehow that he would live for ever.

He really showed me how to look at the world, how to feel the quality of the air, how to look at people and why they say the things they say and how they are saying them.

Sparks flew from under his boots when we walked into town in the evenings. He liked to look in at the lighted shop windows, he marvelled at the ways in which clothes, bread, bicycles, tools and toys could be made to look so desirable. In one shop cream satin cascaded, it was like a waterfall filling the shop and my father explained how he thought the shop woman would have had to come backwards spreading the material right up to the door, moving backwards out on to the pavement. She would then have had to lock up the shop without going back inside.

Back home he took off his boots and studied the soles of them carefully before placing them beside his chair.

'What shall I buy you for Christmas?' I asked my father.

'A lead pencil with a black point please,' he replied.

'What colour?'

'You choose,' he said.

'Red?'

'Yes, but remember the black point.'

And when he asked me what I wanted, 'I'd like some football boots,' I told him.

For the time being I have stopped working in my orchard to come indoors to try to write something from my childhood. It occurs to me that what I am about to write might be disgusting, not amusing and quite untrue. It's hard now to distinguish between the created and the remembered. I come from a household where people wept over Schubert Lieder one minute and tore up pictures of politicians the next. I'd like to be able to make a living picture from the half remembered by writing something from the inside and something from the outside. For me writing is an act of the will.

In this heat and this stillness all life seems withdrawn. This is the longed-for and needed solitude.

I don't cry in the loneliness now but there were times when I did.

Between autumn-berried hedgerows I cried in the middle of a road which seemed to be leading nowhere. Brown ploughed fields sloped in all directions, there were no houses, shops, trams and there were no people, only the rooks gathering, unconcerned, in the leafless trees at the side of an empty lifeless barn. The anxious looks and little words of comfort from the other two girls only brought more fear and I screamed till all three of us stood howling there. And then we made our way back through our tears to what was left of our first boarding-school Sunday afternoon.

I didn't understand then what made me cry. It was only much later that I could put into words something of the shock of discovering the loneliness and uncertainty which is so much a part of living.

The tears of childhood are frequent and children sometimes know why they are crying but hesitate to explain. So when Edith and Amy said to me later in the cloakroom, 'Why are you crying again?', I couldn't tell them it was because there was something about the changing light at the end of the autumn afternoon which reminded me of the time of day when my father would return, knock the carbide from his lamps on the doorstep and bring his bicycle into the safety of the scullery. How could I tell them of this longing for this particular time when he lifted his enamel plate off the hot saucepan and the smell of his pepper rose in the steam.

'It's my father and mother,' I whispered.

'Why what's wrong with them?' Edith asked.

'Oh,' I said, 'they have such dreadful fights.' I looked at my new wrist watch, 'It's just about now that my father comes home drunk and he beats my mother till she's black all over.'

Edith and Amy gazed at me with reverence. And I was so over-come with this new and interesting picture of my family life, I forgot for the time being this illness, this homesickness.

Later I learned more bitterly for myself this thing called home-sickness. But I knew something about it when I was little.

When I lay in bed, long ago at home, I could hear my mother's voice like a stream running as she talked up and down to my father. And every now and then my father's voice was like a boulder in the way of the stream, and for a moment the water swirled and paused and waited and then rushed on round the boulder and I heard my mother talking on, up and down.

I thought I heard my mother crying in the night, her long sighs followed my father creaking on bent legs along the hall.

'What for is Mammy crying?' I called to him. He crawled flick-ering across the ceiling crouching doubled on the wardrobe where there was a fox.

'It is nothing,' he said in his soft voice. 'Go to sleep. It is nothing, she is homesick that is all.' Flickering and prancing he moved up and down the walls big and little and big. The eyes of the fox were amber and full of tears, tiny gold chains fastened its little feet. My hand reached into the soft scented fur touching the slippery silk underneath.

'Go to sleep,' my father folded and unfolded. 'I'm the engine down the mine,' he said, 'I'm the shaft I'm the steam laundry now I'm a Yorkshire ham a cheese a Cheshire cheese a pork pie I'm a mouse in the iron and steel works I'm a needle and thread I'm a cart-wheel turning in the road turning over and over turning and turning I'm the horse the tired tired horse go to sleep go to sleep —'

I went in the dark after his candle had gone and fetched a cup of water. I took it to my mother.

'It's for your homesick,' I told her. 'Drink the water for your homesick.'

The tears of grown-up people seemed to come with such pain. Anti Daisy once sat a whole afternoon crying and my mother, not knowing enough English, tried to comfort her.

Anti Mote cried too. The police often called because of her. She stole the boards on which the tram conductors wrote numbers. These boards rested in slots.

'Very convenient,' Anti Mote said, 'for when I am getting off the tram.' She was brought home too for sunbathing naked in the East Park on cold grey November days. The English policemen wore their cloaks folded and pleated neatly over one shoulder, they had them to wrap round ladies who threw off all their clothes in public.

'Eat my little Duchess,' Anti Mote was on her knees beside my chair. She was knitting a wild cardigan. I turned my face away from the mess of egg, slimy brown, splashed over a silver tray.

'Eat my little Duchess!' she implored. 'It is only that I have scramble in mistaken for fryern, that is all. And in mistake I forget the plate!'

About Anti Mote's tears, she had deep furrows in both cheeks, and when she cried, she cried out of sight and she sounded like a man crying. She was homesick too my father said.

Like my mother Anti Mote was a baroness in her own right. They kept this shared misfortune a secret.

A few days before the move from Flowermead to Mount Pleasant my mother had a party. Her students brought their friends, they came in an old car with shingled heads and pink legs sticking out. They were from the technical college where my mother taught them enough German for their science exams, but she couldn't resist the poetry from her own language so they read Goethe and listened to Schubert with their scientific abstracts.

'*How do you feel when you marry your ideal,*' they sang, '*Ever so goosey goosey goosey.*' And they sang 'The Wedding of the Painted Doll'. My mother danced twirling her beads, strings of them, she danced kicking her feet out to the sides, heels up, toes down and turned in,

'*It's a holiday today! Today's the wedding of the painted doll,*' they sang. Together they all danced across the living room bending their knees and tapping their heads and knees and elbows. My mother had just had all her teeth out because of starving during the war and half starving before the war.

It was the fashion to have all new teeth then and to have the tonsils and the appendix removed. In some families these operations were given as presents at Christmas and birthdays.

In spite of having no teeth I could see by her eyes that my mother was enjoying her party.

They gathered round the piano and sang,

Am Brunnen vor dem Tore,
da steht ein Lindenbaum
ich träumt' in seinem Schatten
So manchen süssen Traum —

My father sat close by shading his eyes with one hand hiding his quiet tears.

I was learning the alphabet and was writing my own stories and poems in long lines of l's and f's and g's copying from a handwriting copybook into an old Boots diary. I loved the feel of the pencil on the smooth paper and as I filled the pages with the sloping letters I showed them to my father and he kissed them.

During the party Grandpa came in having walked all the way from Birmingham to Sutton Coldfield with hazelnuts in his boots. He reached into one boot and brought out some cracked nuts for the guests. To save expense he had carried a second-hand cot on his back. It was for Vera, the miner's child who was staying with us. A great many people were unemployed, it was very bad for the miners, their families had nothing to eat. It was the time of the hunger demonstrations before the great Hunger March which stretched all the way down to London.

My mother tried to feed Vera with a boiled egg but she didn't like it and the egg ran out of her mouth which was all square with her crying. My mother stuffed a toffee in with the egg but this only made it worse.

'Perhaps she's never had an egg,' one of the students said. Anti Mote said a little girl she knew wasted her eggs and I felt ashamed.

'Give her a piece,' the student suggested.

'I want a piecey too,' I said and then my sister wanted one and, in the end, Vera ate several.

As Vera had brought lice with her Grannie tied our heads up in rags dipped in paraffin and sat by us to stop us scratching.

Grandpa took my father on one side and told him if he tried to transplant the six cherry trees they would bleed to death.

All the same, on the day of the removal Grandpa walked over with his hazelnuts, his rupture and his shovel arriving at six in the morning and together they dug up the trees bandaging the roots and earth in sacks. I never saw any blood but, because of what Mount Pleasant was like, the trees died.

It was nearly Christmas and we were leaving. It was a world of jugs and basins and china chamber pots, of castor oil and mousetraps and earache and loose teeth and not knowing whether it would be Anti Mote coming into bed or Anti Daisy. And then there was the hot smell of the curling tongs and singed hair. It was a world of burned-out candles and gas mantles growing dim.

Grandpa always said it was only a matter of time before the horse manure, the great quantities of it, would block and even bury whole streets. Rapidly increasing motor traffic pushed aside the manure and repeatedly he began his conversations in an accusing voice, 'Do you know just how many people are run over and killed every week down there on the Stratford Road —'

When the removal men had finished my father asked, 'Where's Maud?' My mother and Anti Mote were to go in the van to arrive with the furniture. My sister and I were travelling with my father who drove a motor bike and side-car.

'She was picking a bunch of flowers off the front-room wall-paper,' my mother went through the empty house anxiously. But Anti Mote was nowhere to be found.

The removal was then held up by an official from the Tramways Department. A policeman was with him and Anti Mote, penitent but elated. She had for the last time outwitted the conductor on the number seven tram. In Mount Pleasant it was something called trolley buses and Anti Mote was looking forward to them.

'Don't you worry Mr Knight,' Missis Robbins, the neighbour woman said. She poured his tea for him. She gave us red jelly for our breakfast but she made us eat a piece with it.

'Just don't you worry Mr Knight,' she put his tea cup nearer to him.

'What for is Daddy crying?' I asked. Why should my father be crying these fast falling tears? He shaded his eyes with one hand as if to hide his tears. The other hand was clenched on the white table cloth.

Missis Robbins was banging with the iron, she tested it with her spit which flew sizzling across the kitchen. Why should Missis Robbins be telling him not to worry.

'What for is Daddy crying?' I asked. These mysterious tears. 'What for are we leaving Flowermead?' I asked.

'Eat your piecey there's a good girl,' Missis Robbins said. It was time to go.

'Just you mind how you go on the horseway!' Missis Robbins called from her gate and we were on the journey to Mount Pleasant.

In every place, however desolate, there will be some saving quality. Bricks, suddenly warm coloured, and corner stones made noble in an unexpected light from the passing and hesitant sun; perhaps a window catching tree tops in a distant park beyond steep roofs and smoking chimneys. Perhaps it is simply an undefined atmosphere of previous happiness caught and held in certain rooms.

To my mother there was nothing which could redeem the ugly house in Mount Pleasant.

'There is nothing pleasant here at all,' she said.

Grandpa had chosen the name Flowermead and he came there every few days to dig and plant. There was an apple tree, the six cherry trees, a pear tree, red and black currants, gooseberries, raspberries and roses, lawns and grassy banks and flower beds with Michaelmas daisies, larkspur, cornflowers and Canterbury bells. The garden of the new house was a narrow strip of slag from the coal mine. A smouldering pit mound was at the end of the street. Other pit mounds covered with coarse grass and coltsfoot were beyond, and behind them the high wall of the fever hospital. There was a bone and glue factory near and across the street were the brick kilns. Framed on the sky were the wheels and the shaft of the coal mine. The noise of the cage coming up or going down the shaft and the smell of the bone and glue accompanied every action. The heave and roar of the blast furnaces and the nightly glow across the sky became my night light and my cradle song.

Grandpa couldn't think of a name for this house so it was called Barclay after the Bank.

In Flowermead there was a water pump bringing strange draughts from a well deep in the earth. My father was pleased with the new house. Water flowed from taps.

'It's nearer for me for the Central School,' he said, 'and we're the first people to live in it!'

'That's why there are no shelves,' my mother said.

'But electricity!' my father switched the lights on and off.

'And stairs to clean!' my mother was unable to accept the shining invitation from the new linoleum.

'The woodwork's cheap,' Anti Daisy came cream cloched with Grannie to see the new house.

'But look at the grain of the wood,' my father opened and closed the doors.

There's knot holes,' Anti Daisy poked her finger through one in the pantry door. But Grandpa had arrived. To save the fare he'd walked with his hazelnuts, and his rupture and carrying two hens in a box.

'Come upstairs,' my father said to him, 'and see the W.C.'

Through the pantry-door knot hole lay another world, there was a lake of quiet milk, blue as dusk and fringed with the long fern fronds of carrot and celery, jewelled water drops hung sparkling in a cabbage and two apples promised a tub full of fruit.

It was Christmas Eve with frost flowers like lace curtains.

'Guess what I'm giving you for Christmas,' I said to my father.

'I hope it's a lead pencil?'

'Yes, Yes!'

'With a black point?'

'Yes. Now guess what colour it is.'

'Red?'

'Yes.' I couldn't wait to give him the pencil.

'I hope I'm getting some football boots,' I said to him.

'Nice little girls don't ever wear football boots,' Anti Daisy said.

My father suggested that Grannie and Anti Mote should have a little ride in the side-car. There was just room for them both.

'Come upstairs Grettell,' Anti Daisy never pronounced my mother's name properly. She wanted to show my mother the Christmas dolls. They had hair which could be combed, we overheard her telling, and little shoes and socks.

'I still want the boots,' I called up after them. My sister and I went out to look at the hens.

We found Grandpa lying across the cold grey slag, his neck was all bulged over his collar and a terrible noise came from him. I didn't know then that the noise was just his difficult breathing. In terror we rushed up the new stairs. Of course Anti Daisy and my mother had locked themselves in with the presents and wouldn't come out straight away.

Later we sat in the hearth with the dinner plates put to warm. Grandpa sat in the armchair, his freshly combed white hair looked like a bandage.

'Whatever made you have an attack out there!' Anti Daisy came in twitching her dress angrily. 'Whatever made you have an attack now!' she said to Grandpa. 'You frightened these two children,' she accused him. 'D'you hear me?' she shouted at him. 'You frightened the children!'

When Anti Daisy had gone back to the kitchen Grandpa shook his head slowly and tears rolled down to his white moustache.

These mysterious tears? I wanted to put my arms round his neck and kiss his wet cheek and tell him, 'Never mind. Never mind.' But I was afraid of him and shyly I sat there with my sister watching the old man weeping,

The Black Country was a mixture of coal mines, factories, chain shops and brickworks and little farms in green triangles huddled in the shadows of the slag heaps. Rows and rows of mean little houses gave way suddenly to hawthorn hedges and fields. Here, the air was suddenly fragrant.

Grannie enjoyed her side-car ride but couldn't understand why they had stopped in a place where there was no view.

'I seemed to be looking straight into the hedge,' she said. My father explained that the side-car had come off the motor bike and had come to rest in a ditch. While he was fixing it Anti Mote had disappeared.

'I expect Maud is walking home,' he said, 'it's not very far.' His face was white in the dusk when he looked for her up and down the unknown streets. I didn't know then, as I do now, that it seems that a child, a person, has to look both ways and to look along and follow roads which often seem to be going nowhere.

Anti Mote was a little late for the present giving. The living-room door flew open at last, a breath of cold air came,

'*Guten Tag! Grüss Gott und fröhliche Weihnachten*!' she kissed all the anxious faces. 'On the trolley buses,' she announced, 'they have them too! Very neat and nicely made from metal,' and from somewhere in her skirt she brought out the conductor's board from trolley bus eleven.

'*Die mit Tränen säen, werden mit Freuden ernten*,' my father read aloud, 'They that sow in tears shall reap in joy.'

Grandpa and Grannie said, 'Amen! Amen!'

There were no football boots for me. I did get them years later on my ninth birthday. That was in June, by the autumn my feet couldn't squeeze into them.

'I only had time,' Anti Mote said, 'for one Christmas knitting, it is for you!' She had knitted the cardigan for me. Unwillingly I put it on. She smiled happily.

'Is so wide and big,' she said, 'both children can wear it at the same time!'

Paper Children

Clara Schultz lying alone in a strange hotel bedroom was suddenly confronted by the most horrible thoughts. For a woman accustomed to the idea that she would live for ever, having lived, it seemed for ever, these thoughts were far from welcome. For instead of being concerned with her immortality they were, without doubt, gravely concerned about her own death.

Perhaps it was the long journey by air. She had travelled from Vienna, several hours in an aeroplane with the clock being altered relentlessly while her own body did not change so easily. She was on her way to her daughter. She had not seen her since she was a baby and now she was a grown woman, a stranger, married to a farmer. A man much younger than herself and from a background quite unknown to Clara and so somewhat despised by her. She confided nothing of this thought, rather she boasted of her daughter's marriage.

'I am going to visit Lisa, my daughter, you know,' she told her neighbour Irma Rosen. Sometimes they stopped to talk on the stairs in the apartment house in the Lehar Strasse and Clara would impress on Irma forcefully, 'My daughter is married to an Australian farmer and expecting her first child. All these years I have only a paper daughter and now my paper children, my daughter and son-in-law, they want me to come, they have invited me!' And Irma whose smooth face was like a pink sugar cake on the handworked lace collar of her dress nodded and smiled with admiration.

It was only when she was alone Clara despised the farmer husband, she was able to overlook completely that her despising was in reality a kind of fear of him and his piece of land.

'We are in a valley,' Lisa wrote to her mother. Clara tried to imagine the valley. She had in her mind a picture of a narrow green flower-splashed place with pine trees on the steep slopes above the clusters of painted wooden houses, like in the Alps, very gay and always in holiday mood. She tried to alter the picture because Lisa described tall trees with white bark and dry leaves which glittered in the bright sunshine, she wrote also of dust and corrugated iron and wire netting and something called weatherboard. Clara found it hard to imagine these things she had never seen.

No one can know when death will come or how. Alone in the hotel, Clara thought what if she should go blind before dying. She thought of her room at home, what if she had to grope in that familiar place unable to find her clothes, unable to see where her books and papers were. She lay with her eyes closed and tried to see her desk and her lamp and her silver inkwell, trying to place things in order in her mind so that she would find her way from one possession to the next.

What if she should go blind now here in this strange room, not knowing any other person here? In a sudden fear she pushed back the bedclothes and put her small white fat feet out of the bed and stood on the strange floor and groped like a blind person for the light switch.

'Lisa,' she said to her daughter gently so as not to startle the girl. Lisa turned, she had a very white face, she moved awkwardly and her face was small as if she was in pain. She was much younger than her mother expected her to be. Beside her was a little girl of about two years, she had fair hair cut square across a wan little forehead. The child had been crying.

'What a dear little girl,' Clara said as pleasantly as she knew how. 'What do you call her?'

'Sharon.'

'Cheri?'

'No Sharon.'

'Ach! What a pretty name. Come here to Grossmutti my darlink,' but the little girl hid behind the half open door.

'What a pretty place you have Lisa,' Clara tried. 'Pretty! Pretty!' She waved her short plump arm towards the desolate scene of the neglected hillside, cleared years ago, scraped and never planted; patches of prickly secondary growth littered the spaces between collapsing sheds and the tangles of wire netting where some fowls had lived their lives laying eggs.

The house, in decay, cried out for mercy, it was a place quite uncherished. The rust on the iron roof was like a disease, scabs of it scaled off and marked the verandah as if with an infection. Clara wondered why. Poverty perhaps or was Lisa feckless? Clara had no patience with a feckless woman. If they were poor, well she had money, and she would find out the best way to spend it. She wanted to help Lisa. All the tenderness stored up over the empty years was there to be poured forth, now on her child and her child's property.

'Have you hurt yourself Lisa?' Clara tried again, softly, gently, as if speaking in a dream. She had not expected a little girl. She knew only that her daughter was pregnant.

'Lisa wants me to be near when she has her baby, my paper children want me,' Clara told Irma on the stairs and Irma nodded her approval. 'So I burn up my ships as they say in English and go.' Clara had taken many big steps in her life but never such a final one as this one might be. Australia was such a long way off from Vienna, it almost could not exist it was so remote.

'They have fifty cows and sheeps and chickens.' Such space was not to be imagined on the dark stairs of the apartment. 'Such a long way!' Clara said 'But air travel, you know, makes the world so much smaller.'

'Have you hurt yourself Lisa?' Gently she approached the pale young woman who was her unknown daughter.

'Aw it's nuthin',' the girl replied. 'He threw me down the other night, I kept tellin' him "You're hurtin' my back!" but he took no notice. "You're hurtin' my back," I shouted at him!' She rubbed the end of her spine.

Clara flinched with a real hurt.

'Pete, this is my mother,' Lisa said as a short thick-set young man, very sunburned and bullet shaped came round the side of the house. He threw a bucket to his wife. 'Mother this is Pete.'

As they stood together the sun slid quickly into the scrub on the far hillside and long shadows raced one after the other across and along the sad valley. Clara had never seen such a pair of people and in such dreary hopeless surroundings. She felt so strange and so alone in the gathering darkness of the evening.

The little muscular husband shouted something at Lisa and marched off with hardly a look at his new mother-in-law. Clara couldn't help remembering the Gestapo and their friend, they thought he was their friend, the one who became a Gauleiter. That was it! Gauleiter Peter Gregory married to her daughter Lisa.

'This man is my father's friend,' proudly Clara had introduced the friend to her husband only to experience in a very short time a depth of betrayal and cruelty quite beyond her comprehension. Friends became enemies overnight. Lisa's husband somehow reminded Clara unexpectedly of those times.

'Have you something to put on your back?' Clara asked.

'Like what?' the girl looked partly amused and partly defiant.

'Menthol Camphor or something like that,' Clara felt the remoteness between them, a kind of wandering between experience and dreams. She moved her hand in a circular movement. 'Something to massage, you know.'

At first Lisa didn't understand, perhaps it was the unusual English her mother spoke, Clara repeated the suggestion slowly.

'Aw No! Had a ray lamp but he dropped it larst night! Threw it down most likely but he said he dropped it. "The lamp's died," he said. I thought I'd die laughin' but I was that mad at him reely I was!'

'Should we, perhaps, go indoors?' Clara was beginning to feel cold. The Gauleiter was coming back. 'I just have these few packages,' Clara indicated her luggage which was an untidy circle about her. But the young couple had gone into the cottage leaving her to deal with her baggage as well as she could.

Trying to hear some sort of sound she heard the voice of Gauleiter Peter Gregory shouting at his wife, her daughter Lisa, and she heard Lisa scream back at her husband. Voices and words she couldn't hear and understand properly from the doorway of the asbestos porch. She heard the husband push the wife so that she must have stumbled, she heard Lisa fall against a piece of furniture which also fell, a howl of pain from Lisa and the little child, Sharon, began to cry.

Clara entered the airless dishevelled room. Because of all she was carrying it was difficult, so many bundles. 'One cannot make such a journey without luggage,' Clara explained to Irma as, buried in packages, she said goodbye to her neighbour, 'Goodbye Irma. Goodbye for ever dear friend.'

Besides she had presents for Lisa and even something for that husband.

Lisa looked up almost with triumph at her mother.

'I'm seven months gone,' she said 'and he wouldn't care if he killed me!' The husband's sunburned face disappeared in the gloom of the dirty room.

'Oh,' Clara said pleasantly, 'she is too young to die and far too pretty.'

'Huh! me pretty!' Lisa scoffed and, awkwardly, because of the pain in her back, she eased herself into a chair.

'Who's young!' the husband muttered in the dark. Clara didn't know if he was sitting or standing. 'Well, we women must back each other up,' she said, wasting a smile. Whatever could she do about Lisa's pain.

Clara fumbled with the straps of her bag.

'Come Sharon, my pretty little one. See what your Grossmutti has brought for you all across the World.' The child stood whimpering as far from Clara as possible while the parents watched in silence.

And Clara was quite unable to unfasten the bag.

She had never been frightened of anything in her whole life. Dr Clara Schultz (she always used an abbreviation of her maiden name), Director of the Clinic for Women (Out Patients' Department), University Lecturer, wife of the Professor of Islamic Studies, he was also an outstanding scholar of Hebrew. Clara Margarethe Carolina, daughter of a Baroness, nothing frightened her, not even the things that frightened women, thunder and mice and cancer.

Even during the occupation she had been without fear. They were living on the outskirts of the city at that time. One afternoon she returned early from the clinic intending to prepare a lecture and she noticed there was a strange stillness in the garden. The proud bantam cock they had then was not crowing. He was nowhere in sight. Usually he strutted about, an intelligent brightly coloured little bird, and the afternoons were shattered by his voice as he crowed till dusk as if to keep the darkness of the night from coming too soon. The two hens, Cecilia and Gretchen, stood alone and disconsolate like two little pieces of white linen left by the laundress on the green grass.

Clara looked for the little rooster but was unable to find him. His disappearance was an omen.

Calmly Clara transferred money to Switzerland and at once, in spite of difficulties and personal grief, she arranged for her two-year-old baby daughter to be taken to safety while she remained to do her work.

A few days later she found the bantam cock, he was caught by one little leg in a twisted branch among the junipers and straggling rosemary at the end of the garden. He was hanging upside down dead. Something must have startled him Clara thought to make him fly up suddenly into such a tangled place. When she went indoors, missing her baby's voice so much, she found her husband hanging, dead, in his study. She remained unafraid. She knew her husband was unable to face the horror of persecution and the threat of complete loss of personal freedom. She understood his reasons. And she knew she was yearning over her baby but she went on, unafraid, with her work at the clinic. Every day, day after day, year after year, in her thick-lensed spectacles and her white coat she advised, corrected, comforted and cured, and, all the time, she was teaching too, passing on knowledge from experience.

But now, this fearless woman trembled as she tried to unfasten two leather straps because now years later, when all the horror was over for her, she was afraid of her daughter's marriage.

As Clara woke in the strange bedroom, it was only partly a relief. There was still this possibility of blindness before death, because of course she would die. Ultimately everyone did. For how long

would she be blind, if she became blind? Both her grandmothers
had lost their sight.

'But that was a cataract,' Clara told herself. 'Nowadays one can
have operation.'

Again in imagination, she blundered about her room at home
trying to find things, the treasures of her life. But alone and old she
was unable to manage.

And another thing. What if she should go deaf and not be able
to listen to Bach or Beethoven any more? She tried to remember
a phrase from the Beethoven A Minor String Quartet. The first
phrase, the first notes of caution and melancholy and the cascade of
cello. She tried to sing to herself but her voice cracked and she could
not remember the phrase. Suppose she should become deaf now at
this moment in this ugly hotel with no music near and no voices.
If she became deaf now she would never again be able to hear the
phrase and all the remaining time of her life be unable to recall it.

Again she put her small fat white feet out of the bed and stood
on the strange floor and began like a blind and deaf person to grope
for the light switch.

'Travelling does not suit everyone,' she told herself and she put
eau de Cologne on her forehead and leaving the light on, she took
her book, one she had written herself, *Some Elementary Contribu-
tions to Obstetrics and Gynaecology*, and began to read.

This time it really was Lisa, with joy in her heart Clara went towards
her. The real Lisa was much older and Clara saw at once that the pregnancy was full term. Lisa walked proudly because of the stoutness of
carrying the baby. Though Clara knew it was Lisa, she searched her
daughter's face for some family likeness. The white plump face was
strange however, framed in dark hair, cut short all round the head.
Mother and daughter could not have recognised each other.

'Oh Lisa you have a bad bruise on your forehead,' Clara gently put out a hand to soothe the bruise. Supposing this husband is the same as the other one, the thought spoiled the pleasure of the meeting.

'It's quite clear you are a doctor, Mother,' Lisa laughed. 'Really it's nothing! I banged my head on the shed door trying to get our cow to go inside.'

'One cow and I thought they had many,' Clara was a little disappointed but she did not show it. Instead she bravely looked at the valley. It was not deep like the wooded ravine in the Alps, not at all, the hills here were hardly hills at all. But the evening sun through the still trees made a changing light and shade of tranquillity, there was a deep rose blue in the evening sky which coloured the white bark and edged the tremulous glittering leaves with quiet mystery. Clara could smell the sharp fragrance of the earth, it was something she had not thought of though now she remembered it from Lisa's letters. All round them was loneliness.

'Where is your little girl?' Clara asked softly. Lisa's plain face was quite pleasant when she smiled, she had grey eyes which were full of light in the smile.

'Little girl? Little boy you mean! He's here,' she patted her apron comfortably. 'Not born yet. I wrote you the date. Remember?'

'Oh yes of course,' Clara adjusted her memory. 'Everyone at home is so pleased,' she began.

'Here's Peter,' Lisa said. 'Peter this is my mother,' Lisa said. 'Mother this is Peter.'

The husband came to his mother-in-law, he was younger than Lisa so much so that Clara was startled. He seemed like a boy, his face quite smooth and it was as if Lisa was old enough to be his mother.

Peter was trying to speak, patiently they waited, but the words when they came were unintelligible. His smile had the innocence of a little child.

'He wants to make you welcome,' Lisa explained. She took her husband's arm and pointed across the cleared and scraped yard to a small fowl pen made of wire netting. Beside the pen was a deep pit, the earth, freshly dug, heaped up all round it.

'GO AND GET THE EGGS!' she shouted at him. She took a few quick steps still holding his arm and marched him towards the hen house. 'QUICK! MARCH!' she shouted. Gauleiter Lisa Gregory. Clara shivered, the evening was cold already. Her own daughter had become a Gauleiter.

'QUICK! MARCH! ONE TWO! ONE TWO!' Lisa was a Führerin. The valley rang with her command. 'DIG THE PIT!'

The sun fell into the scrub and the tree tops in the middle distance between earth and sky became clusters of trembling blackness, silent offerings held up on thin brittle arms like starved people praying into the rose deep, blue swept sky.

Mother and daughter moved in the shadows to the door of the weatherboard and iron cottage.

'I am very strong, Mother,' Lisa said in a whisper and in the dusk Clara could see her strength, she saw too that her mouth was shining and cruel.

In the tiny house there was no light. Clara was tired and she wondered where they could sleep. In a corner a cot stood in readiness for the baby, there seemed no other beds or furniture at all.

'When my sons are born,' Lisa said in a low voice to her mother, 'it is to be the survival of the fittest!' She snapped her thick fingers. Clara had no reply. 'Only the strong and intelligent shall live,' Lisa said. 'I tell my husband to dig the pit. I have to. Perhaps it will be for him, we shall see. Every day he must dig the pit to have it ready. There will be no mercy.'

Clara reflected, in the past she had overlooked all this, she had taken no part in the crimes as they were committed but, ignoring them, she had continued with her work and because her work was essential no one had interfered. Clara reflected too that Lisa had never known real love, taken away to safety she had lost the most precious love of all. Clara took upon herself the burden of Lisa's cruelty now. She wanted to give Lisa this love, more than anything she wanted to overlook everything and help Lisa and love her. She wanted to open her purse to show Lisa before it was too dark that she had brought plenty of money and could spend whatever was necessary to build up a nice little farm. She wanted to tell Lisa she could buy more cows, electricity, sheds, pay for hired men to work, buy pigs, two hundred pigs if Lisa would like and drains to keep them hygienic. Whatever Lisa wanted she could have. She tried to tell her how much she wanted to help her. She tried to open her purse and Lisa stood very close and watched Clara in severe silence. The cottage was cold and quite bare, Clara longed to be warm and comfortable and she wanted to ask Lisa to unfasten her purse for her but was quite unable to speak, no words came though she moved her mouth as if trying to say something.

She had never been so stupid. Of course she would feel better in the morning. Women like Dr Clara Schultz simply did not fall ill on a journey. It was just the strange bed in the rather old-fashioned hotel. Tomorrow she would take her cold bath as usual and ask for yoghurt at breakfast and all she had to do then was to wait for Lisa and Peter.

The arrangement was that they were driving the two hundred miles to fetch her to their place. Of course it was natural to be a little curious. Lisa was only two years old when she was smuggled out of Vienna. The woman Lisa had become was a complete stranger, and so was the husband. Even their letters were strange, they wrote in English because Lisa had never learned to speak anything else.

Clara knew she would feel better when she had seen them. All these years she had longed to see Lisa, speak with her, hear her voice, touch her and lavish love and gifts on her. She still felt the sad tenderness of the moment when she had had to part with her baby all those years ago.

'Lisa, my bed is damp,' Clara said. 'The walls are so thin. I never expected it to be so cold.'

Lisa had been quite unable to imagine what her mother's visit would be like. In spite of the heat and her advanced pregnancy she cleaned the little room at the side of the house. She washed the louvres and made white muslin curtains. There was scarcely any furniture for the narrow room but Lisa made it as pretty as she could with their best things, her own dressing table and a little white-painted chair and Peter fetched a bed from his mother's place.

Lisa tried to look forward to the visit, she knew so little about her mother, an old lady now after a life of hard work as a doctor. Every year they threw away the battered Christmas parcel which always came late, sewn up in waterproofed calico. There seemed no place in the little farmhouse with its patterned linoleum and plastic lamp shades for an Adventskranz and beeswax candles. And the soggy little biscuits, heart shaped or cut out like stars, had no flavour. Besides they ate meat mostly and, though Peter liked sweet things, his choice of pudding was always tinned fruit with ice cream. The meaningless little green wreath with its tiny red and white plaster mushrooms and gilded pine cones only served to enhance the strangeness between them and this mother who was on her way to them.

Of course her mother was ill as soon as she arrived. She had not expected the nights to be so cold she explained and it was damp in the sleepout.

'My bed is damp,' she said to Lisa. So they moved her into the living room.

'No sooner does your mother arrive and the place is like a C-Class Hospital,' Peter said. He had to sit for his tea in the kitchen because Clara's bed took up most of the living room. She had all the pillows in the house and the little table beside her bed was covered with cups and glasses and spoons and bottles and packets of tablets.

'It is only a slight inflammation in my chest,' she assured Lisa. 'A few days of rest and warm and I will be quite well, you will see!'

Lisa worried that her mother was ill and unable to sleep. She tried to keep Peter friendly, but always a silent man, he became more so. She stood in the long damp grass outside the cowshed he had built with homemade concrete bricks, waiting for him at dusk, she wanted to speak to him alone, but he, knowing she was standing there, slowly went about his work and did not emerge.

From inside the asbestos house came Clara's voice. 'Lisa! Another hot water bottle please, my feet are so cold.'

Lisa could not face the days ahead with her mother there. She seemed suddenly to see all her husband's faults and the faults in his family. She had never before realised what a stupid woman Peter's mother, her mother-in-law, was. She felt she would not be able to endure the life she had. Years of this life lay before her. Fifteen miles to the nearest neighbour, her mother-in-law, and the small house, too hot in summer and so cold and damp once the rains came, and the drains Peter had made were so slow to soak away she never seemed able to get the sink empty. This baby would be the first of too many. Yet she had been glad, at her age, to find a husband at last and thought she would be proud and happy to bear a farmer a family of sons.

'A spoonful of honey in a glass of hot water is so much better for you!' Clara told them when they were drinking their tea. She disapproved of their meat too. She was a vegetarian herself and prepared salads with her own hands grating carrots and shredding cabbage for them.

Peter picked the dried prunes out of his dinner spoiling the design Clara had made on his plate.

'I'm not eating that!' he scraped his chair back on the linoleum and left the table.

'Oh Peter please!' Lisa implored, but he went out of the kitchen and Lisa heard him start up the utility with a tremendous roar.

'He will come back!' Clara said knowingly nodding her head.

'Come eat! Your little one needs for you to eat. After dinner I show you how to make elastic loop on your skirt,' she promised Lisa. 'Always I tell my patients, "an elastic loop, not this ugly pin!"' she tapped the big safety pin which fastened Lisa's gaping skirt. 'After dinner I show you how to make!' Lisa knew her mother was trying to comfort her but she could only listen to Peter driving down the track. He would drive the fifteen miles to his mother and she would, as usual, be standing between the stove and the kitchen table and would fry steak for him and make chips and tea and shake her head over Lisa and that foreign mother of hers.

She listened to the car and could hardly stop herself from crying.

Living, all three together became impossible and, after the birth of the baby, Lisa left Peter and went with her mother to live in town. Clara took a small flat in a suburb and they went for walks with the baby. Two women together in a strange place trying to admire meaningless flowers in other people's gardens.

Lisa tried to love her mother, she tried to understand something of her mother's life. She realised too that her mother had given up everything to come to her, but she missed Peter so dreadfully. The cascading voices of the magpies in the early mornings made her think as she woke that she was back on the farm, but instead of Peter's voice and the lowing of the cows there were cars on the road outside the flat. She missed the cows at milking time and the noise of the fowls. And in the afternoon she longed to be standing at the edge of the paddock where the long slanting rays of the sun lit up the tufted grass and the shadows of the coming evening crept from the edges of the Bush in the distance.

'Oh Liserl! Just look at this rose,' her mother bent over some other person's fence. 'Such a fragrance and a beautiful deep colour. Only smell this rose Lisa!' And then slowly, carrying the baby, on to the next garden to pause and admire where admiration fell lost on unknown paving stones and into unfamiliar leaves and flowers unpossessed by themselves. The loneliness of unpossession waited for them in the tiny flat where a kind of refugee life slowly unpacked itself, just a few things, the rest would remain for ever packed. Only now and then glimpses of forgotten times came to the surface, an unwanted garment or a photograph or an old letter reminding of the reasons why she had grown up in a strange land cared for by people who were not hers.

In the evenings they shaded the lamp with an old woollen cardigan so that the light should not disturb the baby and they sat together. Lisa listened to the cars passing, in her homelessness she wished that one of the cars would stop, because it was Peter's. More than anything she wished Peter would come. Tears filled her eyes and she turned her head so that her mother should not see.

'Oh Peter!' Lisa woke in the car, 'I was having such an awful dream!' She sat up close to the warmth of her husband feeling the comfort of his presence and responsibility.

'Oh! It was so awful!'

She loved Peter, she loved him when he was driving, especially at night. She looked at his clear brow and at the strong shape of his chin. He softly dropped a kiss on her hair and the car devoured the dark road.

'You'll feel better when you actually meet her,' he said. 'It's because you don't know her. Neither of us do!'

Lisa agreed and sat in safety beside her husband as they continued the long journey.

Clara was able to identify Lisa at once. She had to ask to have the white sheet pulled right down in order to make the identification. Lisa had two tiny deep scars like dimples one on the inside of each thigh.

'She was born with a pyloric stenosis,' Clara explained softly. 'Projectile vomiting you know?' The scars, she explained, were from the insertion of tiny tubes.

'Subcutaneous feeding, it was done often in those days,' she made a little gesture of helplessness, an apology for an old-fashioned method.

In the mortuary they were very kind and helpful to the old lady who had travelled so far alone and then had to have this terrible shock.

Apparently the car failed to take a bend and they were plunged two hundred feet off the road into the Bush. Death would have been instantaneous, the bodies were flung far apart, the car rolled. They tried to tell her.

Clara brushed aside the clichés of explanation. She asked her question with a professional directness.

'What time did it happen?' she wanted to know. She had been sitting for some time crouched in a large armchair, for some hours after her yoghurt, wondering if she could leave the appointed meeting place. Outside it was raining.

'Should I make a short rain walk?' she asked herself. And several times she nearly left the chair and then thought, 'But no, any moment they come and I am not here!'

A few people came into the vestibule of the hotel and she looked at them through palm fronds and ferns, surreptitiously refreshing herself with eau de Cologne, wondering, hopeful. Every now and then she leaned forward to peer, to see if this was Lisa at last, and every time she sat back as the person went out again. Perhaps she was a little relieved every time she was left alone. She adjusted her wiglet.

Back home in Vienna she was never at a loss as to what to do. Retirement gave her leisure but her time was always filled. She never sat for long hours in an armchair. Back home she could have telephoned her broker or arranged with her dentist to have something expensive done to a tooth.

'Time? It's hard to say exactly,' they said. 'A passing motorist saw the car upside down against a tree at about five o'clock and reported the accident immediately.'

There were only the two bodies in the mortuary. Beneath the white sheets they looked small in death. Dr Clara Schultz was well acquainted with death, the final diagnosis was the greater part of her life's work. And wasn't it after all she herself who, with her own hands, cut the dressing-gown cord from her own husband's neck. She had to put a stool on his desk in order to reach as she was such a short person, and furthermore, his neck had swollen, blue, over the cord making the task more difficult.

They supported the old lady with kind hands and offered her a glass of water as she looked at the two pale strangers lying locked in the discolouration of injury and haemorrhage and the deep stillness of death.

Clara looked at her daughter and at her son-in-law and was unable to know them. She would never be able to know them now.

'I have a photograph, and I have letters,' she said. 'They were my paper children you know.' She tried to draw from the pocket of her travelling jacket the little leather folder which she took with her everywhere.

In the folder was a photograph of them standing, blurred because of a light leak in the camera, on a track which curved by a tree. And on the tree was nailed a small board with their name on it in white paint. Behind the unknown people and the painted board was a mysterious background of pasture and trees and the light and shade of their land. She pulled at the folder but was unable to pull it from her pocket.

Not being able to speak with them and know them was like being unable ever again to hear the phrase of Beethoven, the cascade of cello. It was like being blind and deaf for the rest of her life and she would not be able to recall anything.

Dr Clara had never wept about anything but now tears slowly forced themselves from under her eyelids.

'My daughter, Lisa you know, was pregnant,' she managed to say at last. 'I see she is bandaged. Does this mean?'

'Yes yes,' they explained gently, 'That is right. Owing to the nature of the accident and the speed with which it was reported they were able to save the baby. A little girl, her condition is satisfactory. It was a miracle.'

Dr Clara nodded. In spite of the tears she was smiling. As well as knowing about death she understood miracles.

As soon as it was decently possible she would ring for the chamber-maid and ask for a glass of hot water. Of course she wasn't blind or deaf and no one had come in with any news of an accident. She was only a little upset with travelling. Her fear of the failure of her body was only the uneasiness of stomach cramp and the result of bad sleep. She would have her cold bath early and then only a very short time to wait after that. Country people had to consider their stock, that was why they were driving overnight to fetch her. It might be a good idea to start getting up now, it would never do to keep them waiting. She put her fat white feet out of the bed and walked across the strange floor to ring the bell. It was a good idea to get up straight away because the telephone was ringing. Dr Clara, in the old days was used to the telephone in the night. Often she dressed herself with one hand and listened to the Clinic Sister describing the intervals between the labour pains and the position of the baby's head. A little breathless, that was all, she sat on the chair beside her telephone, breathless just with getting up too quickly.

'Dr Clara Schultz,' she said and she thought she heard a faint voice murmur.

'Wait one moment please. Long distance.' And then a fainter sound like a tiny buzzing as if voices were coming from one remote pole to another across continents and under oceans as if a message was trying to come by invisible wires and cables from the other side of the world. Clara waited holding the silent telephone. 'Clara Schultz here,' she said alone in the dark emptiness of her apartment for of course she had sold all her furniture.

'I have burn up my ships,' she told Irma. 'Clara Schultz here,' her voice sounded strange and she strained into the silence of the telephone trying to hear the other voice, the message, her heart beat more quickly, the beating of her heart seemed to prevent her listening to the silence of the telephone.

'Lisa!' she said, 'Is it you Lisa?'

But there was no sound in the telephone, for a long time, just the silence of nothing from the telephone. 'Lisa speak!' But there was no voice.

Clara longed to hear her daughter's voice, of course the voice could not be the same now as the laughter and incoherent chatter of the little two-year-old. Now as an old woman, holding a dead telephone she remembered with a kind of bitterness that she sent away her little girl and continued her work at the clinic paying no attention to the evil cruelty of war. She knew she was overlooking what was happening to people but chose to concern herself only with the menstrual cycle and the arched white thighs of women in labour.

'It's a means to an end,' she said softly to her frightened patients when they cried out. 'Everything will be all right, it's a means to an end,' she comforted them.

Clara knew she had neglected to think of the end. Now she wanted, more than anything, to hear Lisa speak. But there was no sound on the telephone. She went slowly out on to the dark stairs of the apartment house. On the second landing she met her neighbour.

'Irma is that you?'

'Clara!'

'Irma you are quite unchanged.'

Irma's pink sugar cake face sat smiling on the lace collar which was like a doily. 'Why should I change?' Irma asked.

Clara took Irma's hand, grateful to find her friend. 'Only think, Irma,' she said, 'I am bringing home my daughter's baby!' she laughed softly to Irma. 'My paper children had a baby daughter,' she said, 'I shall call her Lisa.'

When Lisa and Peter arrived at the hotel they were unable to understand how it was that Clara must have been crying and laughing when she died.

Irma Rosen tried to explain to them as well as she could with her little English, and of course she was very tired with making the long journey by air at such short notice.

'When I find her you know, outside my door,' Irma said. 'I

know, as her friend, I must come to you myself to tell. On her face this lovely smile and her face quite wet as if she cry in her heart! While she is smiling.'

They were as if encapsulated in the strange little meeting in the hotel vestibule. Lisa tried to think of words to say to this neat little old lady, her mother's friend. But Irma spoke again. 'Your mother is my friend,' she said, 'Always she speak of you. Her paper children and she so proud to be preparing to come to you. She would want me to tell you. Now I suppose I go back. Your mother say always "But air travel, you know, makes the world so much smaller." Is true of course, but a long way all the same!' She smiled and nodded, pink, on her lace collar. 'Sorry my Enklisch iss not good!' she apologised. 'Oh you speak beautifully,' Lisa was glad to be able to say something. 'Really your English is very good,' Lisa shouted a little as if to make it easier for Irma to understand her.

The young couple wanted to thank Irma and look after her but as Lisa's labour pains had started during the long journey, Peter had to drive her straight to the hospital.

Bathroom Dance

When I try on one of the nurse's caps my friend Helen nearly dies.

'Oh!' she cries, 'take it off! I'll die! Oh if you could see yourself. Oh!' she screams and Miss Besser looks at me with six years of reproach stored in the look.

We are all sewing Helen's uniform in the Domestic Science room. Three pin-striped dresses with long sleeves, buttoned from the wrist to the elbow, double tucks and innumerable button holes; fourteen white aprons and fourteen little caps which have to be rubbed along the seam with a wet toothbrush before the tapes can be drawn up to make those neat little pleats at the back. Helen looks so sweet in hers. I can't help wishing, when I see myself in the cap, that I am not going to do nursing after all.

Helen ordered her material before persuading me to go to the hospital with her. So, when I order mine it is too late to have my uniform made by the class. It is the end of term, the end of our last year at school. My material is sent home.

Mister Jackson tells us, in the last Sunday evening meeting, that he wants the deepest responsibility for standards and judgements in his pupils, especially those who are about to leave the happy family which is how he likes to think of his school. We must not, he says, believe in doing just what we please. We must always believe in the nourishment of the inner life and in the loving discipline of personal relationships. We must always be concerned with the relentless search for truth at whatever cost to tradition and externals. I leave school carrying his inspiration and his cosiness with me. For some reason I keep thinking about and remembering something about the reed bending and surviving and the sturdy oak blown down.

My mother says the stuff is pillow ticking. She feels there is nothing refined about nursing. The arrival of the striped material has upset her. She says she has other things in mind for me, travelling on the Continent, Europe, she says, studying art and ancient buildings and music.

'But there's a war on,' I say.

'Oh well, after the war.'

She can see my mind is made up and she is sad and cross for some days. The parcel, with one corner torn open, lies in the hall. She is comforted by the arrival of a letter from the Matron saying that all probationer nurses are required to bring warm sensible knickers. She feels the Matron must be a very nice person after all and she has my uniform made for me in a shop and pays extra to have it done quickly.

Helen's mother invites me to spend a few days with Helen before we go to St Cuthberts.

The tiny rooms in Helen's home are full of sunshine. There are bright-yellow curtains gently fluttering at the open windows. The garden is full of summer flowers, roses and lupins and delphiniums, light blue and dark blue. The front of the house is covered with a trellis of flowers, some kind of wisteria which is sweetly fragrant at dusk.

Helen's mother is small and quiet and kind. She is anxious and always concerned. She puts laxatives in the puddings she makes.

I like Helen's house and garden, it is peaceful there and I would like to be there all the time but Helen wants to do other things. She is terribly in love with someone called David. Everything is David these few days. We spend a great deal of time outside a milkbar on the corner near David's house or walking endlessly in the streets where he is likely to go. No one, except me, knows of this great love. Because I am a visitor in the house I try to be agreeable. And I try to make an effort to understand intense looks from Helen, mysterious frowns, raised eyebrows, head shakings or noddings and flustered alterations about arrangements as well as I can.

'I can't think what is the matter with Helen,' Mrs Ferguson says softly one evening when Helen rushes from the room to answer the telephone in case it should be David. We are putting up the blackout screens which Mrs Ferguson has made skilfully to go behind the cheerful yellow curtains every night. 'I suppose she is excited about her career,' she says in her quiet voice, picking up a little table which was in Helen's way.

Everyone is so keen on careers for us. Mister Jackson, at school, was always reading aloud from letters sent by old boys and girls who are having careers, poultry farming, running boys' clubs and digging with the unemployed. He liked the envelopes to match the paper, he said, and sometimes he held up both for us all to see.

Helen is desperate to see David before we leave. We go to all the services at his mother's church and to her Bible class where she makes us hand round plates of rock cakes to the Old Folk between the lantern slides. But there is no David. Helen writes him a postcard with a silly passionate message. During the night she cries and cries and says it is awful being so madly in love and will I pretend I have sent the postcard. Of course I say I won't. Helen begs me, she keeps on begging, saying that she lives in the neighbourhood and everyone knows her and will talk about her. She starts to howl and I am afraid Mrs Ferguson will hear and, in the end, I tell her, 'All right, if you really want me to.'

In the morning I write another card saying that I am sorry about the stupid card which I have sent and I show it to Helen, saying, 'We'll need to wash our hair before we go.'

'I'll go up first,' she says. While she is in the bathroom using up all the hot water, I add a few words to my postcard, a silly passionate message, and I put Helen's name on it because of being tired and confused with the bad night we had. I go out and post it before she comes down with her hair all done up in a towel, the way she always does.

Mrs Ferguson comes up to London with us when we set off for St Cuthberts. Helen has to dash back to the house twice, once for her camera and the second time for her raincoat. I wait with Mrs Ferguson on the corner and she points out to me the window in the County Hospital where her husband died the year before. Her blue eyes are the saddest eyes I have ever seen. I say I am sorry about Mr Ferguson's death, but because of the uneasiness of the journey and the place where we are going, I know that I am not really concerned about her sorrow. Ashamed, I turn away from her.

Helen comes rushing up the hill, she has slammed the front door, she says, forgetting that she put the key on the kitchen table and will her mother manage to climb through the pantry window in the dark and whatever are we waiting for when we have only a few minutes to get to the train.

David, unseen, goes about his unseen life in the narrow suburb of little streets and houses. Helen seems to forget him easily, straight away.

Just as we are sitting down to lunch there is an air-raid warning. It is terrible to have to leave the plates of food which have been placed in front of us. Mrs Ferguson has some paper bags in her handbag.

'Mother!' You can't!' Helen's face is red and angry. Mrs Ferguson, ignoring her, slides the salads and the bread and butter into the bags. We have to stand for two hours in the air-raid shelter. It is very noisy the A.R.P. wardens say and they will not let us leave. It is too crowded for us to eat in there and, in any case, you can't eat when you are frightened.

Later, in the next train, we have to stand all the way because the whole train is filled with the army. Big bodies, big rosy faces, thick rough greatcoats, kitbags, boots and cigarette smoke wherever we look. We stand swaying in the corridor pressed and squeezed by people passing, still looking for somewhere to sit. We can't eat there either. We throw the sad bags, beetroot soaked, out onto the railway lines.

I feel sick as soon as we go into the main hall at St Cuthberts. It is the hospital smell and the smell of the bread and butter we try to eat in the nurses' dining room. Helen tries to pour two cups of tea but the tea is all gone. The teapot has a bitter smell of emptiness.

Upstairs in Helen's room on the Peace corridor as it is called because it is over the chapel, we put on our uniforms and she screams with laughter at the sight of me in my cap.

'Oh, you look just like you did at school,' she can't stop laughing. How can she laugh like this when we are so late. For wartime security the railway station names have been removed and, though we were counting the stops, we made a mistake and went past our station and had to wait for a bus which would bring us back.

'Lend me a safety pin,' I say, 'one of my buttons has broken in half.' Helen, with a mouthful of hair grips, busy with her own cap, shakes her head. I go back along the corridor to my own room. It is melancholy in there, dark, because a piece of black-out material has been pinned over the window and is only partly looped up. The afternoon sun of autumn is sad too when I peer out of the bit of window and see the long slanting shadows lying across unfamiliar fields and roads leading to unknown places.

My school trunk, in my room before me, is a kind of betrayal. When I open it books and shoes and clothes spill out. Some of my pressed wildflowers have come unstuck and I put them back between the pages remembering the sweet, wet grass near the school where we searched for flowers. I seem to see clearly shining long fingers pulling stalks and holding bunches. Saxifrage, campion, vetch, ragged robin, star of Bethlehem, wild strawberry and sorrel. Quickly I tidy the flowers – violet, buttercup, kingcup, cowslip, coltsfoot, wood anemone, shepherd's purse, lady's slipper, jack in the pulpit and bryony . . .

'No Christian names on duty please,' staff nurse Sharpe says, so, after six years in the same dormitory, Helen and I make a great effort. Ferguson – Wright, Wright – Ferguson.

'Have you finished with the floor mop – Ferguson?'

'Oh, you have it first – Wright.'

'Oh! No! by all means, after you Ferguson.'

'No, after you Wright.'

Staff nurse Sharpe turns her eyes up to the ceiling so that only the whites show. She puts her watch on the window sill saying, 'Quarter of an hour to get those baths, basins and toilets really clean and the floors done too. So hurry!'

'No Christian names on duty,' we remind each other.

We never sleep in our rooms on the Peace corridor. Every night we have to carry out blankets down to the basement where we sleep on straw mattresses. It is supposed to be safe there in air raids. There is no air and the water pipes make noises all night. As soon as I am able to fall asleep Night Sister Bean is banging with the end of her torch saying, 'Five-thirty a.m. nurses, five-thirty a.m.' And it is time to take up our blankets and carry them back upstairs to our rooms.

I am working with Helen in the children's ward. Because half the hospital is full of soldiers the ward is very crowded. There are sixty children; there is always someone laughing and someone crying. I am too slow. My sleeves are always rolled up when they should be rolled down and buttoned into the cuffs. When my sleeves are down and buttoned it seems they have to be rolled up again at once. I can never remember the names of the children and what they have wrong with them.

The weeks go by and I play my secret game of comparisons as I played it at school. On the Peace corridor are some very pretty nurses. They are always washing each other's hair and hanging their delicate underclothes to dry in the bathroom. In the scented steamy atmosphere I can't help comparing their clothes with mine and their faces and bodies with mine. Every time I am always worse than they are and they all look so much more attractive in their uniforms, especially the cap suits them well. Even their fingernails are better than mine.

'Nurse Wright!' Night Sister Bean calls my name at breakfast.

'Yes Sister.' I stand up as I have seen the others do.

'Matron's office nine a.m.,' she says and goes on calling the register.

I am worried about my appointment with the Matron. Something must be wrong.

'What did Matron want?' Ferguson is waiting for me when I go to the ward to fetch my gas mask and my helmet. I am anxious not to lose these as I am responsible for them and will have to give them back if I leave the hospital or if the war should come to an end.

'What did Matron want?' Ferguson repeats her question, giving me time to think.

'Oh it is nothing much,' I reply.

'Oh come on! What did she want you for? Are you in trouble?' she asks hopefully.

'Oh no, it's nothing much at all.' I wave my gas mask. 'If you must know she wanted to tell me that she is very pleased with my work and she'll be very surprised if I don't win the gold medal.' Ferguson stares at me, her mouth wide open, while I collect my clean aprons. She does not notice that one of them is hers. It will give me an extra one for the week. I go to the office to tell the ward sister that I have been transferred to the theatre.

> *Had I the heavens' embroidered cloths,*
> *Enwrought with golden and silver light,*

O'Connor, the theatre staff nurse, is singing. She has an Irish accent and a mellow voice. I would like to tell her I know this poem too.

> *The blue and the dim and the dark cloths*
> *Of night and light and the half light,*

In the theatre they are all intimate. They have well-bred voices and ways of speaking. They look healthy and well poised and behave with the ease of movement and gesture which comes from years of good breeding. They are a little circle in which I am not included. I do not try to be. I wish every day, though, that I could be a part of their reference and their joke.

In a fog of the incomprehensible and the obscure I strive, more stupid than I have ever been in my life, to anticipate the needs of the theatre sister whose small, hard eyes glitter at me above her white cotton mask. I rush off for the jaconet.

'Why didn't you look at the table?' I piece together her angry masked hiss as I stand offering a carefully opened and held sterilised drum. One frightened glance at the operating table tells me it is catgut she asked for.

'Boil up the trolley,' the careless instruction in the soft Irish voice floats towards me at the end of the long morning. Everything is on the instrument trolley.

'Why ever didn't you put the doctors' soap back on the sink first?' The theatre is awash with boiled-over soap suds. Staff nurse O'Connor, lazily amused, is just scornful enough. 'And,' she says, 'what in God's Holy Name is this?' She fishes from the steriliser a doll-sized jumper. She holds it up in the long-handled forceps. 'I see trouble ahead,' she warns, 'better not let sister see this.' It is the chief surgeon's real Jaeger woollen vest. He wears it to operate. He has only two and is very particular about them. I have discovered already that sister is afraid of the chief surgeon, consequently I need to be afraid of her. The smell of boiled soap and wool is terrible and it takes me the whole afternoon to clear up.

Theatre sister and staff nurse O'Connor, always in masks, exchange glances of immediate understanding. They, when not in masks, have loud voices and laugh. They talk a great deal about horses and dogs and about Mummy and Daddy. They are quite shameless in all this Mummy and Daddy talk.

The X-ray staff are even more well-bred. They never wear uniform and they sing and laugh and come into the theatre in whatever they happen to be wearing – backless dinner dresses, tennis shorts or their night gowns. All the time they have a sleepy desirable look of mingled charm and efficiency. War-time shortages of chocolate and other foodstuffs and restrictions on movement, not going up to London at night for instance, do not seem to affect them. They are always called by pet names, Diamond and Snorter. Diamond is the pretty one, she has a mop of curls and little white teeth in a tiny rosebud mouth. Snorter is horsey. She wears trousers and little yellow waist coats. She always has a cigarette dangling from her bottom lip.

I can't compare myself with these people at all. They never speak to me except to ask me to fetch something. Even Mr Potter, the anaesthetist who seems kind and has a fatherly voice, never looks in my direction. He says, holding out his syringe, 'Evipan' or 'Pentothal', and talks to the others. Something about his voice, every day, reminds me of a quality in my father's voice; it makes me wish to be back at home. There is something hopeless in being hopeful that one person can actually match and replace another. It is not possible.

Sometimes Mr Potter tells a joke to the others and I do not know whether I should join in the laugh or not.

I like Snorter's clothes and wish that I had some like them. I possess a three-quarter-length oatmeal coat with padded shoulders and gilt buttons which my mother thinks is elegant and useful as it will go with everything. It is so ugly it does not matter what I wear it with. The blue skirt I have is too long, the material is heavy, it sags and makes me tired.

'Not with brown shoes!' Ferguson shakes her head.

It is my day off and I am in her room. The emptiness of the lonely day stretches ahead of me. It is true that the blue skirt and the brown shoes, they are all I have, do look terrible together.

Ferguson and her new friend, Carson, are going out to meet some soldiers to go on something called a pub crawl. Ferguson, I know, has never had anything stronger than ginger beer to drink in her life. I am watching her get ready. She has frizzed her hair all across her baby round forehead. I can't help admiring her, the blaze of lipstick alters her completely.

Carson comes in balancing on very high-heeled shoes. She has on a halo hat with a cheeky little veil and some bright-pink silk stockings.

'What lovely pink stockings!' I say to please her.

'Salmon, please,' Carson says haughtily. Her hair is curled too and she is plastered all over with ornaments, brooches, necklaces, rings and lipstick, a different colour from Ferguson's. Ferguson looks bare and chubby and schoolgirlish next to Carson.

Both of them are about to go when I suddenly feel I can't face the whole day alone.

'It's my day off too,' I say, 'and I don't know where to go.'

Ferguson pauses in the doorway.

'Well, why don't you come with us,' Carson says. Both of them look at me.

'The trouble is, Wright,' Carson says kindly, 'the trouble is that you've got no sex appeal.'

After they have gone I sit in Ferguson's room for a long time staring at myself in her mirror to see if it shows badly that I have no sex appeal.

I dream my name is Chevalier and I search for my name on the typed lists on the green baize notice boards. The examination results are out. I search for my name in the middle of the names and only find it later at the top.

My name, not the Chevalier of the dream, but my own name is at the top of the lists when they appear.

I work hard in all my free time at the lecture notes and at the essays 'Ward Routine', 'Nursing as a Career', 'Some Aspects of the History of Nursing' and 'The Nurse and her Patient'.

The one on ward routine pleases me most. As I write the essay, the staff and the patients and the wards of St Cuthberts seem to unfold about me and I begin to understand what I am trying to do in this hospital. I rewrite the essay collecting the complete working of a hospital ward into two sheets of paper. When it is read aloud to the other nurses, Ferguson stares at me and does not take her eyes off me all through the nursing lecture which follows.

I learn every bone and muscle in the body and all the muscle attachments and all the systems of the body. I begin to understand the destruction of disease and the construction of cure. I find I can use phrases suddenly in speech or on paper which give a correct answer. Formulae for digestion or respiration or for the action of drugs. Words and phrases like gaseous interchange and internal combustion roll from my pen and the name at the top of the lists continues to be mine.

'Don't tell me you'll be top in invalid cookery too!' Ferguson says and she reminds me of the white sauce I made at school which was said to have blocked up the drains for two days. She goes on to remind me how my pastry board, put up at the window to dry, was the one which fell on the headmaster's wife while she was weeding in the garden below, breaking her glasses and altering the shape of her nose forever.

My invalid carrot is the prettiest of them all. The examiner gives me the highest mark.

'But it's not even cooked properly!' Ferguson is outraged when she tastes it afterwards. She says the sauce is disgusting.

'Oh well you can't expect the examiner to actually eat all the things she is marking,' I say.

Ferguson has indigestion, she is very uncomfortable all evening because, in the greedy big taste, she has nearly the whole carrot.

It is the custom, apparently, at St Cuthberts to move the nurses from one corridor to another. I am given a larger room in a corridor called Industry. It is over the kitchens and is noisy and smells of burning saucepans. This room has a big tall window. I move my bed under the window and, dressed in my school jersey, I lie on the bed for as long as possible to feel the fresh cold air on my face before going down to the basement for the night. Some evenings I fall into a deep and refreshing sleep obediently waking up, when called, to go down to the doubtful safety below.

Every day, after the operations, I go round the theatre with a pail of hot soapy water cleaning everything. There is an orderly peacefulness in the quiet white tranquillity which seems, every afternoon, to follow the strained, bloodstained mornings.

In my new room I copy out my lecture notes:

. . . infection follows the line of least resistance . . .

and read my school poetry book:

Through the thick corn the scarlet poppies peep,
And round green roots and yellowing stalks I see
Pale pink convolvulus in tendrils creep;
And air-swept lindens yield
Their scent . . .

I am not able to put out of my mind the eyes of a man who is asleep but unable to close his eyes. The putrid smell of wounded flesh comes with me to my room and I hear, all the time, the sounds of bone surgery and the troubled respiration which accompanies the lengthy periods of deep anaesthetic . . .

Oft thou hast given them store
Of flowers – the frail leaf'd, white anemony,
Dark blue bells drench'd with dews of summer eves
And purple orchises with spotted leaves . . .

. . . in the theatre recovery ward there are fifteen amputations, seven above the knee and eight below. The beds are made in two halves so that the padded stumps can be watched. Every bed has its own bell and tourniquet . . .

St Cuthberts is only a drop in the ocean; staff nurse O'Connor did not address the remark to me, I overheard it.

Next to my room is a large room which has been converted into a bathroom. The dividing wall is a wooden partition. The water pipes make a lot of noise and people like to sing there, usually something from an opera.

One night I wake from my evening-stolen sleep hearing two voices talking in the bathroom. It is dark in my room; I can see some light from the bathroom through a knothole high up in the partition. The voices belong to Diamond and Snorter. This is strange because they live somewhere outside the hospital and would not need to use that bathroom. It is not a comfortable place at all, very cold, with a big old bath awkwardly in the middle of the rough floor.

Diamond and Snorter are singing and making a lot of noise, laughing and shrieking above the rushing water. Singing:

> *Give me thy hand O Fairest*
> *   la la la la la la la,*
> *I would and yet I would not*

laughter and the huge bath obviously being filled to the brim.

> *Our lives would be all pleasure*
> *   tra la la la la la la*
> *   tra la la la la la la*
> *   tum pe te tum*
> *   tum pe te tum*

'That was some party was it not!'

'Rather!' Their rich voices richer over the water.

I stand up on my bed and peer through the hole which is about the size of an egg. I have never looked through before, though have heard lots of baths and songs. I have never heard Diamond and Snorter in there before – if it is them.

It is Diamond and Snorter and they are naturally quite naked. There is nothing unusual about their bodies. Their clothes, party clothes, are all in little heaps on the floor. They, the women not the clothes, are holding hands, their arms held up gracefully. They are stepping up towards each other and away again. They have stopped singing and are nodding and smiling and turning to the left and to the right, and, then, with sedate little steps, skipping slowly round and round. It is a dance, a little dance for two people, a minuet, graceful, strange and remote. In the steam the naked bodies are like a pair of sea birds engaged in mating display. They appear and disappear as if seen through a white sea mist on some far off shore.

The dance quickens. It is more serious. Each pulls the other more fiercely, letting go suddenly, laughing and then not laughing. Dancing still, now serious now amusing. To and fro, together, back and forth and together and round and round they skip and dance. Then, all at once, they drop hands and clasp each other close, as if in a private ballroom, and quick step a foxtrot all round the bathroom.

It is not an ugly dance, it is rhythmic and ridiculous. Their thighs and buttocks shake and tremble and Snorter's hair has come undone and is hanging about her large red ears in wispy strands.

The dance over, they climb into the deep hot bath and tenderly wash each other.

The little dance, the bathroom dance, gives me an entirely new outlook. I can't wait to see Diamond and Snorter again. I look at everyone at breakfast, not Ferguson, of course (I know everything there is to know about her life) with a fresh interest.

Later I am standing beside the patient in the anaesthetic room, waiting for Mr Potter, when Snorter comes struggling through the swing doors with her old cricket bag. She flops about the room dragging the bag:

And on the beach undid his corded bales

she says, as she always does, while rummaging in the bag for her white wellington boots. I want to tell Snorter, though I never do, that I too know this poem.

I look hard at Snorter. Even now her hair is not combed properly. Her theatre gown has no tapes at the back so that it hangs, untied and crooked. She only has one boot on when Mr Potter comes. The unfairness of it all comes over me. Why do I have to be neatly and completely dressed at all times. Why do they not speak to me except to ask for something to be fetched or taken away. Suddenly I say to Snorter, '*Minuet du Salle de la Bain*', in my appalling accent. I am surprised at myself. She is hopping on one foot, a wellington boot in her hand, she stops hopping for a moment.

'*de la salle de bain* surely,' she corrects me with a perfect pronunciation and a well-mannered smile. 'Also lower case,' she says, 'not caps, alters the emphasis.'

'Oh yes of course,' I mutter hastily. An apology.

'Pentothal.' Mr Potter is perched on his stool at the patient's head, his syringe held out vaguely in my direction.

Black Country Farm

Today my house stands open to the spring, and some cornflowers, blue with that intense cornflower blue, crowd the borders. The brick path is almost hidden. I am immediately reminded of the possibility of cornflowers growing in another part of the world where the seasons are not the same as they are here. I am reminded of another time in my life, a long time ago. At that time, using a wooden spatula of the kind used for pressing down the tongue during an examination of the tonsils, I planted out some cornflower seedlings. I am not sure now whether, at the time, I thought of the vivid mass of colour the anonymous seedlings would produce in their maturity. Perhaps it could be said that during my life I have made remarks and carried out various actions, both simple and complicated, without looking ahead to consequences surprisingly pleasant or otherwise. One of the aspects of both sowing and planting is that it is necessary to remember that the work is done with hope.

It is not hard for me to imagine now how cornflowers would look when seen in the soft light of an English summer evening.

The black-out shutters in the hospital, where I worked during the war, were put up every evening so that light would not show from the large building. Because of its many windows the hospital looked like a great ship forever in harbour. Two porters put up the shutters at night and another two took them down in the mornings. The evening porters started on chests on the fifth floor and worked their way down both wings of the hospital through obstetrics, gynaecology, ear nose and throat, orthopaedics, the private wards and so on. Because it was such an immense thing to get done they had to start at about four-thirty, when the afternoon sunlight was pouring into the wards. So, it was like this, coming off duty at five-thirty for an evening off before my day off; the sudden light evening outside, after being in the darkened ward, was a surprise to say the least. This forgotten, unexpected light – it was something which lifted the spirits – this summer evening queening it still through the city and the suburbs. I could not get enough of it. I always sat upstairs on the bus, on the left, so that as we lumbered through the suburb, scraping the summer-green leafiness, I could be as if right in these green trees for the whole journey.

Other memories follow, out of sequence; the red cabbages on my father's allotment, the roan horses on the tow paths pulling barges laden with coal, and a gypsy who cursed the veins in my mother's legs causing her to have phlebitis later on. Perhaps it is the Regency tea party which is uppermost in my mind now, with its promise of Queen Anne cups and saucers, China tea with real cream and yards and yards of chiffon . . .

'You must come,' I told my mother. But she felt too shy to visit my new friends.

About these two people, I thought they were the most perfect people on earth. I admired them. In my eyes they could not make a mistake, could not do a bad thing towards anyone.

'It's going to be Regency,' Felicity said, bunching the chiffon in her large capable hands. 'I'm going to drape the mantelpiece,' she said. 'You'll see, it will be lovely. Do bring your mother.'

My mother was unable to trust these two, Felicity and Noël. She had these feelings of mistrust without even meeting them. Perhaps it was my enthusiasm for them which worried her and the fact that, as soon as I arrived home for my day off, I went at once on my bicycle to their place. I admired their knowledge of music and literature and their ability to conduct whole conversations within quotation marks, if you like to put it that way. They quoted from Shakespeare, Dante, the Bible, from Eliot and Auden, and they sang as if they were characters in an opera.

Den Adigen steht die Ehrenhaftigheit
im Gesicht geschrieben.
Nun, verlieren wir keine Zeit,
augenblicklich will ich dich heiraten.

'*A nobleman's honour,*' Felicity explained the meaning, '*is written in his face. Now, let's not waste time. I'll marry you.*' When she laughed she sang tenor through her laugh.

Their voices, pure and able, were sustained as if with deeply felt love, as if nothing could go wrong with either their voices or with them or with me.

They introduced me to the novels of Virginia Woolf. When my father asked me, one time on my day off, 'Have you got a nice book? What are you reading?' I showed him the book.

'*To the Lighthouse,*' he said. 'That's a good title but I'm afraid it's too highbrow for me.'

'No it's easy,' I told him, nodding wisely. I read all Virginia Woolf's books and discovered later that I had never seen any of the faces of the people in any of the novels. One thing I did see was a plush cloth pulled off a table with a flamboyant movement. I never saw, then, the implication behind that simple action which, I think, was in a sea captain's stateroom. Even the action itself, the reason for it, I realise now, was not clear to me.

'These people are arty crafty,' my mother said. How did they earn a living, she wanted to know. And how did they pay rent? Decrepit as the place was they would not have it for nothing. My mother, being unsure of her own place in a society to which she was not accustomed, based her attitudes and opinions on those of a neighbour, a railway man's widow, Mrs Pugh, who was a dress-maker. Crawling round on the floor with her mouth full of pins while she adjusted a hem, this neighbour, it seemed to my mother, knew all there was to know about human life and how it should be lived.

'You don't never get no pleasure,' the neighbour told my mother. And when the new Odeon Cinema opened on the edge of the hous-ing estate they went to the pictures together, twice a week when the programme changed. They sat in warmth, in the rich golden splen-dour of mirrors, brass light fittings, brass handrails and voluminous red velvet curtains. In the interval they listened to the theatre organ as it rose from its cave in the floor. And they received from maids, in black dresses with white aprons and caps, afternoon tea on little trays made, it seemed, of hand-beaten silver.

So, when my mother agreed to accepting the invitation to the Regency tea party it was on condition that Mrs Pugh could come too. They would catch the bus and walk from the corner and I would meet them at the field path.

It was true, they, my two new friends, were arty crafty. One of them made a skirt for me from cloth woven by them both. Knowing how long weaving takes, a skirt length was a large gift. They rented the place. It was one of those dilapidated farm houses remaining in a small triangle of green meadow right in the middle of an industrial area. There was a coal mine and the brick works to one side, the bone and glue factory on the other side and, behind the house, there was an enormous slag heap partly overgrown with tufted grass and coltsfoot. The field was low lying and enclosed by hedges of haw-thorn and elderberry. To one side of the kitchen door there was a derelict wash house. A potter's wheel, a mess of clay dug from the wet field and a kiln built by themselves was on the other side. They had a cow and some chickens. The cow was found to have TB and, after a while, it was fetched away.

Even now the strong fragrance of elderberry, should I be in a place where it grows, reminds me of the excitement, as it seemed then, of going 'to the country', to be there with them.

As the day for the Regency tea party drew near I began to be anxious about the dirty tumbledown house. They seemed to enjoy writing their names and audacious remarks in the dust. They left dishes and clothes everywhere and never made their bed. I despised myself for wanting to impose my suburban and hospital-trained standards on them. These bits of Black Country farms, left over, brought some prettiness during the seasons; daffodils, the pink and the white mayflowers, buttercups and daisies and, on the slag heap, the yellow coltsfoot. There were dog roses too in the hedges and the flowers heralding blackberries and the shiny fruit itself and, finally, the red hawthorn berries and the rosy wild crab-apples. Theirs was one of those pretty places in the middle of the smoke and dirt, the heave and roar of the iron and steel works and the unforgettable noise of the wheels turning as the miners' cage was going down or coming up.

'Don't they speak nice,' the railway widow, Mrs Pugh, was not able to hide the approval in the face of her disapproval and distaste. She stood with my mother, both of them balancing in their best shoes, on a tuft of grass at the edge of the mud. My mother, as a rule, admired people who, having been to Oxford, as my new friends had, said *barth* and *parth* with that special resonance as the vowel sound is brought down through the nose. *Grass* and *laugh* also, as if an 'n' lurked somewhere in these words. She felt the short 'a' was an unfortunate stigma and was quick to correct people, even strangers in shops. My mother approved of grey flannels and Oxford sandals saying that they were elegant and went well with the haircut which allowed a nice wave to fall across an intellectual forehead.

The only trouble about their clothes was that, when my mother and Mrs Pugh arrived, my two friends were not wearing any.

Nervously I stood with the two visitors listening to the high-pitched little screams which belonged to the way in which my friends talked and laughed. The smoke from the wash-house chimney rewarded us with a sudden shower of sparks and soot. From inside came the sounds of a tin bath being shared.

'Always the accomplished acrobat. You delightful tormenting creature!' a laughing well-bred voice said, causing the visitors to look away from each other and to stare stonily at the generous surrounding of mud.

'Acrobat! Contortionist!' the two-toned laughter contained in its music the sounds of an exchange of playful slappings, of wet hands on wet bare flesh.

'And, whose little bottom is this?' Slap slap. 'And, whose little bottom is this?' Two more slaps.

'Who or what are these so-called friends of yours?' My mother's white hat with its small spotted veil was an inadequate protection.

'Them forrin or what?' Mrs Pugh said.

'They're Bohemians,' I said.

'It's not a question of which country . . .' My mother's lips made a pale thin line. I looked away from her.

'Bohemians,' I tried again. 'You know, *A la Boemm*,' I said, 'as in art, in painting and poetry . . . that sort of thing . . . clay modelling, pottery . . .' I waved a hand towards the kiln. Another high-pitched scream of laughter interrupted my attempt.

'Well,' Mrs Pugh said. 'I don't know much about art but I like a nice picture now and again, you know, something pretty.'

One of the inmates of the wash house had started to blow bubbles. The other was singing, then they both sang from Don Giovanni:

> Give me thy hand, oh fairest,
> I would, and yet I would not . . .

'Sounds like there's two of a kind in there,' Mrs Pugh pursed her lips.

'Really!' my mother's speech was cut short as the wash-house door was pushed open from within and my two friends, sharing a bath towel, stepped on to the plank which bridged the mud between the wash house and the kitchen. The two of them seemed, at that moment, to fly across in a flurry of pink nakedness.

'I'm going for the bus even if I have to stand and wait two hours for it out there on the corner,' my mother began picking her way across the sodden meadow. 'They'll wreck your career, those two,' there were tears in her voice. 'Believe me,' she said, 'between them, those two, they'll wreck your career.'

Unable to look at my mother's white hat I took her arm to steady her across to the next little island of turf. I could see myself quite plainly working my way through bladders and stomach ulcers, gall-stones and various surgical conditions, through the men's private wards and the women's private wards, a never ending path to being a battleaxe of a sister in charge of some God-forsaken place like Radium Therapy or the diet kitchen on the Lower Ground Floor, or, worse, in charge of the ear, nose and throat theatre, with its two humourless and untender surgeons, always at war with each other, and on towards a final triumph – that of being a District Nurse, enormous in navy blue, on a bicycle, visiting patients, admonishing husbands and delivering babies on sheets of newspaper in overcrowded kitchens or bedrooms. I suppose I wanted to be both wrecked and rescued. I saw a tear on my mother's soft, carefully powdered cheek and noticed again her patent-leather shoes being spoiled.

'No!' I said. 'No, no I won't let them . . . I won't let anything wreck . . .'

Just then Felicity, dressed, called to us to come indoors. The kettle, she sang, was boiling. She was making tea.

My mother and Mrs Pugh hesitated.

'I could just do with a nice cup of tea,' Mrs Pugh said.

My two friends, their wet hair brushed back, waited on my mother and Mrs Pugh with charm.

'Thank you very much, ta,' Mrs Pugh held her tea cup and saucer high, level with her proud bosom. 'Well, thank you very much. I don't mind if I do,' she helped herself delicately to a sandwich from Felicity's offered plate.

There wasn't any chiffon and the cups were absolutely not Queen Anne. Felicity must have discarded the Regency idea. While the visitors were being looked after I went outside and, crouching in the rain which was beginning to fall, I planted out all the cornflower seedlings I had brought with me. I used the spatula which I kept in my pocket along with my watch and my nursing scissors. These things, together with my pen, were my possessions; I cherished them.

When I come upon the surprise of cornflowers here I know that there will have been the surprise of them in that other place. I never went back to see. My two friends did not write to me and I never wrote to them. The other day I almost read a Virginia Woolf novel again. And then I put it back on the shelf.

I am afraid that this time I would see the faces and be disappointed.

Motherhood

When I was about six I went with my mother to visit the orphanage where my father taught. It was called the Sir Josiah Mason Orphanage, and it lay somewhere between Erdington and Sutton Coldfield in the English Midlands. My mother was wearing what she called her travelling dress, a long brown skirt and a long brown jacket which had a cape. I was always very fond of sitting in the soft brown folds of this material, close up to my mother, in the bus or in the train.

I remember arriving at the orphanage and a door being opened into a room full of little girls. They all had very short hair and were all dressed in black woollen stockings and blue overalls. While we were just in the doorway a little girl, smaller than I was, suddenly looked up and rushed to my mother and jumped into her arms. I remember my mother's arms round the little girl as she buried her face in the travelling dress cape. And I thought then how the little girl must like the cape as much as I did. She clung there like a monkey and I looked on while someone tried, with quite a lot of trouble, to get the little girl out of my mother's arms.

I asked later in the train, when we were going home, why the girl had jumped up like that. My mother explained it was because she had no mother. This seemed to be unbelievable, being without a mother. 'She is motherless,' my mother said.

I moved away a bit from the travelling dress then and tried to look as if I had no mother, to see what it would feel like to be motherless, and to see if the other people in the compartment would notice that I was all alone. I do not know if anyone noticed but I do remember my mother suggesting I should stop fidgeting.

I suppose my mother can be said to have taken motherhood pretty seriously. I have many half memories of an extra cover being spread over my bed during the night or a cup of cold water being offered at the edge of a feverish dream.

On the day of the orphanage visit I must have slept for the best part of the journey home. I must have forgotten that I had no mother. I remember waking up in the warmth and safety of the cape, an essential and repeated part of the experience recalled now in connection with thoughts on motherhood all these years later on.

Before my first child was born I actually imagined I would be able to sit, nicely dressed, by the window nursing my baby and reading a book. Goethe in his novella *Elective Affinities* describes the young woman, Ottolie, walking peacefully along a path beside a lake, carrying a baby (some months old) and, at the same time reading, with enjoyment, a favourite novel.

After discovering the impossibility of my pre-natal dream of the sweet tranquillity of motherhood, I told my mother of the silly idea I had had. She confessed she, too, had had the same thought years earlier. So perhaps many women, unknown to each other, have had a similar dream of motherhood that has been shattered.

A contemporary Australian poet and mother, Judith Rodriguez, has a poem called 'Rebecca in a Mirror' which starts:

Our little tantrum flushed and
misery-hollow
sits having it out

in a mirror; drawn stiff as it –
till her joke of a body, from flat,
flaps with the spasms of crying.
The small eyes frighten
the small eyes clutching
out of such puffed intensity of rage.

The poem expresses a deep love from the mother towards the baby who is experiencing, as indeed the mother is experiencing as she watches, the first and most powerful of emotions – rage, loneliness and the need to express them. The complete poem shows the understanding, which begins to develop early on in the state of motherhood, of the intricate journey the newly born infant has made from the first stages of growth through to the delivery – and then the awful truth that there is no turning back for the 'hero'. The poem ends with the lines:

past perils vaster than space
she has come –
and can never re-enter
the unasked bodily friendship
of her first home.

The story of the epiphany, the manifestation of the Christ child to the Magi, may be a story which many people do not believe, but the story is acknowledged. Translated into ordinary life, into our own times, the newly born child is shown not to three kings representing foreign territories and customs, but to a whole world of family and friends and neighbours. (By announcing the birth in a newspaper, strangers also are told.) The new mother who has, in the first place, to become accustomed to being called 'mother', has the great need to show her baby to her own mother or to the person who has been 'mother' to her. Women cross continents, they cross the world, in order to share mother and daughter motherhood. Very often the younger woman, in beholding her own mother handling the new baby, sees qualities in the older woman that she, though certainly having experienced these qualities at one time in her life, has never seen before.

Unexpectedly, some ideas about this emerged for me while I was writing the novel *Cabin Fever*, a book which became, during the writing, a sort of homage to mother and to motherhood.

Vera, the character in the book, is visited in the nursing home, where she has just given birth, by her mother who brings lilies-of-the-valley in a small green vase shaped like a stork. Vera almost makes the cruel remark that she supposes her mother is trying to pretend the baby has been brought by a stork. The baby cries throughout the visit and Vera's mother holds the baby and tries to quiet her. Vera begins to see things about her mother that she realises she has not seen before.

Later on when Vera makes a small pilgrimage to her mother's house with the baby this knowledge is increased:

My mother buries her face in Helena's shawl. When my mother looks up at me it is as if my baby has inherited these jewels, my mother's blue eyes. My baby looks like my mother.

'She looks like you,' I tell her.

'Your father will say she looks like his mother,' my mother says.

'He has always said this about babies.'

'Only if they are related.'

'No, not always.'

'All babies look like someone,' she says after a bit. She sits down with Helena and starts to unwrap her. Once again I am seeing something I have not known about before, in my mother, like the time she came the day Helena was born.

'How the child has grown,' she says. Helena's resemblance to my mother is striking and cancels any other resemblance.

'She is like you,' my mother says. 'She looks like you when you were a baby.' Eagerly, like a little girl with a doll, my mother undresses Helena to change her on the kitchen table. I look on, seeing her doing the things I imagined her doing. She bends over Helena who lies kicking on the folded blanket. In their smiling at one another it seems, for a moment, as if they are exchanging the blue brilliance of their eyes.

It was when I was writing this chapter in which Vera and her six-week-old baby journey to visit her mother that I began to understand something about the deep significance of handing on motherhood from mother to daughter and the possibility of the daughter actually *looking back towards her mother*, something that children rarely do; they are looking forward in their lives to the next thing they have to face.

Vera, in the novel, has no husband and no acknowledged father for her baby. The great bond of motherhood, which emerges in the novel and which is a truth about real life, shows that with the birth of a child the qualities of motherhood can flourish and very often families and friends, separated previously, take the opportunity to do some healing and to be healed.

There is perhaps no lovelier poetry than the sweet, soft sounds of discovery between a mother and child. An Indian poet, in 100 BC, said, 'Great is the joy of a mother when a child is born to her. The touch of children is the delight of the body; the delight of the ear is the hearing of their voices.'

All through the ages writers have turned to motherhood as the source of inspiration, and they have turned back to that time of innocence when the newly born child is placed at the breast or put in the lap of the mother. An anonymous medieval poem presents an idyllic and romantic picture:

I sing of a maiden that is makeless;
King of all kings to her son she chose.
He came all so still where his mother was,
As dew in April that falleth on the grass.
He came all so still to his mother's bower,
As dew in April that falleth on the flower.
He came all so still where his mother lay,
As dew in April that falleth on the spray.
Mother and maiden was never none but she,
Well may such a lady God's mother be.

The poem puts forward the idea that in every birth there is a suggestion of the ubiquitous which cannot be denied; that every human individual, seemingly omnipresent, possesses the spirit of Christ and that ultimately the spirit in one individual will seek out and speak to this same spirit in another. The images of the soft, delicate, longed-for baby lying on rose leaves, bathed in raindrops, caressed by sunbeams in gentle arms of the delicate and quiet mother – all are there for the taking. But motherhood is not so simple.

Contemporary fiction also explores contemporary motherhood and fatherhood, showing a disintegration of all that is offered in the above poem. Fatherhood, at the present time, cannot be ignored. William Trevor in his story 'Access to the Children' describes the plight of the lonely divorced father collecting his children for the day, having exhausted all possible 'treats', having to think up fresh things to do and, feeling thoroughly homeless, being turned away in the evening at the door of his ex-wife's new household.

Motherhood for the single mother involves having to place her child in a day care centre and then exercise great discipline of the mind in order to concentrate not on the child's needs but on the work she must do to earn a living.

Contemporary motherhood often has to undergo an expansion as marriages end in favour of new relationships and children of previous marriages, living out of suitcases, are brought together within the bounds of another fresh family and all are expected to 'get on' well together. An aspect of motherhood which emerges is that not all families are made of Brady Bunch material.

Sometimes writers, for the purposes of the story and character exploration, need to dispose of motherhood, or the power of motherhood. For example the motherly letter Mrs Durbeyfield writes to Tess on the eve of her marriage to Angel Clare in Hardy's novel *Tess of the Durbervilles*. Mrs Durbeyfield advises Tess not to tell her future husband of her Fall from Grace earlier, since the resulting baby had died straight away. Tess, turning her back on her mother's advice, having lost her unwanted state of motherhood, tells Angel Clare of her previous downfall. Clare is shocked and says it is impossible for them to live together as man and wife. He goes off to foreign lands, leaving Tess to a life of hardship as she tries to fend for herself working as a labourer on farms, one of which was known as Starvation Acre. Had Tess been able to recognise and respect the bond of motherhood between her mother and herself the novel would possibly have been only half its present length!

Similarly, in the novel *Silas Marner*, George Eliot disposes of motherhood in that Eppie's mother, no longer wanted by her husband, and already overcome by increasingly large doses of opium, falls into a snowdrift where she falls asleep, frozen, forever. Had

Eppie's mother lived, Silas, the lonely weaver, would never have taken on the duties of motherhood which George Eliot gives him.

The novel contains the most touching and lifelike description of motherhood ever to appear on the printed page. All the criteria of wanting what is best for the child are brought forward. Eliot writes, 'The stone hut was made a soft nest for her, lined with downy patience.' The role of motherhood is taken on eagerly by the man, Silas, who has had no experience of bringing up a child. He is not a relative but a stranger into whose warm kitchen the little child has wandered, her soaked little boots pressing painfully on her little ankles.

As far as we know George Eliot was an intellectual rather than a motherly person. She was never a mother herself but, in the novel, has created an unforgettable picture of motherhood.

Fairfields

'Why can't the father, the father of your — What I mean is why can't he do something?'

'I've told you – he's dead.'

'How can you say that? He was on the phone last night. I could tell by your voice that's who it was.'

'He's dead. I've told you.'

At last the day has come when I must leave for Fairfields. It is all arranged. I have been there once already and know it to be a place of grated raw vegetables and children with restless eyes. It is also a place of poetry and music and of people with interesting lives and ideas.

'I simply can't understand you. How could you with your education and your background breed like a rabbit —'

'You're always saying that, for years you've said it. I've told you, rabbits have six, I only one.'

'How can you speak to me, your mother, like that.'

'Oh shut up and remember this. I'm never coming back. Never!'

'And another thing, Helena looks like a miner's child dressed up for an outing!' My mother does not like the white frock and the white socks and the white hair ribbons. I tie Helena's hair in two bunches with enormous bows and do not remind my mother that she bought the white frock, and the white socks and the white ribbons.

'She'll get a headache, her hair pulled tight like that. And why white for a train journey, two train journeys. Oh, Vera!' My mother, I can see, has tears in her eyes. 'Leave Helena here with me, your father and I would like to have her here with us, please! Besides, she is happy with us.'

But I will not be parted from my child. I throw a milk bottle across the kitchen, it shatters on the tiles and I am pleased because my mother is frightened. 'What's wrong with miners and their children and their outings?' I shout at her.

Perhaps Helena *would* be happier with her grandmother. I do not want to think this and it is painful to be told.

My father comes with us to the station.

'That's a nice coat,' he says, carrying it for me. It is my school winter coat, dark green and thick. It would not fit into my case so I have to carry it or wear it.

'It's a new coat, is it?' he says, feeling the cloth with his hands. I don't reply, because I have been wearing the coat for so many years.

We are too early for the train. The platform is deserted.

'It looks like a Loden,' he is still talking about the coat. 'Like an Austrian Loden cloth.' He is restless, my father, very white faced and he holds Helena's hand and walks up and down the platform, up and down, the coat on his other arm.

Always when my father sees off a train he is at the station too soon. And then, when the train is about to leave, when the whistle is being blown and the doors slam shut, one after the other down the whole length of the train, he rushes away and comes back with newspapers and magazines and pushes them through the window as he runs beside the moving train. As the engine gets up steam and the carriages clank alongside the platform my father increases his speed, keeping up a smiling face outside the window. His bent figure, his waving arms and his white face have always been the last things I have seen when leaving. I know too from being with him, seeing other people off, that he stands at the end of the platform, still waving, long after the train has disappeared.

Walking up and down we do not speak to each other. The smell of the station and the sound of an engine at the other platform remind me of Ramsden and of the night several years earlier when I met her train. Ramsden, staff nurse Ramsden, arriving at midnight. There was a thick fog and her train was delayed.

'I've invited Ramsden to come and stay for a few days,' I said to my mother then, assuming a nonchalance, a carelessness of speech to hide Ramsden's age and seniority.

'Why of course Vera, a nursing friend is always welcome . . .' There had been a natural progression from school friend to nursing friend. My father never learned to follow, to keep up with this progression.

'And is Miss Ramsden a good girl?' would be his greeting, a continuation of, 'And is Jeanie a good girl?' He would say it to Ramsden without seeing the maturity and the elegance and without any understanding of the superior quality of her underclothes.

'My parents are looking forward to meeting you.' I invited Ramsden knowing already these other things.

Ramsden, with two tickets to Beethoven, in our Town Hall, prepared herself to make the long journey.

Putting off the visit, in my mind, from one day to the next, reluctantly, at last I was in the Ladies Only waiting room crouched over a dying fire, thin lipped and hostile in the bitter night. My school coat heavy but not warm enough and my shoes soaked.

Ramsden, who had once, unasked, played the piano for my tears, arrived at last. I could see she was cold. She was pale and there were dark circles of fatigue round her eyes. She came toward me distinguished in her well-cut tailored jacket and skirt. Her clothing and manner set her apart immediately from the other disembarking passengers.

'Miss Ramsden will have to share the room,' my mother said before I left for the station, 'your sister's come home again.' Shrugging and blinking I went on reading without replying. Reading, getting ready slowly, turning the pages of my book, keeping one finger in the page while I dressed to go and meet the train.

Ramsden came toward me with both hands reaching out in leather gloves. At once she was telling me about the Beethoven, the choral symphony, and how she had been able to get tickets. There was Bach too, Cantata eighteen. 'Remember?' she said. *'For as the rain cometh down and the snow from heaven,'* she sang, beating time with one hand, *'so shall my word be that goeth forth out of my mouth ...'* In the poor light of the single mean lamp her eyes were pools of pleasure and tenderness. She did not mind the black-out, she said, when I apologised for the dreariness of the station. 'Ramsden,' I said, 'I'm most awfully sorry but there's been something of a tragedy at home. I couldn't let you know ... I'm so most awfully sorry ...'

'Not ...?' Concern added more lines to Ramsden's tired face. I nodded, turning away from the smell of travelling which hung about the woollen cloth of her suit.

'Oh Wright! I am so sorry, Vera.' It was the first time she had spoken my first name, well almost the first time. I glanced at her luggage which stood by itself on the fast emptying platform. The case seemed to hold in its shape and leather the four long hours of travelling, the long tedious journey made twice as long by the fog.

There would be a stopping train to London coming through late, expected at three in the morning the porter said as Ramsden retrieved her case from its desolation.

A glance into the waiting room showed that the remnant of the fire was now a little heap of cold ash. Perhaps, she suggested, even though there was no fire it would be warmer to sit in there.

'I'm so sorry,' I said. 'I shall not be able to wait for your train.' So sorry, I told her, I must get back, simply must get back.

'Is it . . .?' More concern caused Ramsden to raise her dark eyebrows. The question unfinished, I drew my arm away from her hand's touch. I thought of the needlework and embroidery book I had chosen from her room, too nervous to read the titles when, to please me, she said to choose a book to keep, as a present, from her shelf. The badly chosen book I thought, at the time, made me feel sick. I began that day, almost straight away, to feel sick.

We walked along the fog-filled platform. 'I've come to you all the way from London,' Ramsden, drawing me to her, began in her low voice. 'I'd hoped . . .' I turned away from the clumsy embrace and her breathed-out, whispered words, knowing her breath to be the breath of hunger.

'I'm sorry,' I said again stiffening away from her, 'but I'll have to go.'

'To them,' she said. 'yes, of course, you must.' She nodded her understanding and her resignation.

'I am sorry I can't wait till your train comes. I can't wait with you. I'm most awfully sorry!' Trying to change, to lift my accent to match hers.

She nodded again. I knew from before, though I couldn't see them, what her eyes would be like.

I had to walk the three miles home, as there were no buses at that time of night. The fog swirled cold in my face. The way was familiar but other things were not. My own body, for one thing, for I was trying, every day, to conceal my morning sickness.

I turn away, trying to avoid the place on the platform where Ramsden tried to draw me toward an intensity of feeling I could not be a part of that night.

'She wasn't on the train,' I told my mother the next morning standing on purpose behind her flowered smock and keeping to the back of her head which was still encased in metal rollers. She was hurrying to get to the Red Cross depot. Her war effort.

'It was a dreadful night for travelling,' my mother said, not turning from the sink, 'perhaps your Miss Ramsden will send a letter. You can invite her again, perhaps in the spring, we'll have more space then, perhaps by then your sister will be better.'

My father, running now beside the moving train, pushes a magazine and a comic through the window. I, because I feel I must, lean out and see him waving at the end of the platform. Helena, clinging to my skirt, cries for her Grandpa.

Unable to stop thinking of Ramsden I wonder why do I think of her today after all this time of forgetting her. I never write to her. I never did write even when she wrote to me saying that she was still nursing and that she lived out, that she had a little flat which had escaped the bombs and if I liked to stay she would love to have me stay as long as I liked, 'as long as you feel like it'. I never answered. Never told her I had a child. Never let her into my poverty and never let her into my loneliness.

London is full of people who seem to know where they are and to have some purpose in this knowing. I drag my case and the coat and Helena and change stations and at last we are travelling through the fields and summer meadows of Hertfordshire. The train, this time, is dirty and has no corridor and immediately Helena wants the lavatory. I hate the scenery.

At last we are climbing the steep field path from the bus stop
to the school. Fairfields, I have been there once already and know
the way. The path is a mud path after it leaves the dry narrow track
through the tall corn which is turning, waving and rippling, from
green to gold, spotted scarlet with poppies and visited by humming
hot-weather insects. I have seen before that the mud is caused by
water seeping from two enormous culverts among the trees at the
top of the hill. Drains, the drains of Fairfields School.

'Who is that?' Helena stops whimpering. And I see a man standing quite still, half hidden by trees. He does not seem to be watching,
rather it is as if he is trying to be unseen as we climb higher. He does
not move except to try and merge into a tree trunk. With the case I
push Helena on up the steepest part of the path and I do not look
back into the woods.

In the courtyard no one is about except for a little boy standing in the porch. He tells me his Granny will be coming to this
door, that he is waiting to be fetched by her. 'My Granny's got a
gas stove,' he tells me. I think suddenly of my mother's kitchen and
wish that I could wait now at this door for her to come and fetch me
and Helena. Straight away I want to go back.

Miss Palmer, the Principal, the one they call Patch, I know this
too from my earlier visit, carrying a hod of coke, comes round from
an outhouse.

'Ah!' she says. 'I see you mean to stay!' She indicates my winter
coat. 'So this is Helena!' She glances at my child. 'She's buttoned up
I daresay.' I know this to mean something not quite explained but
I nod and smile. Patch tells me that no one is coming to fetch Mar-
tin. 'He's new,' she says, looking across to the little boy. 'He hasn't
adjusted yet.'

She shows me my room which I am to share with Helena. It is
bare except for a cupboard and two small beds. It is bright yellow

with strong smelling distemper. There is a window, high up, strangled with creeper.

'Feel free to wander,' Patch says, 'tea in the study at four. Children's tea in the playroom at five and then the bathings. Paint the walls if you feel creative.' She has a fleshy face and short, stiff hair, grey like some sort of metal. I do not dislike her.

'Thank you,' I say, narrowing my eyes at the walls as if planning an exotic mural.

Helena, pulling everything from the unlocked case, intones a monologue over her rediscovered few toys. I stare into the foliage and the thick mass of summer-green leaf immediately outside the window.

Later the Swiss girl, Josepha, who has the room opposite mine, takes me round the upstairs rooms which are strewn with sleeping children. We pull some of them out of bed and sit them on little chipped enamel pots. There is the hot smell of sleeping children and their pots.

Josepha tells me the top bathroom is mine and she gives me a bath list. The face flannels and towels hang on hooks round the room.

Josepha comes late to breakfast and takes most of the bread and the milk and the butter up to her room where her sweetheart, Rudi, sleeps. I heard their endless talk up and down in another language, the rise and fall of an incomprehensible muttering all night long, or so it seemed in my own sleeplessness.

The staff sit at breakfast in a well-bred studied shabbiness huddled round a tall copper coffee pot and some blue bowls of milk. Children are not allowed and it seems that I hear Helena crying and crying locked in our room upstairs. Patch does not come to breakfast, but Myles, who is Deputy Principal, fetches prunes and Ryvita for her. She is dark-eyed and expensively dressed like Ramsden but she has nothing of Ramsden's music and tenderness. She is aloof and flanked by two enormous dogs. She is something more than Deputy Principal. Josepha explains.

'Do not go in,' she points at Patch's door, 'if both together are in there.'

When I dress Helena I take great trouble over her hair ribbons and let her, with many changes of mind, choose her dress because I am sorry for leaving her alone, locked in to cry in a strange place. I have come to Fairfields to work with the idea that it will give Helena school and companionship and already I have tried to persuade her, to beg her and finally rushed away from her frightened crying because staff offspring (Myles' words) are not allowed at staff meals. I take a long time dressing Helena and find that Josepha has dressed all the children from my list as well as her own. I begin to collect up the little pots.

'No! Leave!' Josepha shouts and, tying the last child into a pinafore, she herds them downstairs. Moving swiftly Josepha can make me, with Helena clinging to my dress, seem useless.

Josepha does the dining room and I am to do, with Olive Morris, the playroom where the smaller children have their meals. Mrs Morris has a little boy called Frank but Helena will not sit by him. She follows me with a piece of bread and treacle and I have to spend so much time cleaning her that Olive Morris does the whole breakfast and wipes the tables and the floor. She does not say anything only gets on with ladling cod-liver oil, which is free from our government, into the children as they leave the little tables.

I discover that Olive Morris has three children in the school and that Josepha feels it is morally right that Olive should work more than anyone else because of this. Josepha is always dragging children off to have their hair washed. She has enormous washing days and is often scrubbing something violently at ten o'clock at night. The smell of scorching accompanies the fierceness of her ironing.

'Do not go in there,' she points to the first-floor bathroom, 'when Patch and Tanya are in there,' she says, 'and do not tell Myles!'

Tanya teaches art. She looks poor but Josepha says she is filthy rich and wears rags on purpose.

Tanya, on my first day at work, was painting headless clowns on the dining-room walls. She stepped back squinting at her work. 'They are going to play ball with the heads,' she explained bending down over her paint pots as if she had been talking to me for years.

'What a good idea,' I said, ashamed of my accent and trying to sound as if I knew all about painting.

That day she asked me what time it was, saying that she must hurry and get her wrists slashed before Frederick came back from his holiday.

Later, in the pantry, she is there with both arms bandaged. 'Frederick the Great,' she says, 'he'll be back. Disinfectant, fly spray, cockroach powder, and mouse traps. He will,' she says, 'ask you to examine his tonsils.'

Olive Morris looks ill. Sometimes when I sit in my room at night with an old cardigan round the light to keep it from shining on Helena's bed I think of Olive and begin to understand what real poverty is; her dreadful little bowls of never clean washing, the rags that she is forever mending and her pale crumpled face from which her worried eyes look out hopelessly.

I have plenty of pretty clothes for Helena. And then it suddenly comes to me that this is the only difference. My prospects are the same as Olive's. I have as little hope for the future as she has. It just happens that at present, because of gifts from my mother, Helena, for the first years of her life, has been properly fed and is well dressed.

One hot afternoon I sit with the children in the sand pit, hoping that they will play. There are only two little spades and the children quarrel and fight and bite each other. It is hard to understand why the children can't enjoy the spacious lawns and the places where they can run and shout and hide among the rose bushes. Beyond the lawns is deep uncut grass bright with buttercups and china-blue hare-bells. I am tired, tired in a way that makes me want to lie down in the long grass and close my eyes. Helena, crying, will not let me rest. The children are unhappy. I think it is because they do not have enough food. They are hungry all the time.

I do lie down and I look up at the sky. Once I looked at the sky, not with Ramsden but after we had been talking together. I would like to hear Ramsden's voice now. It is strange to wish this after so long. Perhaps it is because everyone here seems to have someone. Relationships, as they are called here, are acceptable. And I, having no one, wishing for someone, vividly recall Ramsden. She said, that time in the morning before I went for my day off to sleep among the spindles of rosemary at the end of my mother's garden, that love was infinite. That it was possible, if a person loved, to believe in the spiritual understanding of truths that were not fully under-stood intellectually. She said that the person you loved was not an end in itself, was not something you came to the end of, but was the beginning of discoveries which could be made because of loving someone.

Lying in the grass, pushing Helena away, I think about this and wonder how I can bring it into the conversation at the four o'clock staff tea and impress Patch and Myles. I practise some words and an accent of better quality.

Because of being away from meadow flowers for so long I pick some buttercups and some of the delicate grasses adding their glow-ing tips to the bunch wondering, with bitter uneasiness, how I can get them unseen to my room. I can see Patch and Myles at the large window of Patch's room. Instead of impressing them I shall simply seem vulgar, acquisitive and stupid, clutching a handful of weeds, ineffectually shepherding the little children towards their meagre plates of lettuce leaves and Patch-rationed bread.

In the evening there is a thunder storm with heavy rain. I am caught in the rain on the way back from the little shop where I have tried to buy some fruit. The woman there asks me if I am from the school and if I am, she says, she is unable to give me credit. In the shop there is the warm sweet smell of newspapers, firelighters, and cheap sweets, aniseed, a smell of ordinary life which is missing in the life of the school. Shocked I tell her I can pay and I buy some poor-quality carrots, as the apples, beneath their rosy skins, might be rotten. I will wash the carrots and give them to Helena when I have to leave her alone in our room in the mornings.

The storm is directly overhead, the thunder so loud I am afraid Helena will wake and be frightened so I do not shelter in the shop but hurry back along the main road, through the corn and up the steep path. I am wet through and the mud path is a stream. The trees sway and groan. I slip and catch hold of the undergrowth to stop myself from falling. When I look up I see that there is someone standing, half hidden, quite near, in the same place where the man was standing on that first afternoon. This man, I think it is the same man, is standing quite still letting the rain wash over him as it pours through the leaves and branches. His hair is plastered, wet-sleeked on his round head and water runs in rivulets down his dark suit. He, like me, has no coat. He does not move and he does not speak. He seems to be looking at me as I try to climb the steep path as quickly as I can. I feel afraid. I have never felt or experienced fear like this before. Real terror, because of his stillness, makes my legs weak. I hurry splashing across the courtyard and make my way, trembling, round to the kitchen door. Wet and shivering I meet Olive Morris in the passage outside my room. She is carrying a basin of washing.

Rags trail over her shoulder and her worn-out blouse, as usual, has come out of her skirt.

I tell her about the man in the woods. 'Ought I to tell Patch?' I try to breathe calmly. 'It's getting dark out there. He's soaked to the skin. I ought to tell Patch.'

Olive Morris's shapeless soft face is paler than ever and her lips twitch. She looks behind her nervously.

'No,' she says in a low voice. 'No, never tell anyone here any-thing. Never!' She hurries off to the other stairs which lead directly up to her room in the top gable of the house.

While I am drying my hair, Olive Morris, in a torn raincoat, comes to my door.

'I'm going down to post a letter,' she says putting a scarf over her head. 'So if I see your stranger in the trees I'll send him on his way – there's no need at all to have Myles go out with the dogs. No need at all.'

My surprise at the suggestion that Myles and the dogs might hunt the intruder is less than the feeling of relief that I need not go to Patch's room where Myles, renowned for her sensitive nudes, will be sketching Patch in charcoal and reading poetry aloud. They would smile at each other, exchanging intimate glances while only half listening to what I had to say. Earlier, while Patch pretended to search her handbag for a ten-shilling note as part of the payment owing to me, Myles had looked up gazing as if thoughtfully at me for a few minutes and then had resumed her reading of the leather-bound poems.

Josepha is on bedroom duty and the whole school is quiet. Grate-ful that Helena has not been disturbed by the storm I lie down in my narrow bed.

Instead of falling asleep, I think of the school and how it is not at all as I thought it would be. Helena stands alone all day peering through partly closed doors watching the dancing classes. She looks on at the painting and at the clay-modelling and is only on the edge of the music.

There must be people who feel and think as I do but they are not here as I thought they would be. I want to lean out of a window in a city full of such people and call to some passer-by. I am by my own mistakes buried in this green-leafed corruption and I am alone.

My day off which Josepha did not tell me about till all the children were washed and dressed was a mixture of relief and sadness. A bus ride to town. Sitting with Helena in a small café eating doughnuts. Choosing a sun hat for Helena. Buying some little wooden spades and some coloured chalks. Trying to eat a picnic lunch of fruit and biscuits on a road mender's heap of gravel chips. I can hardly bear to think about it. As I handed Helena her share and saw her crouched on the stones with her small hands trying to hold her food without a plate I knew how wrong it was that she was like this with no place to go home to.

I think now over and over again that it is my fault that we are alone, more so than ever, at the side of the main road with cars and lorries streaming in both directions.

There is a sudden sound, a sound of shooting. Gun shots. I go into the dark passage. From Josepha's room comes the usual running up and down of their voices, first hers and then Rudi's. I am afraid to disturb them. A door further down clicks open and I see, with relief, that it is Tanya.

'Oh it's you Tanya! Did you hear anything just now?'

'Lord no. I never hear a thing m'dear and I never ask questions either so if you've been letting anyone in or out I just wouldn't know darling.'

I tell her about the shots.

'Lord!' Tanya says. 'That's Frederick. Back from his leave.

Frederick the Great, literature and drama. Room's over the stables. Never unpacks. Got a Mother. North London. Cap gun. Shoots off gun for sex. The only trouble is darling,' Tanya drawls, 'the orgasm isn't shared.' She disappears into the bathroom saying that she's taken an overdose and so must have her bath quickly.

I go on up the next lot of stairs to Olive's room. I have never been there. I must talk to someone. Softly I knock on the door. At once Olive opens it as if she is waiting on the other side of it.

'Oh it's you!' Her frightened white face peers at me.

'Can I come in?' I step past her hesitation into her room. It is not my intention to be rude, I tell her, it is my loneliness. Olive catches me by the arm. Her eyes implore. I am suddenly ashamed for, sitting up in bed wearing a crumpled shirt and a tie, is a man. The man I had seen standing with sinister patience in the rain.

'Oh Olive, I am so sorry. I do beg . . .'

'This is Mr Morris, my husband. This is Vera Wright, dear,' Olive whispers a plain introduction.

'Pleased to meet you I'm sure,' Mr Morris says. I continue to mumble words of apology and try to move backward to the door.

The three Morris children are all in a heap asleep in a second sagging double bed up against the gable window. Washing is hanging on little lines across the crowded room, and Mr Morris's suit is spread over the bed ends to dry.

'Mr Morris is on his way to a business conference,' Olive begins to explain. I squeeze her arm. 'I'll see you tomorrow,' I say. We are wordless at the top of the steep stairs. She is tucking her blouse into her too loose skirt. It seems to me that she will go on performing this little action forever even when she has no clothes on.

'No one at all knows that Mr Morris is here,' she says in a breaking whisper.

At breakfast I wish I had someone to whom I could carry, with devotion, bread and butter and coffee. I could not envy Myles because of Patch, or Josepha because of Rudi. Tanya must be feeling as I feel for she prepares a little tray for Frederick and is back almost at once with a swollen bruised bleeding nose and quite quickly develops two black eyes which, it is clear, will take days to fade.

It would be nice for Olive to sail into breakfast and remove a quantity of food bearing it away with dignity to the room in the top gable.

'I suppose you know,' I say to Patch when we meet by chance in the hall, 'that Olive Morris's husband arrived unexpectedly last night and will be with us for a few days.'

Patch says, 'Is he dear?' That is all.

Mr Morris, who is a big man, wears his good suit every day thus setting himself somewhat apart from the rest of us. He comes to supper and tells us stories about dog racing. His dogs win. He tells us about boxing and wrestling. He has knocked out all the champs. He knows all their names and the dates of the matches. He knows confidence men who treble their millions in five minutes. His brothers and sisters teach in all the best universities and his dear old mother is the favourite Lady in Waiting at Buckingham Palace. Snooker is his forte, a sign, he tells us, of a misspent youth. He sighs.

Patch comes to supper every night. Josepha stops shouting at Olive. Mr Morris calls Olive 'Lovey' and reminds her, for us all to hear, of extravagant incidents in their lives. He boasts about his older children regaling us with their exam results and sporting successes. Olive withers. She is smaller and paler and trembles visibly when Patch, in a genial mood, with mockery and amusement in her voice, leads Mr Morris into greater heights of story telling. While he talks his eyes slide sideways as he tries to observe us all and see the effects of his fast-moving mouth.

Mr Morris, we have to see, is the perfect husband and father. During the day he encourages his children and the other children to climb all over him. He organises games and races, promising prizes. He gives all sorts of presents, the table in the kitchen is heaped with chickens and ducks ready for the oven, jars of honey and expensive jams and baskets of apples and fresh vegetables. Patch prepares the meals herself. Our diet was vegetarian only because the local butchers, unpaid, no longer supplied the school.

Frederick, refusing to come to meals, refusing to leave the loft, has a bucket on a string into which Josepha, he will not take from anyone else, puts chicken breasts and bread and butter and a white jug of milk. Tanya says if there is any wormy fruit or fly-blown meat Frederick the Great will get it. He, she explains, because of always searching for them, attracts the disasters in food.

'Where is Mr Philbrick?' Patch asks correcting quickly what she calls a fox's paw, a slip of the tongue. 'Mr Morris? Why isn't he here?' She is carving, with skill, the golden chickens and Myles is serving the beans and baby carrots which shine in butter. Olive can hardly swallow a mouthful.

'What's keeping Mr Morris?' I ask her loud enough for Patch's ears. 'Anything wrong?' devouring my plateful. 'Is someone ill?'

'No. No – it's nothing at all,' she whispers.

Toward the end of the meal Mr Morris comes in quietly and sits down next to the shrinking Olive. Patch, with grease on her large chin, hands a plate of chicken to him. Thick-set, stockily at the head of the table, she sings contralto as if guarding a secret with undisturbed complacence.

There is a commotion in the hall and the sound of boots approaching.

'It is the Politz!' Josepha, on bedroom duty, calls from the stairs.

Mr Morris leaps up.

'Leave this to me dear Lady,' he says to Patch. And, with a snake-like movement, he is on his way to the door.

We follow just in time to see Mr Morris, suddenly small and white faced, being led in handcuffs to the front door and out to a car which, with the engine running, is waiting.

I want to say something to Olive to comfort her.

'It's better this way,' she says, 'better for him this way, better than them getting him with dogs. And the children,' she says, 'they didn't see anything.' I don't ask her what Mr Morris has done. She does not tell me anything except that Mr Morris finds prison life unbearable and that he has a long stretch of it ahead.

Patch walks about the school singing and eating the ends off a crusty loaf. When the bills come addressed to her for all the presents from Mr Morris she laughs and tosses them into the kitchen fire.

One of the little boys rushing through the hall stops to glance at Tanya's latest painting.

'How often do you have sexual intercourse?' he pauses long enough in his flight to ask.

'Three times a week.' Tanya steps back to squint at her work. 'Never more, never less,' she says.

Tanya says that Frederick the Great is coming down from the loft and will be at supper. I wash my hair and put on my good dress and go down to the meal early rejoicing that it is Olive's night to settle the children. I am looking forward to meeting Frederick. Perhaps, at last, there will be someone for me. Olive scuttles by with her tray which she must take upstairs. I hear the uproar from the bedrooms and smile to myself.

Frederick is bent in a strange contortion over the sink in the pantry. He is trying to see into his throat with a torch and a small piece of broken mirror stuck into the loose window frame. I am glad to be able to meet him without Josepha and Tanya.

'Would you mind looking at my throat?' he says straightening up. He is very tall, and his eyes enclosed in gold-rimmed spectacles do not look at me. 'I've been trying a new gargle.' He hands me the flashlight and I peer into his throat.

'Is it painful?' I feel I should ask him.

'Not at all,' he says, taking back the torch.

In the dining room Frederick has a little table to himself in the corner. He eats alone quickly and leaves at once. I sit in my usual place. One of the children is practising on the pantry piano. I listen to the conscientious stumblings. Ramsden played Bach seriously repeating and repeating until she was satisfied and then moving on to the next phrases.

In my head I compose a letter to Ramsden . . . *this neck of the woods*, this is not my way but it persists, *this neck of the woods is not far from London. Any chance of your coming down one afternoon? Staff tea is at four. I'd love to see you and show you round . . .*

There is so much I would tell Ramsden.

For as the rain cometh down, and the snow from heaven, and returneth not thither, but watereth the earth, and make it bring forth and bud, that it may give seed to the sower, and bread to the eater: So shall my word be that goeth forth out of my mouth:

I want to write to Ramsden. After that night and after almost five years how do I address her? Dear Ramsden? Dear staff nurse Ramsden? She might be Sister Ramsden. She might not be nursing now though she did go on after the end of the war. She might be married though I think that is unlikely, perhaps she is on concert platforms . . .

Dear Ramsden I have no way at all of getting away from this place. Please Ramsden can you come? Please?

Patch and Myles come in to supper. Ignoring me they devotedly help each other to mountains of grated raw carrots and cabbage.

A Small Fragment
of the Earth

Not everyone seeing the bits of dried grass, the twigs and little sticks of straw in a bird's nest will also see that 'the nest is a cup, shaped by the beak of desire and the breast of love', as the Australian poet Kenneth Mackenzie once described a wagtail's nest. It is the ability in the reader to match the personal note of the poet's sensibility that makes the difference.

I came to Western Australia in 1959, in the middle of my life. I looked, on the morning of arrival, across from the ship towards the flat land that lay beyond the wharf and the Customs sheds. The rail of the safely berthed ship bobbed slowly above the horizon, and slowly below the horizon. There was no way then of knowing, while waiting for disembarkation, what life here would be like.

On a clear day, and most days are clear, the light in Western Australia is more brilliant than anything I have encountered elsewhere. During my first weeks, I felt lost in its intensity. The light comes from the sky and is reflected back from rock or stone or water. Water is the last thing to get dark, and its reflection has the quality of highly polished silver. The reflected light lends, to even the most solid building, an insubstantial air, as if it is part of a theatrical setting.

From the port of Fremantle, the flat sand plains, encompassing the city of Perth, stretch for about 30 kilometres to an escarpment.

Over and beyond the escarpment there is a mixture of rural land that has been cleared for farming, and the bush.

Farther inland, for about 500 kilometres east towards the rabbit-proof fence – a great double fence at the edge of the Nullarbor desert, made of wire and designed to keep out rabbits and emus – there are endless paddocks for sheep and wheat (sheep feed on the stubble of the wheat).

The city of Perth lies in a half-circle around the edge of a wide saucer of blue water that is the Swan River. Like the bush, the river takes its colour from the clear sky. During the winter, heavy rain, bringing topsoil from the vineyards, makes the water a purple–brown colour. Black cockatoos fly screaming across the choppy waves. When I came here, I thought the sandy beaches and the grassy places shaded by pepper trees were a sort of paradise for the children.

'You must be English,' a passer-by said to me on that first afternoon by the river. 'No Australian children would go in the water on such a cold day.' I had been thinking how hot it was. It was mid-November.

Winter in the south of Western Australia is interspersed with clear days when the wind is still and the sun shines and sitting outside is pleasanter than it would be in an English summer. But such days are in a minority. The winds from the Southern Ocean are bitter, and the existence of the state depends upon long periods of rain.

Summer is hot and dry, apart from the occasional storm that may help to fill dams but is otherwise harmful. There are two springs: one at the end of the long winter and the other after the heat of the summer. At both times, growth begins again. The new leaves of the eucalyptus show red and gold and bright green. There is no autumn. It is in the intense, still heat of January that, in the bush, the leaves fall silently.

Years ago, the buildings in Perth seemed to be built of pink and green sugar and piped with white icing. They had charming balconies of wrought iron. And there were shops that looked temporary (but were not), with wooden-board verandahs and posts, as if set up for a shoot-out in a Western. To me, it seemed that the shutters on the windows were an ominous sign of the attempts people had made to ameliorate the discomfort of the great heat of summer. Since that time air-conditioning and high-rise buildings have transformed Perth and, to some extent, the little town of Claremont, where I live.

Claremont is an old township halfway between the port of Fremantle and Perth, between the Indian Ocean and the Swan River. (There is a letter box on the Stirling Highway, which runs between Fremantle and Perth, that marks the exact spot where the post runners, coming from opposite directions, exchanged their mail bags.)

There was in Claremont, once, a corner shop, an emporium, where it was possible to buy – with your groceries and vegetables – hair ribbons, socks and stockings, birthday cards, candles, soap, saddles and harnesses, chicken feed, 44-gallon drums of kerosene, yesterday's bread cheap and any amount of gossip – which was free. Now we have a supermarket and a great many expensive shops (perhaps boutiques is the name for them). And no gossip.

There is now also a restaurant on the river in the place where an old swimming hole – made of a fence of round poles driven into the riverbed – once was. The fence was to keep out any sharks that might come up the river. Hundreds of children had swimming lessons every summer in the river, but now new swimming pools have taken the place of the old swimming holes with their jetties and pole fences.

The latest new buildings on the river are a hotel and an enormous casino. Tourists are hoped for. An enterprising person has opened a pawnshop not far away, and it is said that he is doing quite well.

Surrounding Claremont is a suburb of mainly one-storey houses, many with iron roofs. In spring there is everywhere the lightness and excitement of the coming summer. There is the warm garden scent of freshly mown lawns and the cut grass drying in little brown heaps. There is the fragrance of tall grasses, uncut, waving feathered heads. There is the perfume of unnamed flowers, and of roses and nasturtiums and of the flowers of weeds.

Everywhere in the suburb there is also a piling up of colour. From the green and yellow and orange of the leaves and the brave trumpets of the nasturtiums, vivid splashes of colour climb into the golden lantana and up into the scarlet bottlebrush flowers. Pink and purple bougainvillea hang sprawling in all directions, over fences and over the roofs of sheds and over neat brick walls. In some places, the creeper reaches up into the powdered rain cloud of the cape lilac.

There is a caressing warmth and lightness in the air, even first thing in the morning. Magpies, crooning all night because it is spring, fill the quietness with their carolling notes. Hundreds of doves, grey and silver, pink-edged with tender feathers, fly upward with a soft clapping of wings, a tiny, scattered applause.

In 1970 we bought a piece of land 65 kilometres from Claremont.

COUNTRY TOWNS AND PROPERTIES

For sale. Five acres virgin bush, partly cleared and fenced with round poles for horses; one acre alfalfa; abundant power available; tin shed for tools; septic system; possible pig licence; suitable stone fruit, goats and almonds. GPO 58 kilometres.

Neighbour Woman on the Fencing Wire: 'So you've bought this place well let me tell you straight away your soil's no good all salt even 160 feet down and up on the slopes is outcrops of granite and dead stumps of dead wood nothing'll grow there we know we've tried what the crows don't take the rabbits and bandicoots will have your creek floods in winter and in summer it's dried the water's all salt there too your sheep'll either starve or drown and if a calf gets born it'll not be able to get up that's the kind of place this is and what's more you've poison weed all over your block so if you put stock you'll lose the lot and another thing there was a snake on our place last year and its shot through into yours and I daresay it's still there and where there's one snake there's sure to be another and there's been some terrible accidents round here only last a week a man just married a week thought he'd fix his roof and fell through the rafters and his wife only a young thing found him hanging dead and then there was that pig ate a woman's baby right in front of her door mind you I always say . . .'

As the neighbour woman says, the five-acre virgin, though beautiful, with grass trees, wildflowers and enormous ancient trees – wandoo and jarrah – is not the ideal place for growing an orchard. But that is what we are trying to do there. We keep geese, too, and Rhode Island Red chickens . . . In spite of the neighbour woman it is the place I think of, and I try to go there as often as possible.

There are always those who tell you that the Australian landscape is monotonous and that one part of the bush is indistinguishable from another, even though separated by a few thousand miles. From 30,000 feet, or whatever height the new planes fly at, the different parts of Australia, seen through clouds, may well look alike.

But here on the ground, and travelling slowly, there is a constant and subtle variation. A distant township near the rabbit-proof fence seems to be a desolate, scattered poverty, a shabbiness of weather-blistered little houses, with stacks of poles and empty drums gathered near a closed filling station.

There is also a wheat silo alongside the deserted, overgrown railway. Generators reverberate in a tin shed that stands up against the hotel. Suddenly, after leaving the township, a different landscape is revealed. On both sides of the main road there are endless paddocks with far-off patches of gold where the sun, shining from between distant clouds, catches with its brightness the curve of the land as it falls towards the horizon.

All these miles of wheat in all directions, folded and mended in places, are pulled together, as if seamed, by little dark lines of trees, as if they are embroidered with rich green wool or silk on a golden background. In the design of the embroidery are some silent houses and sheds. Narrow places, fenced off and watered sparingly, produce a little more of the dark green effect. At the intervals, there are unsupervised windmills, turning and clicking with a kind of solemn and honest obedience. But the landscape is not always wheat.

The phrase 'grey–green bush' is encountered all too frequently and is mainly false. The bush is like the sea. It changes with the sky. It changes with the seasons. At the beginning of the summer it is possible to see not merely the varying shades of greens but, by the extravagance of the new growth, these greens run into excesses of gold and red.

It is difficult to convey in words a description of grass trees (blackboys) to someone who has never seen them. Perhaps it is their movement that makes the best picture – a small delicate shivering of hundreds of green stalks, which is attractive, especially when it has been raining and the sunlight causes spider webs and quivering raindrops to shine and sparkle.

In a dry country, water, either the lack of it or sudden floods, can be uppermost in one's mind. My journeys into the wheat country have provided me with images I would otherwise never have known. Many different flowers grow in the places where water runs off rocks. In other places, quite near but without this collected water, there are none.

Because of the water and its movement, one end of a paddock can be deep purple, like a plum, and within that single paddock, from one end to the other, the colours can range from the deep purple prune plum through the pale pearly green of the unripe satsuma.

To walk barefoot on the fragrant sun-dried grass and eucalyptus leaves is another new experience. In the extreme dry heat of summer all life seems withdrawn. It is as if some wisdom is hidden in the bush. To sit on the warm earth with closed eyes, to breathe in the fragrance and to listen to the liquid song of the magpies and the strange cries of parrots and the pink-and-grey galahs, and the wild mad laughter of the kookaburras, is to realise, yet again, that this is indeed a foreign country where human life can be of very little account.

In the middle of the nineteenth century, the Benedictine monk Rosendo Salvado wrote, 'Bishop Brady was well aware that if a European ventured into the bush and lost contact with the towns, or the outlying settlers' homes, he had no hope of coming back alive.' The same is true today.

Because of my work conducting creative writing workshops, I have driven alone through the remote areas. There I have often experienced an extraordinary phenomenon – brought about, I suppose, by fatigue – seeing old, grey, bent men and women waiting indefinitely on green, misleading corners, and then becoming part of the scrub and the roadside undergrowth as soon as I stopped to investigate. Or noticing comfortable, inviting tracks in the twilight, lined with soft sand and leaves, appearing to lead off easily to the right as the main road curves to the left.

On one occasion, emerging from bush and forest and travelling once again through land that had been cleared for farming, I found myself pulling off onto the gravelly shoulder of the road to allow a ship to cross in front of me, from one moonlit paddock to another.

In a country where a 10-centimetre-scale map would produce sheets of blank spaces, the emptiness and the silence are impressive.

At times, in this silence, the traveller is tempted to stop the car with the idea of walking. To get out of the car and to walk. The road between empty paddocks is quiet and deserted. When walking it would be possible to accept a different view of time and journey. It would be possible to feel small and safe, walking and then pausing to stand still.

The occupation of a small fragment of the earth is known only to the person who is alone on it. It is possible to imagine the feeling of being unseen and not known about while standing alone in one isolated place, low down under the immense, clear blue sky. It might even be possible to think that all anxieties and fears will disappear. They might dissolve, dissipate themselves into the silence.

THE LAND

Sun stroked slopes
Waist high wild oats
Shadow splashed.
Light gravel loam
White with frost,
Summer warmed
Winter washed.

The Pelican

I am sitting on a bench watching the children on the merry-go-round. I can't stop myself from thinking of something that happened a whole year ago. People are walking by, talking and laughing and eating fruit and ice creams, and I wish I could see everything as I once did see it. As the children wave to me from the little painted horses I wave and smile and, for a moment, forget that I am frightened.

The day we went for the Barbecue was very hot and we were quite a crowd, four couples and eighteen children between us. Molly and Tom have only two, small-boned little girls with fair skins and far too many dresses. Most of the children were mine because I had my sister's two boys staying with me while she was in hospital waiting for an operation.

What happened that day is so much on my mind I have to make an effort to think of something else. Bessie, Molly, Betty and myself were all at school together and when we married, much about the same time, we all went on a Barbecue. Every year since then, we have all met and gone to the same place. And every year there have been more children, mostly mine as I have had a child every year.

So on that hot day we all piled out of the cars in a curve of sandy scrub and the spiky green and brown and grey country stretched quietly out away on all sides. We soon filled the silence with our noise, gathering wood for the fire, pouring drinks and handing round thick slices of egg-and-bacon pie. Bessie's man, Hartley, is the first to do everything. He wears thick-rimmed glasses and, when he swears in five languages, everyone admires him. Of course he organised the cooking and fixed up the billy for making the tea. I don't think I ever saw sausages and chops disappear so quickly and all the great basins of salad were empty in no time.

Hartley, showing off, seized one of Molly's girls and swung her round and up in the air. Her fair skin flushed and she looked pleased to be chosen by Hartley. When suddenly he set her down and cried out that something from her had stuck a splinter in his finger. He looked at her accusingly and sucked his finger, complaining about the pain. Everyone rushed to help him, he is like that. Draws every bit of attention. Not mine because I saw Molly's Cynthia standing flushed and dizzy, her eyes full of tears, because of being blamed.

Molly bandaged Hartley, fussing and telling Cynthia she was a wicked child to hurt her Uncle Hartley. I felt really mad at Hartley but Fred, that's my husband, said if we wanted to get to the Pelican in time we should put out the fire and go.

Our car was full of children so two of my girls went in with Molly and Tom. It was quite a long drive and the children sang all the songs they knew.

I better explain The Pelican is a rock which looks like a pelican, especially at dusk for then the outline is dark against the sky as if a great Bird was turned into stone on coming down to the earth. We always try to arrive at dusk to watch the Bird appear out of the rocks. We all touch the Pelican in turn and wish for every one of us health and happiness and success. Even the hands of the babies are put to touch the Pelican. It has become a real ceremony to us.

It was very lonely on the road, only our cars. At last we were there, there was a beautiful moon and there was our Pelican strong and majestic and unchanged. We all said our words of good wishes and Hartley, who made his sound like a prayer, was first to put his hands on the rock. He called Bessie and she called her children.

'Arthur, Harry and Mary!' They went up to the Pelican and Mary called Betty and William. And Betty called her children.

'Simon, Archie and little Arthur.' Little Arthur in his reedy voice called,

'Tom and Molly!' and Molly called,

'Cynthia and Rosie!' and Molly called,

'Cynthia!' again. Rosie stood back in the quiet dark evening waiting for her sister. But there was no sign of Cynthia.

All the time the Pelican seemed bigger and blacker as the moon raced up the sky.

'Cynthia be quick! It's getting late!' Molly called into the silence. 'She travelled with you, didn't she?' Molly asked me, her voice sharp with fear.

'No,' I said. 'We only had the boys and baby, my girls went with you.' I could hardly speak for the fear I felt. It seemed cold suddenly. Rosie began to cry and Molly shouted at Tom, and Tom, who is always as quiet as a refrigerator box, shouted back at Molly. Then Fred said we must all go back and look for Cynthia. The children were all very subdued with what had happened, we counted them all into the cars.

We had to drive back all those miles of dark winding road to look for Cynthia. I kept thinking of the little girl alone in the bush afraid of witches and ghosts and afraid, if we find her, of our anger. And gradually that fear will have turned into a more terrible fear with the coming night as she is all alone with no one there except what she thinks is there lurking in the scrub.

At last we were there. It was as if we had come to the wrong place, it was so dark and strange. The children sat quietly in the cars while we spread out to try to find Cynthia. I peered into the frightening mysterious undergrowth. Twigs and leaves crackled under our feet and when we called her name, our own voices frightened us. It was as if a strange silent person was watching us stumbling about. I felt I couldn't stand it and then Molly began to run wildly falling down and screaming.

Fred said it was no use to look. We must get Molly home. Perhaps, he suggested, Cynthia walked along the road and was picked up by a passing car. This quieted Molly.

We didn't find Cynthia on the way and the Police did not have her or any news about her. There was nothing about Cynthia for us.

Molly and Tom came to our place and we put the children to bed, Rosie in with our two girls. We didn't go to bed ourselves, I tried to persuade Molly to lie down but she kept going to the window to stare out into the darkness.

'Remember, Liz,' she said to me, 'remember last year, Cynthia never touched the Pelican when we all did. Remember she was naughty, she pretended to fall, and took so long and Hartley sent her back to wait in the car. I stopped her from touching the Pelican, I was so angry, and now —' Molly began to cry, the most weary hopeless crying I have ever heard. And I knew we should never see Cynthia again. That was what happened last year.

Everything was done to try to find the little girl. The bush was searched but she was never found, not even a piece of clothing or a shoe. Nothing was ever found. Nothing.

All that was a year ago but I am not able to get it out of my mind. I suppose if you feed thoughts like this they will grow, but you see not one of us, neither Fred nor myself nor my children, nor my sister's boys, who are still with me, not one of us touched the Pelican last year.

At the River

'Don't suck your thumb here, Eric!' Isobel spoke sharply to the boy Eric who sat hunched in the shade of one of the trailing peppermint trees.

'Isn't it strange how the women from Italy, who have come here, wear black dresses?' Isobel spoke in a different tone. She was watching the people going by. 'I mean, them wearing black dresses when everyone else is in bathing costumes and shorts, because it's Sunday I suppose, not that it matters, just looks odd. Some of them, that one there,' Isobel nodded her head to indicate, 'she is very handsome, very striking, not what you would call pretty though, don't you agree?' Denis, her husband, murmured a reply without looking up from his Henry James. He had a list of serious reading for the holidays and was already embarked. Both he and Isobel were irritated by Eric hunched up, hot and thumb-sucking and refusing to go into the water with their other two children, Denise and Jose. Jose was a square-shaped child and happy, still a baby, and able to ride on her big sister's back in the shallow kind-hearted river. Denise was thirteen. Isobel had never liked the name Denise. At the time of her birth Denis's mother had been staying with them and everyone had been so sure the baby was to be a boy. There was nothing Isobel could do about it and within half an hour of the baby's arrival Denis and his mother had started calling her Denise.

Isobel waved to the two girls.

'Eric!' she said, 'change into your bathers and go in the water and get cool!' Her voice was sharp with suppressed anger and weariness with the boy. 'Please!' she pleaded. 'You will love it in the water, here, let me help with your bathers!' Isobel used the word 'bathers' self-consciously as she had only recently learnt to use it. Eric hunched himself up even more. She would have liked to slap him.

'Slap him hard!' said Denis; immediately he said this Isobel felt tenderness for the boy, he was such a shrimp, lately grown too tall and thin, his head egg-shaped and vulnerable with close-cropped hair and large red ears.

'Please Eric!' she said with an anxious glance at Denis, but the boy only laid his head in her lap.

Denis put his book down with a bang and lost his place, his face was ugly with anger.

'Take the boy home!' he said irritably, 'Go on, take him home at once! At once!' His tone implied it was all her fault. Denis blamed Isobel. He blamed her always, everything which was not right was her fault. She had not realised this for years but now she found herself amazed daily at his capacity for finding her at fault, especially over the children.

'Oh, he will go in a minute, won't you dear?' Isobel said, but Eric shook his head.

'Do as I say!' said Denis. 'Here, take the car keys; take him home and leave him there.' He flung the keys at his wife and stared angrily across the water. The river was blue and wide, the bridge and the city in the distance looked like a pastel drawing on a back drop curtain. Little boats with white sails hurried to and fro in some kind of race near the far bank. Every now and then a motor boat roared by with a bronzed water skier attached behind. The colours were tranquil and clean. But there was nothing pleasant in the scene for Denis as he sat staring in his anger. Isobel stood up slowly, her dress was faded and crumpled and the hem uneven. She was not a bit sun-tanned and her shoulders stooped drearily, one dingy shoulder strap flapped on her arm. Nervously she patted her hair.

'Come along Eric, she said and started to walk across the grass to the car park. She did not look back for the boy but picked her way miserably through the untidy groups of people scattered with their rugs and towels and picnic food. The foreshore was crowded today, mostly families with their old ones carefully seated on folding chairs and their babies in wicker cradles covered with fine white or green mosquito netting. Here and there lay sun-bronzed youths entangled with their girls, but only in a drowsy heat-tumbled embrace. Everywhere transistor radios bleated advertisements and jangled out the Hit Parade. Children were laughing and shouting and crying, the air was heavy with the smell of the river and orange peel. Isobel stood in the heat in the middle of it all and wished things were not as they were.

She had to take Eric home. Denis was always punishing the children in this sort of way so that it was really Isobel who was punished. Suppose Eric cried and clung to her when she tried to leave him at home. Suppose she couldn't get the car out from the crowded car park and safely across the main road. Suppose Eric was not following her at all. The situation and the noise and the heat were unbearable. She looked around; there was Eric just behind her, thin and tired and unhappy-looking. Perhaps he was not very well and so did not like the idea of the water. At nine years he must know what he wanted to do, it was unjust to force him into the water. Sometimes you saw people forcing their children to bathe, a

dreadful sight of thin shuddering bodies, of heaving ribs and clinging hands – and then afterwards, thin and huddled and shivering,
red-eyed and sobbing. An ordeal.

Eric liked to bathe as a rule, this is what made Denis angry. Eric
could spoil the whole day for them if he chose to, Isobel knew this.

They stood by the gap in the hedge, the car park scintillating just
beyond.

Isobel held Eric's hand. They would have to be careful moving
the car through all these other cars.

'What's this smell?' Eric asked his mother. Isobel looked about
her.

'Honeysuckle!' she said. 'Look the hedge is full of it.' They
breathed the fragrance. Isobel hated Denis for the situation she was
in. Still holding Eric's skinny hand, she turned and marched back
through all the unconcerned people to where Denis was reading
under the tree.

'Eric is going to bathe.' Isobel's voice quavered. She hated her
own voice especially when it shook. Without looking at her, Eric
began to take off his shorts.

'Help me Mum,' he whined. Isobel could not help him fast
enough and then she sat nodding and waving and smiling as he went
slowly down to the shore and slowly edged his way into the river to
join his sisters. Denis read and Isobel relaxed and peered about, she
wore spectacles for short sight. After a while she said, 'How about
if I go home and bring some lunch down for us all?'

'What could you bring?' said Denis doubtfully.

'Oh, salad and cold meat. I could put lettuce and things into my
big pastry bowl; that is what people seem to do here.' Isobel was
enthusiastic.

'That would be very nice,' Denis was agreeable. Isobel hastened
to the car and in a few minutes she was at home.

Christmas had collapsed in the heat. The little house was not big enough for them and for Christmas and the heat. The small sitting room was burdened with coloured streamers and lanterns, balloons and greetings cards. Denise had hammered up festoons of paper and had pasted gold paper angels on the doors and windows. And the tree, laden with memories from previous Christmases, leaned heavily to one side. As they had unpacked the little carved decorations, the coloured balls and faded tinsel, Isobel and the children had experienced the bittersweet nostalgia for another place where they had known Christmas, and for the people they had been with, and for all the things that go with Christmas in a cold winter climate. They had made dozens of mince pies; they ate a few of them and the rest were wrapped in newspaper in the dustbin. Silently they were all longing to clear up the sitting room.

Isobel paid no attention to all the mess. She let the flyscreen door bang and went swiftly through the sitting room to the kitchen. She sang softly as she washed a lettuce and peeled and cut up a magnificent carrot and an even more magnificent cucumber. She had radishes and tomatoes and spring onions in the refrigerator and fresh butter and cold meat. She ate a bit while she prepared it. The pickled beef, or corned beef as they called it here, was delicious. She wrapped up two bottles of iced water in sheets of newspaper and filled a big bag with ripe peaches, plums and apricots. The kitchen was fragrant with the fruit. She must remember to write home about the fruit and the smell of it. Finally she cut up a loaf and wrapped it in a cloth. Hurriedly she took everything to the car and very soon was walking carefully over the crowded grass, the pastry bowl nearly slipping from the crook of her arm and the string bag cutting her fingers cruelly, to where Denis lay reading.

This was Denis's first University appointment, he was lecturing in English and he was very pompous and serious over the whole thing.

One of the causes of the failure of Christmas was that he regarded the sitting room as a study and had the whole room littered with books and papers during the entire holiday, thus spoiling the effect of any decorations and adding considerably to the atmosphere of oppressive clutter in the room. Every day Isobel and Denise begged him to tidy things away so they could sit and have carols and games, but in sorting out his papers he only spread them more around on the floor and mantelpiece. And in the end, Denise cried and then, feeling ashamed for crying in front of the two little ones, slammed off to her bedroom. Denis blamed Isobel and said the children were rude to him. A dreary evening had followed.

But Isobel was not thinking of all this now. She set the food down laughing and called the children to come. They were surprised at the picnic and Denise couldn't believe that her mother could have been home and fetched the food unaided. She looked at everything.

'The salt, Mother,' she cried, 'you've forgotten the salt!' Her voice was triumphant. Water dripped from her all over everything. She was offended and sulky when Denis growled at her to move away a bit.

'Oh, so I have.' said Isobel, dismayed. They all ate a lot of salt, Isobel from choice and habit, and the children because she had trained them to. Denis took a lot of salt because he knew it was a good thing in a hot climate.

'Ah well,' said Isobel 'we'll have to manage.' It took some time to get them sitting round as they liked, there was quite a bit of disagreement and Denis growled again at Denise and at Eric. Isobel thought Eric would cry, Denis could not stand the children crying in public.

'Here Eric,' Isobel said quickly, 'I'll make you a sandwich.'

Jose jumped up suddenly and sand cascaded from her fat bottom.

'Oh, the salad!' Isobel wailed. Denise shrieked and Denis growled.

'I don't want any meat,' whined Eric.

'We can't eat the stuff all covered in sand,' Denis was irritable again.

'Oh Jose you silly fool!' Denise shouted at her little sister. Jose began to cry. People around might notice. Isobel felt so hot. She tried to comfort Jose who was howling.

'Oh shut the kid up!' Denis said. Really Isobel was a fool.

Isobel jumped up. 'Come on Jose, we shall wash the salad. I remember seeing a tap by the hedge.' The situation was saved. Isobel came back breathless and smiling and waving the pastry bowl.

'The flies have been on the meat,' Denis said.

'Oh no!' Isobel scrutinised the delicious pink slices, really she was short-sighted even with her spectacles.

'Oh stop peering at it,' Denis said crossly. 'Better not eat it, let's have the salad. Here, that boy's got all the radishes!' Anger changed to amazement.

Eric flushed terribly. Tempted by the colour he had tried a radish and, finding it agreeable, had selected them all from the bowl while the meat inspection had taken place. He stood awkwardly holding them in both hands.

'No radishes! Eric's having the radishes,' Denis said.

'Please, Denis,' begged Isobel. Eric's eyes were filling with tears, he held the radishes out to Denis.

'Not when you've handled them, thank you very much,' said his father.

'Please, Denis,' Isobel begged him. Denis shrugged and filled his mouth with bread and lettuce, and the meal went on.

When they went home Denis had to use two handkerchiefs to hold the steering wheel, it was so hot. He blamed Isobel for parking the car in the full sun. He blamed her because the car was so hemmed in by other cars.

They got through the rest of the day in the untidy house. Denise began to dismantle the tree as it was Twelfth Night. Jose teased and Eric grew paler and paler and finally Isobel found him hunched in a basket chair on the verandah. His face was ashy pale and his breathing difficult. Tenderly she gathered him up and put him to bed. She gave him all the pillows in the house and prepared poultices and the steam kettle.

Denis spread his books and papers all about him and tried to take no notice of Denise and the Christmas tree. He ignored the domestic uproar. He ignored Isobel.

Late that night when everyone was asleep, even Eric, at last, Isobel took the washing out to hang up. Night time was best for this, it was an ordeal in the heat of the day, even at nine in the morning. There was no shade in their back yard. The moon was full and low and hung in the gum leaf lace in someone else's yard. There was quite a breeze and Isobel could smell the river. So Eric was ill again and that was why he did not want to bathe. Isobel reproached herself. She shook out the clothes and pegged them up on the wires. It was peaceful, if only it could always be peaceful so that they could enjoy living here. She would be peaceful looking after Eric till he was well, three or four weeks perhaps. She would get the house tidy, and maybe unpack some of the material she had brought with her and even do some sewing.

'Eat, my pretty one. My little Duchess, I implore you to eat!' Isobel wriggled on her chair and Tante Marthe threw herself down on her knees on the worn carpet. A small white cloth had been spread over one end of the green velvet plush table cover and, in front of Isobel, in a carefully laid place, was a little dish. A tiny silver spoon was slowly turning black in the mess of egg.

'But it's not nice,' whispered Isobel.

'Oh my little princess, I am sorry!' Tante Marthe on bended knees begged to be forgiven. 'I have scramble in mistaken for boiling,' she explained. But Isobel could not eat the egg.

'There are many children in the world starving for an egg!' Tante Marthe pleaded, she ate a little herself. 'Even if scramble it is still good, please eat!' Later Isobel wandered about the kitchen, aimless and hungry, wanting her mother. Rose was good to her and so was Cook, and Tante Marthe was in despair about her appetite and the state of her bowels.

There were marks everywhere of the recent flooding of the Thames. The basements of many houses in Kew had been filled with muddy water. Tante Marthe showed Isobel her table mats all discoloured and warped, she pointed to dreary patches and dark blotchy lines on the wallpaper and told Isobel about the smell of the flood waters in an effort to distract her. She put the distasteful egg into a surprise sandwich, which sat at Isobel's elbow for most of the afternoon while they sat in the crazy little summer house endlessly cutting out paper dolls and flowers from scraps of coloured paper. 'Now a red one, now a blue one,' Tante Marthe patiently pasting them into a book with sweet-smelling homemade paste, her voice going gently up and down, 'Now a red one, now a blue one.'

That night Isobel's mother, after some weeks of illness, died in hospital. Her father had been killed the year before in an accident so Isobel stayed with Tante Marthe in the tall old-fashioned London house and was looked after in turn by Rose and Cook and Tante Marthe and sometimes by all three at once. Tante Marthe's husband, Uncle Otto, was keeper of the Herbarium in Kew Gardens. He was white-haired and elderly and kind. He was away a great deal, or quietly shut up in his book-lined study on the first floor. He sometimes read to Isobel or patted her on the head.

Some years later Uncle Otto died from pneumonia and Tante

Marthe locked herself in her room for three days. Rose and Cook and Isobel, now a thin pale girl of eleven, tiptoed about the dark house whispering to each other and waiting anxiously to see what would happen next. At the end of the third day Tante Marthe emerged from her room very pale but quite calm. She decided at once to send Isobel to boarding school and set about the preparations immediately. They visited the doctor and the dentist and it was discovered Isobel needed to have three teeth stopped and she had to wear spectacles. Tante Marthe bought the necessary uniform and sat with Rose and Cook and sewed name tapes on all the clothes.

Isobel was a quiet school girl, short-sighted, and homesick for her life with Tante Marthe and Rose and Cook. She quite liked her lessons and the other girls and looked forward with quiet eagerness to her holidays, which were spent in the dark old-fashioned house. Tante Marthe sent parcels to school, untidy paper packages bulging with home-knitted mittens for chilblains and hard-boiled eggs and toffees. The parcels embarrassed Isobel. On the Parents' Days at school Tante Marthe arrived in her strange old-fashioned clothes with a Dutch basket made of wickerwork stuffed with useful oddments for Isobel from Rose and Cook – a handworked canvas calendar, for one thing. Quickly Isobel hid it in her locker. Once Tante Marthe brought Isobel a hockey stick. Isobel could never thank her enough, and she wondered endlessly how Tante Marthe knew about hockey sticks and what weight to get and so on.

School finished, Isobel went to training College and became a quiet teacher with dark untidy hair. She was still short-sighted. Tante Marthe, now very old, came with Rose and Cook, now quite old, to see Isobel's school and her class of little children. Tante Marthe inspected their cut-out paper dolls and flowers and nodded her head with approval.

Later Isobel brought Denis Farr to visit Tante Marthe and in six months she and Denis, also a teacher, were married and went to live in Newcastle-upon-Tyne where Denis had a teaching post. They lived in middle-class suburbia, three bedrooms and an outside water closet, semi-detached and in an ugly street of houses, every one the same. They had two more children after rather a long interval (Isobel had been back teaching), Eric a boy and soon after, Jose a lovely baby girl, serene and thriving on inward merriment.

When Denise was thirteen, Eric six and Jose four, Denis applied for and was accepted for this University appointment in Australia.

They spent an hour visiting Tante Marthe in the tall old-fashioned London house. Tante Marthe, now very very old, dug about in her trunks and found a hideous floral garment that she put on so that Isobel's dear little ones should not be frightened of her dressed like an old witch, always in sombre black and several years out of date. Isobel and Denis and the children arrived and had afternoon tea solemnly in the drawing room. Tante Marthe boiled several cups to ensure there were no germs and let the children choose their own. Eric and Jose were very pleased, and later they explored the stuffy old house and Tante Marthe proudly showed them the flood marks in the basement. Denis was a bit pleased with himself and talked about his new appointment with unconcealed pride. Tante Marthe was very impressed about the University and talked gaily about her young days when Uncle Otto was studying at the University in Vienna. The children were delighted to see the summer house.

When it came time to leave Tante Marthe, Isobel felt herself quietly full of grief and, in spite of herself, her eyes filled with tears. True she had not seen Tante Marthe much since her marriage, what with teaching and the children and Denis's mother living in the same street. She wished she had come down to London more often. Denis was surprised at her grief and the children were more so, Denise had snorted and Eric, not used to seeing his mother cry, had sobbed aloud and Denis had been annoyed. Rose stuffed sugar lumps into Eric's pocket and Tante Marthe assured Isobel she would come out to Australia on a visit as soon as they were settled. They had to go. It was time to leave.

'Mind out about the snakes over there!' Tante Marthe called to them. The two old women stood together in the November afternoon gloom and waved after the taxi.

'What a ghastly frock your great-aunt had on!' Denis said. Isobel had nothing to say.

That night in the cheap dingy hotel bedroom, Isobel experienced the bitter wastes of homesickness. The house sold and her final goodbyes said, this was a time of feeling alone and homeless. And she regretted bitterly not going down to see Tante Marthe more often; this was a point of no return.

'What are you homesick for?' Denis said impatiently. Really Isobel was getting impossible. 'Where we're going will be your home,' he said.

'Yes Mother,' Denise said, 'you've got all of us!'

Isobel dried her eyes and tidied her wisps of hair. What they said was true and it was not their faults that they knew nothing of the years with Tante Marthe in the tall dark house in Kew. And it was not their faults that she had left it too late.

It was a very hot summer. Eric slowly recovered from the illness and on these hot airless nights when there was no sea breeze, they came to the foreshore with rugs and cushions and rested there in the space-laden darkness under the little peppermint trees. Sometimes Eric and Jose fought each other but mostly they enjoyed being there. They could see the lights of cars going along on the other side of the river, and they could lie back and look at the stars and see two silver searchlights, fan-shaped and graceful, as they swept the distant reaches of the hot night sky. The soft little waves flopped

on the shore at their feet and a thousand lights danced on the water
and edged the curving ripples with liquid gold. All around them
were families isolated on rugs, children laughed and babies cried
and voices talked on unceasingly in Italian and Dutch and English.

On the voyage Isobel had been impressed with the Australian
mothers. They had well-cut hair and smooth competent thighs.
They had plenty of suitable holiday clothes for the ship and wore
them quite unselfconsciously. They remained calm and smiling
during the domestic uproar and repeated disaster of mealtimes in
the children's dining room. Isobel lacked all this confidence and
blushed painfully when Eric refused to eat his teatime egg or when
Jose upset her soup.

Here on the foreshore from her corner of the rug Isobel peered
at the dark bunches of people. There was something romantic and
mysterious in these dark shapes especially those gathered around
the light of a storm lantern. The women's thighs in the circles of
lamplight were more smooth, more competent and really beautiful, even women with grown-up children. Isobel's own legs were
flabby and white, hidden for years from the sun, and she had never
known what to do with her hair. Her few summer dresses had been
purchased before Jose was born and were entirely out of fashion.
In the city here you never saw a drearily dressed woman, they were
all so smart and so clean, lots of colour and lots of white. White
shoes, white gloves, white handbags and white hats, all so fresh and
so clean you could have eaten your dinner off any of them. Isobel shrank timidly from them. She shrank from their smartness and
from the unknown expression in the eyes behind the dark glasses
they all wore. It was as if they had, somewhere between these darkened unseen eyes and the slender red-tipped fingers and the tightly
closed bright lipsticked lips, tangible boundaries of women, some
secret knowledge of personal cleanliness.

Isobel had to go and buy clothes for the children for school and shirts for Denis, he needed two a day in this heat. And she had to go and buy clothes for herself. Spending money worried her in any case and the heat and strangeness of a new city added to her unhappiness. Faced with this she submitted herself to the kindly scorn of the shop girls, and stood in her dingy slip trying on dresses, sweating and embarrassed and each dress more elaborate and expensive and not a bit what she liked. A battlefield of well-dressed hostesses awaited them. Denis was enjoying it, he managed very well, he wore his shirt open at the neck and had acquired a nasal drawl and talked about 'Art', bringing the word down his nose just as if he had graduated from Oxford. The English department were determined to be 'Arty' and talked painting and pictures with large P's, bringing the letter out heavily almost like a B. Isobel was amazed at the change in Denis, she felt lonely when he was like this, silly of her really, when everyone was so warm-hearted and friendly. It was really this determination to be 'Arty' in talk, clothes and attitude, and she felt Denis was leaving her out. She dreaded the invitations, especially the Buffet Dinner so popular with hostesses, when more people than chairs were being entertained.

Isobel stood in the little fitting room surrounded by the impossible dresses. Finally she chose one as being the least impossible. A few alterations were needed to make it fit; the dress was meant for someone with a bosom, the saleswoman said. The dress was too long, the saleswoman insisted that Isobel had it shortened. Isobel wanted to hide in the dress and here they were taking inches of it away, shortening it, nipping it in a bit here and a bit there, the tailoress was kneeling beside Isobel her mouth full of pins, scoop out the neckline a bit more and tighten the sash. The saleswoman and the tailoress had quite a conversation together, nothing to do with Isobel, in spite of the pins.

Isobel didn't like her new dress very much, Denis said she must wear it as her others were hopeless, and hurry up do.

'You're not going out dressed like that,' Denise regarded Isobel with disapproval. All those guineas, they weighed on Isobel.

The Buffet Dinner exposed one horribly but Isobel faced it bravely. Everyone talking and helping themselves, a sort of Chinese or Indian curry thing, a mountain of rice and a tossed salad, difficult to handle a tossed salad in these circumstances, and everyone talking and laughing and eating and nowhere to sit. Isobel found herself drearily thinking about the money she had spent and worrying about it. Someone gave her a chair.

'Oh, thank you!' she said and sat down, her dress did not cover her enough. She ate a little of her food. Someone was describing a visit to someone, she tried to look attentive.

'Of course, she paints very badly!'

'Oh, Isobel!' everyone used Christian names, it had no meaning being called Isobel.

'Oh, Isobel,' her hostess smiled over her, 'you haven't got nearly enough, let me give you more,' the spoon ladled over the plate and the gravy splashed all down Isobel's dress.

'Oh, Isobel, I'm sorry!' the voice of laughing apology rang out. 'What a good thing it's just one of your little cottons.' The colour rushed up Isobel's hot face, everyone was looking at her, and the gravy grease was spreading, she could feel the warmth of it. Her face ached with trying to smile. The guineas doubled their weight, just one of her little cottons! The only one. The guineas sat on her like lead.

'That reminds me Isobel,' the voice continued ringing lively, full of life, 'you must let me take you shopping, we'll look around the shops and find you something to wear.' And then forgetting Isobel, 'Has anyone heard if the Cullens are back from leave yet?'

There was a hot breeze stirring in the long-leaved peppermint. The children complained it made their eyes sore. Isobel sat with her skirts flapping round her knees, her eyes ached too with the hot wind and the lights twinkling on the water and with some unshed tears, she was still going over in her mind the Buffet Dinner.

'Perhaps we better take them home to bed,' she said to Denis. The little house would be hot and stuffy, these nights were unbearable. Eric would not get to sleep for hours. They sat a while longer on their rugs as if on an island even though there were people all around them. Somewhere quite near music trickled from a transistor radio.

'Better not think too much about last night!' Isobel told herself sharply. Tomorrow she would go out first thing and get her hair cut short, she would wash it under the shower instead of using the tiny hand basin. There were certain changes to be made, she was slow to make them.

Tomorrow she would wear the new dress right from when she got up and she would wear that kind of dress from then on and get used to the short hemline and the skimpiness, the low neck, the lack of sleeves and the nipped-in waist. Really all these things were right. How this old dress flapped round her like a tattered sail on an old ship. Tomorrow she would tear it up into dusters. They all began wearily to collect up their things to go home.

A TENDER WORSHIP

When you came here
It was the time for the acacias
The winter was warm and sweet
With the promise of their flowering.
Old trees, massed dark and green
Bursting suddenly bright yellow
Enriching the valley
Changing with every change
of the sky and the sun.
You are still here
This morning tender tributaries
Swell the plentiful earth.
When you are here
Everything I am doing is for you.
Everything is part of a tender worship
The shining water of the stream in flood
Flowing over flat banks and over the bridge
of weathered railway sleepers. Jarrah trimmed
Long quiet paddocks clover strewn
Orchard ripening pears and sturdy quince
Velvet first fruits and grape bunches
Hanging secretly.
All the blossom and all the fruit
All the harvest when it comes
Even the constant changing of the season
Is yours.

Pear Tree Dance

No one knew where the Newspaper of Claremont Street went in her spare time.

Newspaper or Weekly as she was called by those who knew her, earned her living by cleaning other people's houses. There was something she wanted to do more than anything else, and for this she needed money. For a long time she had been saving, putting money aside in little amounts. Every morning, when she woke up, she thought about her money. The growing sum danced before her, growing a little more. She calculated what she would be able to put in the bank. She was not very quick at arithmetic. As she lay in bed she used the sky as a blackboard, and in her mind, wrote the figures on the clouds. The total sum came out somewhere half way down her window.

While she was working in the different houses she sang, '*the bells of hell go ting a ling a ling for you and not for me*'. She liked hymns best.

'Well 'ow are we?' she called out when she went in in the mornings. 'Ow's everybody today?' And she would throw open windows and start pulling the stove to pieces. She knew everything about all the people she cleaned for and she never missed anything that was going on.

'I think that word should be clay, C-L-A-Y.' She helped old Mr Kingston with his crossword puzzle.

'Chattam's girl's engaged at long larst,' she reported to the Kingstons. 'Two rooms full of presents, yo' should just see!'

'Kingston's boy's 'ad 'orrible accident,' she described the details to the Chathams. 'Lorst 'is job first, pore boy! Pore Mrs Kingston!' Weekly sadly shook the tablecloth over the floor and carried out some dead roses carefully as if to keep them for the next funeral.

'*I could not do without Thee Thou Saviour of the Lorst*,' she sang at the Butterworths.

She cleaned in all sorts of houses. Her body was hard like a board and withered with so much work she seemed to have stopped looking like a woman.

On her way home from work she always went in the little shop at the end of Claremont Street and bought a few things, taking her time and seeing who was there and watching what they bought.

'Here's the Newspaper of Claremont Street,' the two shop girls nudged each other.

'Any pigs been eating babies lately Newspaper?' one of them called out.

'What happened to the man who sawed off all his fingers at the timber mill?' the other girl called. 'You never finished telling us.'

No one needed to read anything, the Newspaper of Claremont Street told them all the news.

One Tuesday afternoon when she had finished her work, she went to look at the valley for the first time. All the morning she was thinking about the long drive. She wondered which would be the shortest way to get to this place hidden behind the pastures and foothills along the South West Highway. It was a strain thinking about it and talking gossip at the same time, especially as she kept thinking too that she had no right really to go looking at land.

All land is somebody's land. For Weekly the thought of possess-ing some seemed more of an impertinence than a possibility. Perhaps this was because she had spent her childhood in a slaty backyard where nothing would grow except thin carrots and a few sunflowers. All round the place where she lived the slag heaps smouldered and hot cinders fell on the paths. The children gathered to play in a little thicket of stunted thornbushes and elderberry trees. There were patches of coltsfoot and they picked the yellow flowers eagerly till none was left. Back home in the Black Country where it was all coal mines and brick kilns and iron foundries her family had never had a house or a garden. Weekly had nothing behind her not even the place where she was born. It no longer existed. As soon as she was old enough she was sent into service. Later she left her country with the family where she was employed. All her life she had done domestic work. She was neat and quick and clean and her hands were rough like nutmeg graters and she knew all there was to know about people and their ways of living.

Weekly lived in a rented room, it was covered with brown lino-leum which she polished. The house was built a long time ago for a large family but now the house was all divided up. Every room had a different life in it and every life was isolated from all the other lives.

Except for the old car she bought, Weekly, the Newspaper of Claremont Street, had no possessions. Nothing in the room belonged to her except some old books and papers, collected and hoarded, and her few washed-out and mended clothes. She lived quite alone and, when she came home tired after her long day of work, she took some bread and boiled vegetables from the fly-screen cupboard where she kept her food, and she sat reading and eating hungrily. She was so thin and her neck so scraggy that, when she swallowed, you could see the food going down. But as she had no one there to

see and to tell her about it, it did not really matter. While it was
still light, Weekly pulled her chair across to the narrow window of
her room and sat bent over her mending. She darned everything.
She put on patches with a herring-bone stitch. Sometimes she made
the worn out materials of her skirts firmer with rows of herring-
boning, one row neatly above the other, the brown thread glowing
in those last rays of the sun which make all browns beautiful. Even
the old linoleum could have a sudden richness at this time of the
evening. It was like the quick lighting up of a plain girl's face when
she smiles because of some unexpected happiness.

It was when she was driving out to the country on Sundays in her
old car she began to wish for some land, nothing very big, just a few
acres. She drove about and stared into green paddocks fenced with
round poles for horses and scattered in the corners with red flame-tree
flowers and splashed all over with white lilies. She stopped to admire
almond blossom and she wished for a little weatherboard house,
warm in the sun, fragrant with orange trees and surrounded by vines.
Sometimes she sat for hours alone in the scrub of a partly cleared
piece of bush and stared at the few remaining tall trees, wondering at
their age, and at the yellow tufts of Prickly Moses surviving.

The advertisements describing land for sale made her so excited
she could hardly read them. As soon as she read one she became so
restless she wanted to go off at once to have a look.

'Yo' should 'ave seen the mess after the Venns' Party,' she called
to Mrs Lacey. 'Broken glass everywhere, blood on the stairs and a
whole pile of half-eaten pizzas in the laundry. Some people think
they're having a good time! And you'll never believe this, I picked
up a bed jacket, ever so pretty it was, to wash it and, would you
believe, there was a yuman arm in it . . .' The Newspaper of Claremont Street talked all the time in the places where she worked. It
was not for nothing she was called Newspaper or Weekly, but all

the time she was talking she never spoke about the land. Secretly she read her advertisements and secretly she went off to look.

She first went to the valley on a Tuesday after work.

'Tell about Sophie Whiteman,' Diana Lacey tried to detain Weekly. Mrs Lacey had, as usual, gone to town and Diana was in bed with a sore throat.

'Wash the curtains please,' Mrs Lacey felt this was a precaution against more illness. 'We must get rid of the nasty germs,' she said. 'And Weekly, I think the dining-room curtains need a bit of sewing, if you have time, thank you,' and she had rushed off late for the hairdresser.

'Well,' said Weekly putting away the ironing board. 'She got a pair of scissors and she went into the garding and she looked all about her to see no one was watching and she cut up a earthworm into a whole lot of little pieces.'

'What did her mother do?' asked Diana joyfully, knowing from a previous telling.

'Well,' said Weekly, 'she come in from town and took orf her hat and her lovely fur coat, very beautiful lady, Mrs Whiteman, she took orf her good clothes and she took Sophie Whiteman and laid her acrorss her lap and give her a good hidin'.'

'Oh!' Diana was pleased. 'Was that before she died of the chocolate lining in her stomach or after?'

'Diana Lacey, what have I told you before, remember? Sophie Whiteman had her good hidin' afore she died. How could she cut up a worm after she died. Use yor brains!'

Weekly was impatient to leave to find the way to the valley. She found a piece of paper and scrawled a note for Mrs Lacey.

'Will come early tomorrow to run up yor curtings W.'

She knew she had to cross the Medulla brook and turn left at the twenty-nine-mile peg. She found the valley all right.

After the turnoff, the road bends and climbs and then there it is, pasture on either side of the road with cattle grazing, straying towards a three-cornered dam. And, on that first day, there was a newly born calf which seemed unable to get up.

She saw the weatherboard house and she went up there and knocked.

'Excuse me, but can yo' tell me what part of the land's for sale?' her voice trembled.

The young woman, the tenant's wife, came out.

'It's all for sale,' she said. They walked side by side.

'All up there,' the young woman pointed to the hillside where it was steep and covered with dead trees and rocks and pig sties made from old railway sleepers and corrugated iron. Beyond was the light and shade of the sun shining through the jarrah trees.

'And down there,' she flung her plump arm towards the meadow which lay smiling below.

'There's a few orange trees, neglected,' she explained. 'That in the middle is an apricot. That over there is a pear tree. And where you see them white lilies, that's where there's an old well. Seven acres this side.'

They walked back towards the house.

'The pasture's leased just now,' the young woman said. 'But it's all for sale too, thirty acres and there's another eighteen in the scrub.'

Weekly wanted to stay looking at the valley but she was afraid that the young woman would not believe she really wanted to buy some of it. She drove home in a golden tranquillity dreaming of her land embroidered with pear blossom and bulging with plump apricots. Her crooked feet were wet from the long weeds and yellow daisies of the damp meadow. The road turned and dropped. Below was the great plain. The neat ribs of the vineyards chased each other towards the vague outlines of the city. Beyond was a thin line shining like the rim of a china saucer. It was the sea, brimming, joining the earth to the sky.

While she scrubbed and cleaned she thought about the land and what she would grow there. At night she studied pamphlets on fruit growing. She had enough money saved to buy a piece of land but she still felt she had no right.

Every Sunday she went out to look at the valley and every time she found something fresh. Once she noticed that on one side of the road was a whole long hedge of white wild roses. Another time it seemed as if sheep were on the hillside among the pig sties, but, when she climbed up, she saw it was only the light on some greyish bushes making them look like a quiet flock of sheep.

One evening she sat in the shop in Claremont Street, sucking in her cheeks and peering into other people's shopping bags.

'Last week yo' bought flour,' she said to a woman.

'So what if I did?'

'Well you'll not be needing any terday,' Weekly advised. 'Now eggs yo' didn't get, yo'll be needing them! . . .'

'Pore Mr Kingston,' Weekly shook her head and addressed the shop, 'I done 'is puzzle today. Mr Kingston I said let me do your crossword – I doubt he'll leave his bed again.'

Silence fell among the groceries and the women who were shopping. The silence remained unbroken for Weekly had forgotten to talk. She had slipped into thinking about the valley. All her savings were not enough, not even for a part of the meadow. She was trying to get over the terrible disappointment she had just had.

'If you're prepared to go out say forty miles,' Mr Rusk, the land agent, had said gently, 'there's a nice five acres with a tin shack for tools. Some of it's river flats, suitable for pears. That would be within your price range.' Mr Rusk spoke seriously to the old woman even though he was not sure whether she was all right in the head. 'Think it over,' he advised. He always regarded a customer as a buyer until the customer did not buy.

Weekly tried to forget the valley, she began to scatter the new land with pear blossom. She would go at the weekend.

'Good night all!' She left the shop abruptly without telling any news at all.

On Sunday Weekly went to look at the five acres. It was more lovely than she had expected, and fragrant. A great many tall trees had been left standing and the tin shack turned out to be a tiny weatherboard cottage. She was afraid she had come to the wrong place.

'It must be someone's home,' she thought to herself as she peered timidly through the cottage window and saw that it was full of furniture. Disappointment crept over her. Purple pig face was growing everywhere and, from the high verandah, she looked across the narrow valley to a hay field between big trees. There was such a stillness that Weekly felt more than ever that she was trespassing, not only on the land, but into the very depths of the stillness itself.

Mr Rusk said that it was the five acres he had meant.

'I've never been there myself,' he explained when she told him about the cottage. 'Everything's included in the price.'

Buying land takes time but Weekly contained herself in silence and patience, working hard all the days.

She began to buy things, a spade, rubber boots, some candles and groceries and polish and she packed them into the old car. Last of all she bought a pear tree, it looked so wizened she wondered how it could ever grow. Carefully she wrapped it in wet newspapers and laid it like a thin baby along the back seat.

On the day Mr Rusk gave her the key, Weekly went to work with it pinned inside her dress. She felt it against her ribs all morning and in the afternoon she drove out to her piece of land.

The same trees and fragrance and the cottage were all there as before. This time she noticed honeysuckle and roses, a fig tree and a hedge of rosemary all neglected now and waiting for her to continue what some other person had started many years ago.

She thought she would die there that first day as she opened the cottage door to look inside. She looked shyly at the tiny rooms and wandered about on the land looking at it and breathing the warm fragrance. The noise of the magpies poured into the stillness and she could hear the creek, in flood, running. She sank down on to the earth as if she would never get up from it again. She counted over the treasures of the cottage. After having nothing she seemed now to have everything, a bed, table, chairs and in the kitchen, a wood stove and two toasting forks, a kettle and five flat irons. There was a painted cupboard too and someone had made curtains of pale-blue stuff patterned with roses.

Weekly wanted to clean out the cottage at once. She felt suddenly too tired. She rested on the earth and looked about her feeling the earth with her hands and listening as if she expected some great wisdom to come to her from the quiet trees and the undergrowth of the bush.

At about five o'clock the sun, before falling into the scrub, flooded the slope from the west and reddened the white bark of the trees. The sky deepened with the coming evening. Weekly forced her crooked old feet into the new rubber boots. She took the spade and the thin pear tree and went down to the mud flats at the bottom of her land.

Choosing a place for the pear tree she dug a hole. It was harder to dig in the clay than she thought it would be and she had to pause to rest several times.

She carried some dark earth from under a fallen tree over to the hole. Carefully she held the little tree in position and scattered the dark soft earth round the roots. She shook the little tree and scattered in more earth and then she firmed the soil, treading gently round and round the tree.

For the first time in her life the Newspaper of Claremont Street, or Weekly as she was called, was dancing. Stepping round and round the little tree she imagined herself to be like a bride dancing with lacy white blossom cascading on all sides. Round and round the tree, dancing, firming the softly yielding earth with her new boots. And from the little foil label blowing in the restlessness of the evening came a fragile music for the pear tree dance.

PEAR TREE DANCE

All day the sun wrapped colour
On bleeding bark and polished stone
These old great trees were growing
Before men made this place their home.
The light is fading from the northern hills
All day it was the second planting,
Kind feet stepping on soft earth dancing
Firming the fresh soil's hopeful face.
In a shower of promised leaf and flower
Will stand a bride blossomed in living lace.
And from the tinfoil label
Comes a fragile music
For the pear tree dance.
Winter nourished
Summer cherished
The secret flesh of sweet fruit whitening
Beneath the glow of fragrant ripening.
Just now, the hungry heron flies alone.

Only Connect!

Only Connect! That was the whole of her sermon. Only
connect the prose and the passion, and both will be
exalted . . .

E. M. Forster

The whole time (a few years) while I was a door-to-door salesman
I had a sinking feeling, a sense of failure which descended as soon
as I woke up and yet I persisted. I cannot explain this persistence
unless it is that I seem to have developed, during my life, the power
to endure. A great deal of life consists of endurance whether it is
some kind of pain, anxiety about children, the company of boring and even malicious people – people endure all kinds of things.
Hardship is in different forms for different people. I went on with
this work even when the small bedroom at home was stacked up
with a particularly dreary green (but good quality) soap, bottles of
coconut-oil shampoo to which the family (and friends) developed
an allergy, packets of jelly crystals and liquid manure (also in packets which looked like jelly crystal packets). Change was supposed
to be given in the form of these packets, the customer could choose,

and this was a way of getting that extra little sale while the foot was still in the door. The air in the little bedroom and in the car was fragrant, perhaps heavy is a better word, with the overpowering redolence of bath salts, packaged in pink and blue plastic urns, and of spices – ginger, cinnamon and so on. Every morning I felt tired and hungry and defeated before I had even reached my selling area which was a sprawling suburb between the railway line and the sea. I longed for work where I carried out certain duties and received regular payment. This seeking for customers and maintaining their interest is one of the hardest ways of working. It belongs to another era really when people waited for the salesman to bring his little case of treasures from which they could make their selection and place their orders. The toothpaste (good quality) which I was selling cost more wholesale than the toothpaste in the supermarket.

I did meet some very nice people as well as the awful ones. I did have doors banged in my face, not very often, but once is enough! Mostly the houses were empty, the whole family being out at work and school. At one house there was an old woman with a bedridden husband; it became a part of the week that I stopped there and helped her give him a blanket bath. In another house was a 'woman in a dressing gown' who really needed my company for a bit. I saw quite a lot of misfortune and loneliness and a certain unexpected poverty hidden behind solid house fronts, venetian blinds and pot plants. At the time I never thought that so much of this would appear in my fiction; in the stories 'The Travelling Entertainer' and 'Two Men Running' and the novel *Milk and Honey*. My concern was to earn a little money to pay for the typing of manuscripts and for postage for repeated submissions. My writing was mostly unaccepted then. Thirty-nine rejections in one year and a failing door-to-door salesman . . .

I preferred to go with Mother on her cleaning job. She had all these luxury apartments in South Heights to do. We got a taste of the pleasures of the rich there and it had the advantage that Mother could let people from down our street in at times to enjoy some of the things which rich people take for granted like rubbish chutes and so much hot water that you could have showers and do all your washing and wash your hair every day if you wanted to. Old Mrs Myer was always first in to Baldpate's penthouse to soak her poor painful feet.

'Five Acre Virgin'

It might have seemed eccentric, in the eyes of people we knew, for me to work as a Flying Domestic but, again, this was work which could be done in hours when I did not need to be at home. It had the advantage of being the kind of job where you worked for a number of hours and received payment. I had always envied cleaning ladies; their opinions seemed to carry weight. They seemed to me to be strong and their children got on well in the world. The children of my mother's cleaning ladies were always held up as an example of perfection during my own childhood. Perhaps I felt some secret blessing would fall on me and on my family if I went out kneeling on acres of vinyl tiles cleaning them minutely with fragments of steel wool and dusting countless ledges covered with ornaments in countless rooms. Perhaps the blessing was there in that the hard physical work cured me of backache and, without realising it at the time, gave me material for the Discarder stories, later published in *Five Acre Virgin and Other Stories,* and enhanced too the character of Weekly for the novel *The Newspaper of Claremont Street.*

Being a Flying Domestic took me into all sorts of houses – and even to the races at Pinjarra to cut sandwiches. Slowly I managed to have all my cleaning work in one block of apartments. This proved to be useful as I worked between the apartments replacing a broken ashtray in one with a good one from another, drying one person's clothes in the clothes dryer on another floor to pay that person back for washing done the previous week in his washing machine and so forth. I never saw any of the people in these apartments but could imagine quite a lot from clothes and possessions, from the state of the kitchen or the bathroom and so on. In one apartment there were some books, an edition of the complete works of Jane Austen beautifully bound. Not having seen the edition before, I took down one book and then another to have a look. Every book contained a set of three wine glasses. I have not used this example of intellectual ingenuity yet in a story. The apartments had all been supplied with the same items of culture, Eros in plaster made to look like bronze, and reproductions of the Mona Lisa and the Laughing Cavalier suitably darkened to look like antiques. All the floors had the same shaggy oatmeal-coloured carpet, wall to wall and including the toilet. Sometimes it was difficult to remember whose apartment I was cleaning at a particular moment.

Cleaning someone else's house is unemotional and the mind is left free for the development of ideas . . .

GOOD SEASON

It's like a quartet, the four seasons
Taking up and passing on the growth and work of the land
All four seasons make the whole
cherishing and nourishing
of the seed, the root, the leaf and the flower.
The seasons changing, the sowing and the growing
And the harvest brings an explanation from the earth.
Until the boundary there is no feed
Once on my land the pasture's in good heart
Stocked about two sheep to every acre
Which has ever been my policy.
A good season, the sheep are sold
And the fat lambs, a good price.
Already I miss the lambs I miss their crying
And the ewes' tender deep replying.
From across the valley comes a quiet consolation
An indifference of angry stallions and reluctant mares.

BAD SEASON

My feckless neighbour fired
His long grass and my orchard.
Scorched dead trees haunt
Hot slopes. Hot wind unwanted
Salt crystals sparkle
Infection in rye grass staggering sheep
And congenital deformity in lambs.
Opening Rains, old water courses
Reopen on wet slopes
Frost crystals crackle
Cold wind invading
Crop of castor oil and cape weed
Sour sob wild oats and stink wort.
In the night the water pipe freezes
And bursts in three places.
I'm thinking
In the summer I sometimes have a shower.

Wheat Belt Smash

Miss Alma Porch, snug in her battered Volkswagen, drove with pleasure through the peaceful surroundings. Enjoying the delightful feeling of escape she sang tunelessly, something operatic, and nodded her head in time to her own aria. She was on the way to Cheathem East. Occasionally she stopped singing to listen, from habit, with some anxiety to the rattle of her engine. This noise being sustained as usual she let her mind race ahead. She hoped Trinity College would live up to her expectations. She thought about sunflowers. Sunflowers with heads as big as dinner plates, golden sunflowers in the corners of old buildings and by crumbling walls. She hoped they would be growing in Cheathem East.

With failing confidence she thought of the death of Chekhov in her briefcase and other unsuitable things remembered and stuffed in at the last moment. She wondered how the students would respond. Cheathem West, she reflected, was positively a forest of television aerials. The aerials were very tall, probably, she thought, because of some geographical and unchangeable error in the choice made by the first settlers who naturally would not have had television in mind when selecting and clearing their land. The thickets of these aerials, all the same, showed unmercifully the tastes of the community, especially as the antennae were possibly capable of picking up only the less desirable programmes.

Frowning, Miss Porch urged her noisy way between the paddocks of golden stubble now spreading on both sides of the road. The aerials, she told herself, were simply a dark wood through which she had passed. She was a little tired that was all. It was a very good thing, she thought, that she was travelling on this long unfamiliar road during daylight. It was still early in the afternoon. It would not get dark for several hours.

Nel mezzo del cammin di nostra vita
mi ritrovai per una selva oscura . . .

'In the middle of the journey I came to myself in a dark wood where the straight way was lost . . . Alas!' Miss Porch sighed, 'I can only misquote a translation made by someone else.

'*I' non so ben ridir com . . .* my pronounciation is so awful, really appalling! It's fortunate that I am travelling alone. Let me see, something like . . . I cannot rightly tell how I entered it. So full of sleep was I about the moment that I left the true way . . .'

Miss Porch's sturdy waggon approached the beginning of a long curve, the first in a very straight road. She was more than a little anxious to finish her journey before nightfall.

The first part of the drive had not been without incident. Foolishly driving through the city when everyone else was intent on getting to work she had been suddenly aware that she was being followed. In her rear mirror there appeared plainly a car exactly like her own with a greyish-green shabbiness and about the same number of dents. Whichever way Miss Porch went the other car followed. In the uneasiness of this she told herself that the driver had mistaken her for someone else. A hard-working wife had obviously left her cut lunch on a suburban kitchen table and the devoted husband was weaving in and out of the lanes of traffic trying to catch her. Perhaps a neat package would sail across the cars and drop into her lap. Miss Porch wondered whether to have her window open in readiness.

Later it became quite clear that the other car was actually, with curious leaps and jerks, following her car. Perhaps, she told herself, feeling indulgent, the two cars were, unknown to both drivers, acquainted. After all, they were roughly the same hideous colour and they looked almost the same age. Perhaps in some car yard they had endured months of waiting side by side, perhaps during a whole winter of endless rain. Or they might actually have followed each other on the same paths of the assembly line sharing the experience of being put together at exactly the same moment.

At some point on the edge of the city Miss Porch's car lost its follower and the rear mirror reflected only the lengths of empty road which gradually lost width as it became embedded in the apparent tranquillity of a more rural landscape.

She knew that what seemed like an incident had not really been one. She wondered whether machinery was capable of feeling excitement and then, of course, after excitement the possibility of disappointment . . .

Using a little ordinary language Miss Porch told herself to pull herself together and to concentrate on the road.

There are strange things about driving alone on long lonely roads through the wheat. Old, grey, bent men and women wait indefinitely on green misleading corners, becoming part of the bushy roadside undergrowth as soon as the helpful traveller stops to investigate. Comfortable inviting tracks in the twilight, lined with soft sand and leaves, appear to lead off easily to the right as the main road curves to the left. And, as dusk advances, more gnarled old men march in formation, keeping up a remarkable speed, alongside, in the shadowy fringes of the saltbush. Occasionally a solitary driver pulls off on to the shoulder of the road to allow a ship to cross in front of him from one moonlit paddock to another.

Miss Porch had her foot flat to the floor. She sang with more fullness perhaps to urge her way with greater speed. She had been driving for several hours and seemed to be penetrating, as she said to herself, the back of beyond.

An ancient bus, once the property of a reputable boarding school for young ladies from good families, still bearing an uplifting motto and emblazoned with crests and colours, travelling in an easterly direction some distance ahead and, because of starting to round the long bend, out of sight, stopped to pick up an elderly woman who was proceeding slowly on foot in the same direction.

The woman, who was dressed in respectable black, Miss Porch thought in the briefest possible time for any thought, must have walked a tremendous distance to be in that remote and lonely place. As she was about to raise a heavy and obviously weary foot to the iron step, Miss Porch, reaching top G, took the first part of the bend in a style suitable for a *prima donna* and crashed into the substantial fender at the back of the bus.

Another phenomenon connected with travelling through the wheat is that motor vehicles remain spaced with considerable distances between them, thus causing the driver to feel he is the only person on a deserted road passing through an entirely empty landscape. Should it be necessary to stop, it becomes evident very quickly that other people are on the road too. An uncanny concertina-like closing of the long-distance spacing occurs. Cars in a hitherto unrealised succession pass the halted one if it is off the road. If the car is standing on the road, there is every chance that the next one, coming more quickly than expected, will run into it.

As soon as Miss Porch's chariot crumpled up on the back of the bus, a second car with a frantic yelping horn and an ineffectual squeal of brakes crashed into the back of Miss Porch. After a few moments a blue Mercedes, purring along on the bitumen, smoothly rounding the bend, crushed the second car. The Mercedes was unharmed. The same could not be said of the other two, sandwiched as they were between the greater strengths.

Miraculously, as if in anticipation of at least two prayers, a tow-truck manned by two muscular men emerged from the shade of the only trees along that part of the road. There was a convenient smooth patch of gravel beneath these trees. It was here the drivers gathered to inspect the damage, shake their heads and exchange names and addresses and insurance companies.

Fortunately, though the drivers were badly shocked and bruised, they were not seriously hurt. Perhaps relying on their shocked state, the bus driver stated simply and quickly that he was not insured and neither was his vehicle. He could, he told them, fully recommend Finch's Smash Repair Yard in Cheathem West, its excellence being out of this world. He would advise them to let the two lads here with the truck take their little problems in hand.

'In tow, I should say,' he added wittily. He suggested that he would then drive them all to where they wanted to go.

'It's the least I can do for youse.' He gave Miss Porch a wink which was startling in its suggestion of familiarity. She noticed his eyes were a clear china blue and very steady like the eyes of a white goose.

'Seeing as there's only the one place to go to along this route,' he pronounced it *rowt*, 'I shan't be goin' out of me way if I take youse all for a ride.'

Gratefully the car drivers and the two passengers belonging to the second car climbed into the bus where the stout woman in black was sitting in an attitude of resigned patience, as if this sort of encounter was an everyday event in her life.

That the bus was there, they all agreed, was an incredible piece of good fortune.

One of the tow-truck men approached the driver of the Mercedes. 'That's a great roo bar you've got there' – he indicated the solid ornament.

'Yes,' the owner of the Mercedes said, 'I like to think of it and this great big bonnet between me and the next man, especially if, inadvertently, I am driving the wrong way in a one-way street.' The tow-truck man nodded in good-natured agreement and suggested that the Mercedes would benefit from a check up over in Finchy's Yard. 'It's more'n likely,' he said, 'that with her being new, still wet behind the ears, so to speak, she'll need respringing for country driving. How's about we run her along with the other two while we're about it . . .'

'A perfectly splendid idea,' the owner of the Mercedes boomed pleasantly. 'I would simply love to finish my journey in good company. Oh! Yes, please do put my luggage, I'm afraid there's rather a lot of it, up on the racks there. Thank you so much.'

The old bus rattled off along the road carrying the travellers and their boxes and bags and cases to Cheathem East.

Miss Porch, leaning her forehead against the cool window of the bus, felt sure she heard Mr Miles, he had told them he was called Miles, talking in a low voice to the woman in black. She heard him say quite distinctly, 'We're in Business! What did I tell you! We're in Business. I'm telling you, three cars orf to the smash yard just in the one trip, not three trips but one. Yo'll get your share never youse worry, after all you done your bit 'anging about for the arternoon. You'll 'ave a nice lay-down soon as we get in. Could do with a kip meself.' It seemed to Miss Porch that Mr Miles, yawning, leered at her. She suddenly felt extraordinarily tired. Sensibly she told herself she was suffering from shock.

During the warm afternoon Miss Porch, turning over on the narrow bed in the small room, knew she had not been asleep. A few bruises seemed to be aching and, as she said to herself, it is hard to actually rest and sleep in a strange place without unpacking and making some sort of territorial investigation and establishment. Usually on arrival in a new place she inspects the cupboards and makes a point of discovering as soon as possible the more strategically placed bathroom.

Half-sitting up she remembered that on one occasion she had been forced to dust the window ledges before being able to feel comfortable. She had really no idea where in the College this room was.

'You'll be having arternoon tea with Miss Peycroft,' Miles had said, 'arternoon tea tit-a-tit with Miss Peycroft.' Simply, after being conducted to the room with her luggage carried up by Miles, she first sat on the bed and later lay on it as if needing to recover from the journey. Shortly she would need to tidy herself. The thought of the tea was comforting. It was quite an ordeal to have to wait until the appointed hour for it.

There was a rustling and a whispering as if people were trampling on the dried-up herbaceous border immediately beneath her window. It was a gruff conversation, the voice being lowered almost to a growl.

'Of course Rennett, you understand, I am not able to offer you marriage. Naturally as we are, er, of the same sex we are not in a position to marry but I have been entertaining the idea for some time, ever since I met you for the first time, here, ten years ago wasn't it, that you should share all that I happen to have the good fortune to possess.'

After a silence, quite brief and with a feeling of embarrassment transmitted through the quiet afternoon stillness, the gruffy talk continued. 'I do hope you will consider my offer, Rennett.' Another silence, and then in an even gruffer, almost inaudible tone: 'I want you to know, Rennett, I do offer my sincerest apologies for my beastly behaviour when I arrived earlier today. I was and still am somewhat overwrought, you understand, the travelling – the mishap on the road and the excitement of being here at last, you know I look forward to it all tremendously – and then seeing you again, well, it was all too much. I hope you will shake hands, Rennett? Please? You will? Oh thank you, you are a dear! A dear old sossidge.'

Miss Porch was conscious of another short silence and then the low growlings of half-spoken endearments, tinged with self-conscious noises of affection, floated upwards through the warm drowsy afternoon. The gruff voice, almost a hoarse whisper, said, 'There's absolutely no need for you to make up your mind in a hurry, Rennett. I know you're settled for the time being. It's just that I'm a lonely old thing wanting to share the comforts I have. I'm thinking of you for later on, when you're ready. Do you see?'

Miss Porch, cautiously leaning over the cracking wood of her unpainted window sill, heard a remnant of a song, a deep throaty singing:

> *Madam will you walk*
> *Madam will you talk*
> *Madam will you walk and talk with me . . .*

The words were soon lost in a droning humming sound. The singer and the object of the song appeared momentarily blocked solid in an unmagical meeting of denim and heather tweed supported on sturdy legs planted wide apart among the small weeds and flowers. Almost at once the vision disappeared and Miss Porch, leaning out a little farther, saw that a door leading into the house was under her window. She drew back into her room. She was too tired to rest. She supposed the lover and the beloved would be a part of the class, her class. Her heart sank. It rose too, for the voice was an excellent one, even if the figure was all wrong. Miss Peycroft had, in her initial letter, stressed imagination and invention as being essential for creativity. Miss Porch felt sure she would be able to use this voice . . .

NEIGHBOUR ON THE OTHER SIDE OF THE VALLEY

The lonely man has fenced his golden crop
And white flowers fall from his honey tree
Spreading flowers where they drop
Down on the flowerless bushes of the scrub.

The lonely man whose name is still not known
Has burned the stubble of his crop
Into the earth, and harrowing the soil
Has made a heap of stone.

The Goose Path:
A Meditation

Along the ridge ran a faint foot-track ... Those who knew it well called it a path; and while a mere visitor would have passed it unnoticed even by day, the regular haunters of the heath were at no loss for it at midnight. The whole secret of following these incipient paths, when there was not light enough in the atmosphere to show a turnpike road, lay in the development of the sense of touch in the feet, which comes with years of night rambling in little trodden spots. To a walker practised in such places a difference between impact on maiden herbage, and on the crippled stalks of a slight footway, is perceptible through the thickest boot or shoe.

Thomas Hardy

Three people, after giving me good advice, died. I don't mean that they dropped dead in front of me as soon as their wisdom fell from their lips. But it seemed as if death followed soon after their parting with certain useful suggestions. Of course other people, now dead, have uttered warnings and promises of conditional success, my father and mother for example, and a succession of governesses and, later, teachers.

Mrs Morton, I always think of her when I'm walking up this part of the firebreak on the Morton's side of the property; Mrs Morton, who was always watching to see what I was doing, told me to burn the broken handle of the mattock.

'Throw it on the fire and burn it out,' she said. I would never have thought to do this and would have worked a long time at the split wood trying to cut it away. It's when I come alongside her old duck pens that I always think of her and how she used to appear at the fence. She was already sick then. Her kidneys were all shrivelled up, she often told me. As she became more seriously ill her face, normally gaunt, looked round. Puffed with fluid I suppose. The roundness made me see something of the child she must have been and I remember this too and feel sorry. To be reminded that there was once a child, with all the shy hopes of childhood, and, who is still a part of the adult, is sad.

The second person was an old woman, a long time ago, a patient in a hospital in Glasgow. She said to tap a tin, all round tap tap tap on its side on the edge of a table, the sort of tin with a screw lid, and then it would unscrew easily. Vaseline or boot polish, she said, that sort of tin. She died the night she told me this. I, as the recipient of the advice, did not die. I do not remember now what sort of tin it was I was trying to open, certainly not boot polish. Vaseline perhaps. It used to be in tins.

The third person. I am not able to remember at all, who it was and what sort of advice. And every time, going uphill on this soft ploughed earth of the firebreak, on a level with the empty Morton duck pens, I try to remember what this third piece of good advice was, who gave it to me and the subsequent death of the person giving it. All I can think of just here is that when Mr Morton told me that Mrs Morton had died he could hardly speak for his grief. His eyes were red and swollen with weeping and I understood that I was face to face at this fence with someone who really loved another person and that he would never get over something which is often brushed aside in the word bereavement. Sometimes now, after all this time, he speaks about Mrs Morton and the tears well up in his innocent elderly eyes and it is as if she has just died all over again and left him alone in his paddocks here at the edge of the bush for ever. Because of this it is possible to know that love exists where the idea of it may be overlooked. Love is not just something for the beautiful and the rich, or between the intellectually refined or the more poetic people.

It does not matter not remembering the third piece of advice for if I did I should not tell it here as I am of the opinion that something should always be held in reserve. Everything should not be told, it is better to keep some things to yourself. It might be too that one day, on this soft warm earth I shall recall the third wise remark and, forgetting the habit of secrecy, perhaps tell it to someone right here by the duck pens . . .

This bit of fence is made like a kind of gate. The wire can be unhooked to let a fire truck or a flock through if necessary. Looking at it you would not see straight away that it can be opened to make a way through. Once a ram belonging to Mr Morton was caught by the horns in the ringlock. I tried to get the ram off. He was mad at being caught and kept pushing against the fence. His pushing and his horns being so curled made his freedom impossible. I kept going away trying to forget him and trying to get on with some work but all the time wondering how to get him free. In the end I thought the only way would be to cut the ringlock and ruin the fence. I came back up here with the wire cutters to find that, by some miracle, the ram had freed his own horns and had gone right away across the Mortons' paddock.

When walking I seem to stop by this bit of fence inadvertently recalling these same random events rather like the recollecting of a sequence of unrelated thoughts and experiences in the ritual of falling asleep. Mrs Morton fell through here once when she was trying to bring me a gift, a cake smothered in cream which, having to be held carefully, caused her to lose her balance. I was all morning painting her wounds with a yellow antiseptic and bandaging the worst ones. The cake, lying where it fell, was an intrusion.

The bleached long grass of my orchard pursues me as if on fire already as I make my way up the slope. I often stop by this particular part of the fence because part of the orchard is up here. My plum trees are here on the left and often I am doing things to them, the things with a sharp pruning knife, which are supposed to be done for fruit trees at different times of the year. The plum trees are satsuma, president, golden drop and the blue prune plum. There are peaches and nectarines in this part too. The long grass from the cultivated places spreads a little more, every year, into the bush, and the bush invades the orchard. Some of the fruit trees have grass trees, or blackboys as they are called, growing close to them without harm to either.

Perhaps, really, it is better to take a walk in a place where there is no responsibility. To keep on up the firebreak, which is what I usually do, is to be concerned about the places where it is not of the regulation width, though in a real fire even the correct width is of little use. A bush fire, rampant, leaps across the tops of trees, across roads and rivers and it races over the baldest paddocks. It is usually a sudden change in the direction of the wind which is the saving thing.

To stop here between the Morton duck pens and my fruit trees is to see again the extraordinary fairytale, picture-book loveliness of the intense blue of the prune plums hanging secretly in the deep green of the leaves. An enticing and surprising mixture of blue and green reminding me of the extravagant colours in the feathers of some exotic bird. The bloom on these small vividly coloured plums gives the impression of a delicate mist hovering about the trees.

Higher up the slope here where there is no orchard there is the bush. The bush grows quickly across a firebreak if it is not freshly ploughed every year. From up here I can look all the way down and across the shallow ravine to a horse stud. I used to call it the Tolstoy country because, across there, they have hay fields and a long paddock fenced with round poles for horses. I like to watch the horses running and not have to worry about the things they can have wrong with them.

The most lovely wildflowers, in their season, appear unexpectedly up here in this part of the bush. I won't list them all as in a catalogue or as in some footage for a film on Western Australia. It is enough to mention the red and green kangaroo paws, at their best when the sun shines through them, and the china blue leschenaultia, the strong but fragile blue like the clear blue of the eyes of a white goose. There are flowers as if enamelled on the prickly undergrowth, some in clusters and some in wreaths and, this last year, the surprise of some delicate orchids in the hollow of the burned-out tree where the firebreak turns and the descent begins.

To follow the fence is to discover where it has been damaged, either pressed down from above or humped up from underneath by kangaroos making their way down to the dam.

To take this walk is to reflect upon time passing and on time standing still. There are places in the bush which seem as if there has been no change over a great many years. The constant changing of the seasons is a relentless movement of time and the silence seems to make the pause. In the still silence and the great heat of summer, in this remote place, it is easy to forget where you came from, where you are going and, in a moment of remembering, to wonder why you are here at all. There is too the strange hope, at times, that out of the hot dry fragrance and the stillness some wisdom will come. This hope during the walk, over the years, has not faded.

The way down on this far side of the bush is rougher and often there are fallen branches on the firebreak. I try to move a branch but it has embedded itself in the hard ground. It has fallen from a great height. Branches fall, not in a gale as would be expected, but during the stillness of a very hot day like this day. The leaves of the eucalypts fall all the year round. The fresh green new leaves often glow with a sort of golden red colour and this makes them look as if they are made of a very thin, beaten metal.

It is on the way down that the unwanted thoughts of inability rise to the surface. Walking is a time for thinking. It is as Hamlet says: *For there is nothing either good or bad but thinking makes it so* ... A fallen branch too heavy to move and the memory, the thought, which is accompanying the walk is the realisation of the ways in which, after tremendous hopes and activity, life in the little cottage and in the orchard seems to have come to a standstill. In the cottage there are a dozen or more Christmas cards all from Mr Morton, curling up, crammed along the kitchen mantelpiece; on the walls are a series of calendars, one year after another, with pictures of poultry feed and farm machinery. There is a heap of out-of-date telephone directories; there are newspapers, lining cupboards and shelves with dates too far back for cleanliness, all with pages of impossibly cheap 'specials'. In the orchard several trees have not had nets put over them, others have not been pruned and yet others have reverted. The place is a paradise for parrots and crows. There are rats in the shed. I have put rat poison in the sprawl of rosemary round the poultry pens ...

From this part of the firebreak I can look down to the dam. To have this ugly dam the winter nelis pears had to be sacrificed. Well, not a sacrifice really, that is just a way of complaining. The winter nelis, the trees (small sweet russet pears), travelling from South Australia had to be fumigated and the white ants, finding moribund roots, were soon inside every tree. The winter nelis were simply an unsuccessful part of the dream.

Instead of keeping to the firebreak there is a wild place which can be crossed. It is rough and suggests the wilderness. Here – *There is a path which no fowl knoweth and which the vulture's eye hath not seen*. It is here that I remember Mrs Morton's speech of welcome on the day, all those years ago, when I took possession and wandered across the warm fragrant earth hardly daring to step one step after another, not believing that land could really belong to anyone. Mrs Morton, appearing suddenly, said the rabbits would eat everything I tried to grow. She went on with frightening fire-talk, snake-talk, dried-up-creek-talk, dead-calf and still-born-lamb-talk, poison-weed-killing sheep-talk, crows stealing eggs, salt in the ground and in the water. All the same I planted tomatoes and seed potatoes, melons and pumpkins. Of course Mrs Morton knew what she was talking about. She was even correct about kangaroos not eating sweet corn but liking to roll in it so that the whole crop could be crushed in one night.

From this wild place there is a track through to the poultry pens. I shall not gather up the dead rats. I have discovered that, in the heat, they disappear quickly. It is here that I think of the word Islam, a foreign word to me. I did not know what the word meant but I understand now that the word means to resign oneself, to submit to something which is greater, is beyond oneself. To bring the wider philosophical belief down to a tiny scratched-out place where I am walking, the submission can be applied to egg-stealing rats and snakes, to a heap of wood which should have been stacked, to a broken old chair propped against a collapsing shed, to the passion vines and the honeysuckle which, growing wild and entangled, have wrapped round the bamboo. There is a staircase here for the fox. The fox, a vixen I feel sure, will have climbed up here using the vine as a sort of ladder. The goose-pen fence is smothered in the flowers of the passion vine. The vixen, it must have been a vixen who, leaving her cubs briefly, bit off the heads of all the geese. She, in her raid, took all the goslings and the unhatched eggs undermining the nests with her industrious digging. This morning the gander stood perplexed in the unnatural silence. All round him the geese lay in a wide semi-circle, their white feathered wings and bodies spread like ballet dancers in formal attitudes of contrition pressed to the ground. Their stage had no proscenium and there was, for their finale, no music. A fox hunts alone like this and this one probably made her visit, single mouthed, in the moonlight shortly before dawn.

Resignation is powerful but perhaps optimism is the stronger power. Can a person be both resigned and submissive and an optimist as well? I think so. I have already arranged to buy some more geese later on today to start the flock once more.

The gander, unslaughtered, left out by some vixenish oversight, calls out occasionally and holds himself in an alert position, very still, waiting for the once familiar reply. It is clear he has lost his sense of direction and has no idea where to go. He has lost the goose path.

This morning early, in that uncanny silence which seemed to hang over the land in the wake of the dead geese, I burned them all. The cremation used all the dry firewood and the kindling stored for next winter. And a great deal of precious water had to be poured to prevent the funeral pyre from being another kind of fire. And now I stop during the walk and begin, too late, the work of searching out the thick coils of the vines. I spoil the pruning knife hacking at these fleshy ropes. The giant reeds (bamboo) in places are strangled and dead and have to be cut and broken off and dragged out. It is a terrible tangled mass this staircase for the fox. The long leaves rustle, sounding like a stream running in a place where water never flows. This is one of the deceitful things, like the unhurried whispering of human voices as the wind moves through certain parts of the bush in places where there are no people. Perhaps these sounds belong to mysterious rites taking place in these small hollows of the land some centuries earlier.

It has been said that *poetry that sings of 'the enshrined past' cannot answer the demands of the new age*. It feels a little bit like this to walk in the bush being deeply attached to something which has existed for a timeless time and at the same time to have to plough up parts of it and to cut other parts of it away. The passion vine is not really a part of the bush, it has been brought here. Some of it must be cut away. It curls snake-like round boots and it springs into the small of the back as if to fell an intruder. It gives the uncanny feeling that someone, not a friend, is hidden close by.

To pause and to look down and across the varying light and shade, down and across the slope of the land is to see each time, with a fresh clarity, the different shades of green from the transluscent pearl green to a deep purple green. To stand in this place at a certain time of the afternoon is to feel the slight change in the air, the *feeling* of the air. Some times the gully winds race in from the east and at other times there is a west wind with its caressing coolness. Thinking about this place when I am not able to be here brings a consolation. Perhaps Thomas Mann felt this same sense of solace when he wrote about the misty edges of the blue–green sea at that magic place, Travemünde. The solace and the consolation can never be entirely pure. The magic is often injected with the tincture of human suffering and anxiety. Travemünde, the place for youthful joy and freedom, has its row of old men worrying whether they will be able to rid themselves satisfactorily of the food eaten the previous day ...

Like a novel, a certain kind of novel, which is a storehouse of observation and experience, thought and feeling, this walk becomes a meditation on human wishes. This meditation is a part of imaginative creation and, to me, is necessary for living and for writing. During the walk the realisation of this, like a prayer against despair, outweighs any sense of inability and failure.

The goose path. It is about the width of one boot. The thin bleached grass is pressed lightly down between the stretches of tall pale grass. When I first saw this tiny track I could not think who could have made it. It is made by the firm flat treading of geese, one goose following one after another, single file, in a long line as they make their way across the meadow at the bottom of the slope to the dam.

To go on with the walk I take the heavy-handled rake and, holding it out horizontally with the shadow of it over the perplexed gander, I walk him down the winding path, down the slope between the orchard trees to the meadow. It is here that he will need to be guided on to the goose path. (An aside, cows and geese walk downhill when they are not sure of the way. To find lost cows and geese it is best to go as far downhill as possible before beginning the search.)

The gander, under the shadow of the rake handle, sets off along the goose path in the direction of the dam. Carefully placing one booted foot after the other I follow him on the fragile path. The walk here must be serene and unhurried.

The apple trees and the pears and quince are down here. The clay soil of the meadow is salt and is flooded in winter. It is a good thing for pears to have their feet in water sometimes and these trees can tolerate a fair amount of salt. Early in the morning and again at the end of the afternoon flocks of rosy-breasted pink and grey parrots fly across here. At other times the screaming black cockatoos swoop and pause and fly on in their marauding search. Just now it is quiet and in the silence the crows cry loneliness along the narrow valley.

The gander, in the shadow of the rake handle, walks obediently placing one sensitive foot in front of the other. His clear blue eyes seem to take in the familiar surroundings. If I remove the shadow of the rake he pauses and does not know which way to go. I guide him on towards the dam. Further down the meadow the creek bed is dry except for one or two oily pools. It was always the custom for the geese to pause and sample this water which lies in the cracks of the clay. The goose path has, for this purpose, a well-defined loop which we follow before making for the final straight track which climbs the white clay slopes of the dam wall.

I watch the gander take to the water. He slides in silently and moves as if without any effort out across the unrippled surface. A few slowly widening rings spread round his gliding movement. I walk round the edge of the dam as if to encourage him but instead of diving and flapping his wings, beating them hard on the water, showing himself off as he has been doing before when courting one or more of the geese he simply makes for the far side and clambers out. He stands on the slope just above the water and makes no attempt to preen his feathers. No sound comes from him. As a rule his voice is the kind of cello with organ-like qualities in the full orchestration of the flock. The geese use their voices like instruments in a well-trained orchestra and without them he seems to have no voice.

It is clear that when the new geese arrive I shall have to help the gander to lead them to the goose path. Perhaps for a few times and then he will lead his small new flock himself. First he will have to wait till they have done gossiping and whispering among themselves. They will preen themselves, pirouetting, stretching out first one leg and then the other. They will taste the water drinking daintily from the bowls in the goose pen. His flock will be small for the whole year for geese only lay eggs and nest at a particular time of the year. Meanwhile the never-ending walk must end here for me. The fox's staircase must be demolished before nightfall. After her hunt the golden eyes of the vixen will be bright still and cunning. They hold in their glassiness a knowledge of things not understood but which have to be forgiven. It is as though the ways of the vixen, her energy, her swift stealthy movements, her thoughts and her freedom are still sewn into the tangled vines of her staircase. She is ancient and thin from her nightly expeditions and she will never lie on the creamy neck and plump shoulders of a concert-going woman. Her rough red-gold pelt will not be stroked lovingly by a child allowed to dress up, fondling the pretty but useless little feet of the fox fur lovingly, in her mother's finery before being sent to bed . . .

The unmistakable perfume, the scent of fox, hangs in the silence. It is heavy and aromatic recalling something predatory and womanly with the rich overpowering sweetness of an older charm, an experienced passion accompanying the strength and the determination of the ageing huntress.

I guide the gander back along the goose path. He walks delicately and is unhurried, perplexed still. I keep the shadow of the rake above him and under this protection he continues up the slope between the fruit trees and across to the goose pen.

I have written 'I' throughout. This land in the bush with its tiny area scraped and conquered for cultivation does not belong entirely to me. It belongs to both of us. While writing I found it difficult to say

'we'. It is because of a certain smugness contained in the pronoun
'we'. I once visited some people who kept on, '*we* do this', '*we* have
this', '*we* like it this way', '*we* like it here' – it seemed to me to be
an impregnable wall of we and us. 'I' seems more vulnerable and
so is more in keeping with how I feel in the bush. I work alone in
the orchard and I walk alone in the bush. I am temporary here and
vulnerable and in this must only speak for myself.

FUNERAL

The shoutings of my neighbour woman which used to fill the valley
Are silent
A goanna lies in the middle of the firebreak still and motionless
For ever.
She, when she strode around her conquered paddocks demanding
The havoc of order seemed gigantic
A goanna suddenly in the thicket of the grape vine appears
so large.

When they carried her box into the crematorium chapel
It was so little I burst into tears
The goanna on the firebreak is so shrunken and small.

As I sit writing little lizards run up my naked legs
And through the hollow arms of my chair
To them I am only a branch which moves lacking stability
They are not aware of my useless benevolence
And no load of guilt drops from my neck.

The goanna in the grape vine and on the firebreak
And the live lizards and the fence wire woman dead
They are all in a different world and I cannot reach them
If my groping hands found them would they find
Terror or serenity.

The Will to Write

If you turn the imagination loose like a
hunting dog, it will often return with the
bird in its mouth.

William Maxwell in 'The Front and Back Parts of the House',

New Yorker, 31 September 1991

Writing for me is an act of the will. Though I want to write I have to make myself sit down and write. It is very slow work and, to me, hard work but, at the same time it is both enriching and illuminating. Perhaps I can explain something about writing and being a writer.

I never called myself 'writer' until I was called 'writer' from outside.

I have always wanted to write. When other girls and boys at school were taking photographs with their box cameras I preferred to write a few words to describe a person, a building or a view, even though my aunt had given me a camera.

I remember when I was about five being given a new clean exercise book. I began at once to 'write' in it, not just on one page, but scribbles on every clean page. My pencil was taken away, my sleeve was pushed up and I received a quick sharp slap on the wrist. I don't think I was ever able to explain to anyone how the smooth white pages had *invited* me to fill them.

Reading has always been a great pleasure for me. At Christmas and on Birthdays the presents I received were books. My sister and I had a dolls' house each. These were on the floor next to each other. The little dolls in the houses were characters for a story that went on from one day to the next for years. We spoke the dialogue aloud and often continued the story on trams or in the train. If we were not able to sit next to each other we shouted the actions and the conversations of our characters to each other, sometimes the length of a crowded tram. I do not remember if anyone else in the tram objected.

I think the games with the dolls' house people encouraged our imaginations and at the same time made us aware socially. Our characters resembled people we knew and others we simply saw passing in the street or in shops. We created dramatic incidents which were often suggested by items in the newspapers or on the radio. But we heightened everything, a burglar had two wooden legs, for example. The fiction writer heightens an everyday experience when creating a dramatic incident in the novel or the short story.

Writing can be regarded as a gift to be cherished as other gifts are; things like an ability in mathematics, excellence in swimming or in other sports, being able to draw horses and dogs or being clever at dressmaking or cooking, the list is endless. Sometimes the wish to write does not show itself at first. I found that I loved words and I enjoyed the long and complicated sentences my English mistress gave me for punctuation exercises. I enjoyed translating from French and German and finding the best words in English for a good translation.

From the age of twelve I have kept diaries and journals. I always advise people who want to write to keep a journal. The important thing to remember is that it is best to write what you want to write and not to try to record things simply because you feel you ought to record them.

Imagination cannot be taught but it can be encouraged. Observation can be taught and the ability to make the quick note can be developed. It is a good idea to carry a small notebook and pencil for the quick note, which can then be written at greater length in the journal. The journal becomes a working place for the writer. Writing consists of a great deal of rewriting and in each rewriting more detail emerges. It is true to say that writing unlocks more writing. A book will not write itself. Time has to be made for writing. It is useless to say, 'I'm going to write a novel *when I've got time.*'

A folder with loose pages makes a good journal because the pages can be moved. It is a good idea to devote some pages to describing books that have been read, stage plays, films, radio and television programmes. Writing about these and having opinions (which must be supported with reasons) are a help towards writing fiction, essays and poetry well.

Other pages can be filled with ideas for stories, little descriptions of characters and samples of their dialogue, and descriptions of their clothes and possessions and of landscapes and settings. Often one of these small descriptions will lead into a story or a novel. It is never necessary to start a story with the title and the first sentences, these may come later. The journal becomes a storehouse of experience, observations and opinions. Opinions can often be given to characters.

All kinds of people offer the writer 'a good title' but they do not say what should be under the title!

Another nice thing which the writer can do is to have a good quality notebook with smooth pages into which especially liked poems or passages of prose can be copied *by hand*. Writing by hand does convey to the writer something of the magic between hand and brain and the beauty in our own language. It is advisable to include the names of the authors and the dates when the pieces were selected. This will, in years to come, prevent a mistake being made about the original authorship. It is a good idea too to write a few lines describing why the particular poem or passage of prose was chosen. I think it is interesting to look back to earlier years to see what choices were made at a certain time and why.

It is unrealistic to expect to leave school and to earn a living as a film star or as a writer. Writing, to start with, should accompany the training or the job. It is important to be with other people, books are not really written in isolation – in a freezing attic or on a desert island. Ideas, little fragments of conversation, human behaviour, other people's thoughts and opinions, even disliking a job – all these things can provide material for a story.

I find the work of writing rewarding and valuable because it helps me in my attempts to understand myself and other people. Creative writing, as it is called for want of a better phrase, is a good way in which to approach reading: literature, poetry, biographies, autobiographies, various books of non-fiction and especially newspapers. The student who understands a little more about himself or herself will have more understanding of other people and this, in family life and in the workplace, is very useful. To have more understanding is to have more resilience to adversity.

Literary works should never be described as dated and then dismissed. Through the ages writers all over the world, as well as offering entertainment, have provided thought-provoking reflections on human life and circumstances. Contemporary writing provides a mirror for us and for others to come. We need the young people who want to write to come forward now to continue the reflections.

FORRESTER

All night I felt I would live for ever
While you slept against my side
I listened to the rain
Thinking of the places where water collects and flows.

All day I worked carrying earth and bark
Making islands
In the rushing flood of the rising stream
To hold the roots of the tender young trees.

All night I felt I would live for ever
While you slept the frogs filled the dark
Night pillows with their music
Under the pale green cradles of the willows.

Almond apple and vine
Planted and growing
Cottage barn and path
Shaped and showing
Details of our living
Determined
Before our time.

This morning tawny flocks of doves
Are flying up into the light
Sudden dropping of golden dust from the rising sun.
A soft clapping of wings and a tiny scattered applause.
All night I felt I would live for ever
This morning I know I will not see the trees when they are old.

Welcome to the Brave New World

If recent developments are endangering the pleasure of reading . . . let me suggest one thing which may help to maintain it. It is this: Plan reading beforehand: have always in mind three or four books which you have decided you want to read; have the books at hand so that when the opportunity comes for reading, the choice may be readily made; otherwise you might be staying in a country house, and something, not reading, may have been planned for the afternoon; stormy weather causes that plan to be cancelled, and two or three hours are thrown into your lap – a little tumble-in of time – an unlooked-for-opportunity for reading. We may, any of us, with such a chance, find ourselves in the middle of a good library, and yet, if we have not already thought to ourselves and determined on some book we wish to read, when the opportunity comes, the greater part of the time may be lost in the difficulty of making a choice. I offer this as a practical advice, and it is easy to apply it.

So writes Edward Grey, Viscount Grey of Fallodon, born 1862 and died 1933. He was educated at Winchester and then Balliol College, Oxford. As Sir Edward Grey, he was Foreign Secretary from 1905 to 1916. Scholar, statesman and sportsman, he is described at the time as the type of literary figure that was, by the 1930s, dying out, 'though Mr Baldwin still remains a striking example'. The Viscount's prose is described as a model of quiet and scholarly dignity.

The situation described in Viscount Grey's essay *The Pleasures of Reading* – the possibility of being *not prepared* for spending a quiet afternoon reading in the comfortable library of a country house during a weekend house party – reads rather like the opening for a romantic novel or a mystery story. You can imagine, from the words of the advice, a howling gale across the moors, causing guests to hurriedly select books and then to sit as close as possible to the library fire, which is piled up with logs . . .

WELCOME TO THE BRAVE NEW WORLD

With these words an advertisement announced that the brave new world has reached two of the giants of the English-speaking world of words and literature.

Encyclopaedia Britannica has stopped printing books because its multimedia CD-ROM version is a far greater reward with sales. And the Oxford English Dictionary has launched its complete revision with an $87 million, ten-year rewriting.

The ending of a tradition for Encyclopaedia Britannica, reaching back more than two hundred years, has come about because the company sells only a minimal number of books compared with 150 thousand compact discs every year in Europe.

A full set of volumes costs $1400 while the computerised version containing the same information costs $140.

It is more profitable for the company to concentrate on the electronic publishing. Though a spokesman has said that this heralds a revolution of change that, at present, no one fully understands, the

45 million words of educational material have not changed. Simply, the computerised version is more easily used. What has changed? What has changed is the way in which people use it.

Up until the late 1960s the well-known encyclopaedia was sold door-to-door. This meant that volumes were brought by salesmen to people in their own homes. In this way books were described by salesmen who knew their goods (the contents of the books) and the circumstances of their clients (or hoped-for clients). In this way books were sold to people who did not possess books and would not naturally buy books, their own reading interests being mainly confined to the sporting pages of the newspapers. They were persuaded to purchase (paying off the debt in instalments) a whole set of volumes, believing that the books would give their children a great advantage and the promise of a better education. The salesmen targetted a certain class of people and did not try to sell books to those who already purchased and read books. They often sold books in the evenings when the man of the house, the father, was at home. Much was made of the educational value of the books.

It is not possible to know how many sets of volumes remained unopened in the households of non-readers or would-be-but-didn't-make-it readers. People either read or they don't. Strangely, many people who love to read and to discuss books will say how guilty they feel if they read during the day instead of waiting till the evening.

Television has been accused of taking people away from books and reading. But I believe television encourages people to read as much as it discourages them. Small children, growing up in front of television programmes, may have attention and reading problems if they are not encouraged to read material they can understand. To suggest that the book will disappear because of television and computers is not profitable. Children, at an early age, love books if they have access to them. They like to collect books, in a series or separately. This habit usually persists, bringing an enrichment to the individual throughout his or her life.

New inventions have happened through the years and will go on happening. It is interesting that people distrust all changes, expecting that the change will be for the worse, that it will spoil the way in which we live. Who now regrets the disappearance of turnpike roads, of thatched roofs and their residential rats, or of the well from which water had to be fetched? Who wants, now, to put heavy washed sheets through the mangle? Or to stand at the sink washing up endless dishes?

In his essay, *The Pleasures of Reading*, Viscount Edward Grey presents a series of changes that threaten books. Changes that will divert people from books and reading. In a rather peevish but well-mannered way he complains that the introduction of the Penny Post has already begun to make a change, the cheap postage causing people to consume a vast quantity of time in correspondence. Correspondence that is *unnecessary, trivial and irksome*.

The railways must take some of the blame, Viscount Grey argues. The railways are altering the lives and habits of the people, causing them to move about more. Though he does allow that a long railway journey has the compensating advantage of affording a first-rate opportunity for reading.

The advent of the motor car is more seriously harmful. The motor car is completely unfavourable to reading. People are consuming even more time in the motor car. Even for people with good eyesight, reading in a motor car is impossible.

The telephone is a *deadly disadvantage* to books and reading. The telephone *minces time into fragments and frays the spirit* . . . (I think we know what Sir Edward means!)

The wireless too, with all its delights, *is a dreadful distraction* from the book. People will have no use for books and reading and conversation. The wireless will be seen to take over the opinions of the educated and the cultured and push them into silence.

The cinematograph is even more disastrous, an absolute change for the worse, causing people to become passive ('passive receivers', as we know them today).

And then, the Viscount has not finished with the problem, there is the previously unthought of threat, a setback for the book and for reading. This is the development of *picture papers and magazines of coloured pictures*, which are diverting people not only from books and reading but from thought. It is almost possible to see Sir Edward's indignation rising hot on the page. *People will stop thinking!* People getting into a railway compartment would, at one time, have been armed with a book or two, and would start reading straight away. But now they come with an armful of picture papers and they sit looking at the pictures with a transient amusement, one after another, to pass the time! Completely empty-headed, vacant and mindless.

There are always those who predict an outcome that will prove to be the worst. But perhaps something saves the worst from happening. Years ago my grandfather maintained, in moments of gloom, that because of the rapid increase in the population of Sparkbrook, an industrial extension of Birmingham, there would be more horses and carts and the streets would be blocked with straw and horse manure. Fortunately the motor car was being developed and, before long, the all-encompassing horse manure disappeared.

THE SILENT AND INTIMATE COMPANION

The statement that technology has threatened the existence of books as we know them physically is followed by the question: will the novel of tomorrow exist only on a screen? Or is the paper and the binding tangibly important enough to make books in the future able to continue in their present format?

The novel – that silent and intimate companion – offers reflections on various aspects of human life about which people are interested to read and to discuss. This applies as well to the short story, the poem and the drama for radio and for stage. These reflections can be in the past, the present or the future. The writing can be factual or fictional, a mixture of the writer's own observation and experience, imagination, and the knowledge of the different structures needed to best show characters, places, events and ideas.

The size and the appearance of the book are very important. A great deal of thought and work are put into the covers of books. The design or picture used will, as a rule, contain a symbolic or metaphorical suggestion towards the material within the book.

I do not know enough about computers. They are very expensive and useful. The only unfortunate thing about them is that because of their tremendous usefulness and the ability of people able to use them, a number of people have become unemployed. This applies of course to all new discoveries that involve work passing from people to some sort of machinery.

It is not possible to halt new discoveries. We should be grateful that such clever changes are taking place and we should try, at the same time, to preserve things that we need and admire.

For myself, pen and ink are here to stay. Reading aloud is a wonderful music and the voice is the instrument. Being read to is a luxurious pleasure second only to the pleasure and enrichment of reading quietly to oneself.

There is no better decoration for a room than a wall of books. In the presence of books it is possible to feel their companionship, especially if the books have travelled with their owners from school and then, later on, accompanied them on long journeys, perhaps from one part of the world to another.

It must be remembered that many people do not want books in their houses and the computer is there for other reasons, not to replace books. Though it might be that some people feel the need for a few nice-looking books – as well as the well-known treasures.

Some years ago I worked as a house cleaner. In one very luxurious flat there were some bookshelves complete with glass doors and some very handsome books, bound in soft leather with titles and authors in gold. Not having seen the editions before, I carefully took down two volumes of Jane Austen and two of Dickens, holding them with reverence. When I opened the Jane Austen there was no book, but instead there were three wine glasses. Similarly there were three wine glasses in every volume. Wine glasses, brandy balloons, little punch cups, champagne glasses – for every occasion the right glasses . . .

The touching thing is that the young man whose apartment it was wanted the appearance of books to show that he was cultured – he could have had books *and* wine glasses!

I still have my copy of *Robinson Crusoe*. It was given to me in 1927.

It is a thick book, 328 pages. A book bound in green linen with the pages firmly stitched in with linen thread. There are sixteen illustrations in full colour with vivid captions. The best part for me was the diary that Crusoe kept when he was completely alone on the desert island after being shipwrecked. He describes how he builds himself a shelter and how he hunts for food. He records faithfully his prayers to be able to overcome his fear. The diary makes the events realistic and close to the reader. At the time, I never read on after the diary but read these pages over and over and kept a diary myself. This diary-keeping closely affects my own written work and has taken its place in the vague area between fact and fiction and autobiography.

Robinson Crusoe is about a man who from his boyhood has known what he wants to do, and that is to go 'away to sea'. And that is what he does. His father tells him that the travelling should be more than 'just a wandering'. It should be a way of 'rising to the top' and every attempt should be made to 'improve a very poor situation'.

SANCTUARY

Sanctuary, The Library. The Public Lending Library. Its name suggests that this is a place where people are welcome, a place of Sanctuary.

Frank McCourt writes of the young Irishman who, lately coming to New York, is lonely. The bartender in Costello's bar tells the boy to quit drinking and go to the library. He does go and the librarians are very friendly. He is given a library card and he can borrow four books at a time.

The sight of the Main Reading Room, North and South, makes me go weak at the knees. I don't know if it's the two beers I had or the excitement of my second day in New York, but I am near tears when I look at the miles of shelves and know if I live till the end of this century I'll never be able to read all those books. There are acres of shiny tables where all sorts of people sit and read as long as they like, seven days a week, and no one bothers them unless they fall asleep and snore. There are sections with

English, Irish, American books, literature, history, religion and it makes me shiver to think I can come here any time I like and read anything, as long as I like, if I don't snore.

He takes the books to his lodgings and sits up in bed reading until his landlady, Mrs Austin, knocks on his door telling him that it's eleven o'clock and she's not a millionaire and lights must be out at eleven to keep down her electricity bill.

In my novel *The Orchard Thieves* there is a grandmother who is always ready to condemn someone or to be really kind and helpful to someone.

In her purse the grandmother had fourteen lending-library tickets.

'Take one,' she said. 'Most of these people are dead,' she explained, offering the intimacy of the bulging compartments of her purse to a stranger who, undecided and holding books in both hands, was standing in front of the shelves in the fiction section. 'Please do have a ticket,' the grandmother said. She went on to say that she knew how awful it was to get all the way home only to discover that the books were familiar, having been read before. This way, she explained, with an extra book or two there was more chance of having something completely fresh to read.

On the way home the grandmother thought about the special kind of wealth there was in the possession of library-book tickets. These were reassuring and steady like the pension cheque. She never went anywhere without her purse. You could never know in advance what the day had in store. There might come a time when it would be necessary to offer all she had to appease an intruder. She knew of women who spread crumpled and torn newspapers all round their beds every night so that they would hear the intruder coming closer. Or, she might be held at knife point by someone in the street. She would offer all she had in her purse, small change, pension cheque and the library-book tickets. There would be absolutely no need for a villain to either strangle or stab her in order to snatch her purse. She would hold it out to him and tell him he could have it and be off. She would tell him this in plain words. The library-book tickets might even make a changed man of him, especially if he had never had a chance to use a public lending library during a life with all the deprivation brought about by being on the run.

We read to refresh and exercise our own creative powers. Because of the creation, the use of language and the expression of feeling and thought within the covers, the familiar framework of the book, people are not going to give them up. The physical art of the covers and the setting of the print enlightens and endears the reader to those who have made the book. And it is the idea of the (relatively) small space holding so much that urges us towards ownership. The CD-ROM is small and convenient too; there is a place for both – why give up one for the other? Why not have them both?

The Little Dance
in Writing

I think that a story can illustrate a truth without telling it. How can the author present the material, which is in itself depressing, frightening, cruel, inhuman? The writing can lift the subject with a small dose of kindness, optimism, gentle humour, or rough black comedy. Or perhaps kindness between characters. The little dance in writing – the alleviation of suffering, an improvement of some sort. This is something that helped me in my writing, helped me to see around my characters, to not overdo one aspect of their lives.

I rely on my observations, people really say and do the most extraordinary things. It is the small details that I try to capture. Even the most boring conversation between people can yield a jewel towards a character, as he or she emerges on the page. Knowing and writing facts about a real person does not always work well for the fiction writer. I would never attempt to write directly about another person. For me it is important, essential really, to have an active imagination and, above all, a fondness, a deeply felt fondness, an affection for people . . . even the most impossible.

These simple rules are in my mind when I teach. Teaching has helped me to write in that I have learned to read and to be aware of overwriting or of writing in a particular style that is not brought to a satisfactory state. I feel the world is full of evil things and that in writing one perhaps can find acceptance. The little dance in writing is very important.

Students, if they become involved with the problems of the world, may stay there and not see beyond the pain and suffering. I have found that students like to 'put the world right' in their writing, and so I use exercises to help them to understand the little dance in writing. One exercise is Lady with a Handbag.

I ask the students to imagine a woman with a handbag, a woman in a hurry. She falls, and the contents of her bag spill out. I ask them to list and describe the contents, concentrating on the one item that tells the most about the woman. They can only use a few words because we move fairly swiftly through the exercise.

Then I ask them to describe the place where the woman has fallen, and to tell what she thinks about the place, using only a few words. She might say something angry or frightened – this is the students' chance to get in a few expletives. Or the woman's thoughts might show her distress about her ruined clothes, being late, or the place where she has fallen. In this way students practise both description and internal monologue.

Sometimes I develop the exercise further to teach about the structure of the short story. I ask the students to introduce another character, someone who offers to help her. The woman does not accept help. The students write the woman's reply.

This leads to practising packed dialogue . . . Fade, change of scene. Describe two women cleaning offices, watching the woman as she fumbles to make herself respectable after the fall. Some rich phrases from the cleaning women – perhaps critical, perhaps not. The gossips enjoy talking, even to the fallen woman's ruined stockings.

Then there is a lesson in closure. In the structure of the short story the writer has to come round to what is more important than the opening event. So I might ask the students to return to the character of the woman, and again develop an interior monologue. This is their chance not only to develop the character further after the gossip of the cleaning women, but also to bring closure. Perhaps the woman thinks about taking off her ruined clothes, promising herself a hot shower. She'll feel better, a lot better then; she'll be glad there is no one in the house. She thinks how nice it is that the hot shower is working.

Teaching has always been important to me. I come from a family of teachers. We used to say that our daddy made everything into a lesson. I find reading very helpful to my writing, and I ask my students to read, not just each other's work, but also the work of great writers. I ask them to make short written comments on what they read, and to share them in a symposium at the start of each class. The rhythm and energy of prose is important. The prose should be exquisite as well as functional. And students can feel and enjoy that rhythm when they read well-written literature.

I love teaching. I like stepping into my classroom and seeing all the students ready with their assignment, having enjoyed the writing of it, ready to listen to each other's work.

Quick at Meals,
Quick at Work

'Look a little, also, at the labours of the teeth, for these correspond with those of the other members of the body . . .' William Cobbett travelled in the south-west of England, early in the nineteenth century, offering advice on almost everything from growing backyard mustard, baking bread in home-built ovens and collecting the right grasses for making sun-bonnets to the choosing of the most suitable wife. In addition he gave detailed advice to the would-be lover.

Cottage thrift and exemplary moral principles, in his philosophy and in his writing, were on the same level as love. He describes how he came to choose his own wife. One cold day in the middle of winter he was walking in the snow. It was hardly light, being very early in the morning, when he passed a house and saw a young woman, out of doors in the snow, scrubbing out a washing tub. He decided immediately that she was the right woman to be his wife.

'Look a little, also, at the labours of the teeth . . .' he writes. 'Get to see her at work upon a mutton chop, or a bit of bread and cheese; and if she deal quickly with these, you have a pretty good security for that activity, that stirring industry, without which a wife is a burden instead of a help. And, as to love, it cannot live for more than a month or two (in the breast of a man of spirit) towards a lazy woman . . .' He goes on to say that the woman who walks with quick and heavy steps, leaning forward, eyes and feet intent on their destination will make a good wife. It is not possible, in his opinion, to expect ardent and lasting love from a woman who *saunters*. 'No man ever yet saw a sauntering girl, who did not when married, make a mawkish wife, and a cold hearted mother . . .'

Cobbett looks at all aspects of the qualities needed for love and for subsequent marriage. He warns that the woman who adorns herself with 'hardware' (he means ornaments and jewels not sauce-pans and tools) 'will not spare the purse when once she gets her hand into it'. He has something to say too about the lack of cleanliness, '. . . dirty sluttish women; for there are some who seem to like filth well enough'. Apparently, men in love can be careless about dress and habits but they do not relish this in the beloved. She must have charm; '. . . charm and filth do not go together'.

The Book of Ruth is described as the perfect idyll, the perfect pastoral setting for a poem of love. It seems harmful to this deli-cate and transparent perfection to go on to say that as well as being simply a love story it is also a story of the need for survival and the manipulation necessary for survival. The story is about sudden widowhood, a widespread famine, the subsequent close friendship between a mother-in-law and her daughter-in-law, a harvest, a cer-emonial transfer of land, and the achievement of a contrived sexual union resulting in a pregnancy and the birth of a baby boy. The story also supports the historical lineal descent of David.

On first reading the story of Ruth, the theme of love and devo-tion is striking and overpowering. Ruth's reply to Naomi (her mother-in-law) on being told to leave and go back to her own people is unforgettable:

Entreat me not to leave thee, or
    to return from following after thee:

for whither thou goest, I will go;
   and where thou lodgest, I will lodge:
thy people shall be my people,
   and thy God my God:
where thou diest, will I die,
   and there will I be buried:
the Lord do so to me,
   and more also,
      if aught but death part thee and me.

On a later and perhaps more hard-boiled reading it can be seen that the love is tempered by the need for food and shelter and for a position in society. The object of Naomi's attention and her method of manipulation is Boaz, a wealthy landowner who seems to be an unobtrusive lover, perhaps shy? Ruth, as a devoted and loving daughter-in-law, does all that Naomi tells her to do. Boaz directs his harvesters that they should not molest Ruth, they should let her dip her bread in their water and they must be sure to leave some gleanings in the fields for her to take home. This is the kind of thrift which, according to Cobbett, should accompany real and lasting love. 'Quick at meals, quick at work.'

On Naomi's competent advice, Ruth, on the night of the harvest festival, approaches the threshing shed where Boaz is sleeping off his merry-making, and there she creeps under the skirts of his coat and makes herself known to him. There is no mention of love, of falling in love, but love is apparent in all the speech, the actions and in the attitudes described. The final scene of love is shown by Naomi as she takes Ruth's newly born baby to her breast.

Love is sometimes where it is least expected. I remember hearing Miss Clayton, my aunt's lady companion, reading aloud one long light summer evening when I was upstairs in bed. I was still at school then and visiting for the weekend. Miss Clayton was reading aloud to my aunt:

> When she rises in the morning
> I linger to watch her;
> She spreads the bath cloth underneath her window
> And the sunbeams catch her
> Glistening white on the shoulders,
> While down her sides the mellow
> Golden shadow glows as
> She stoops to the sponge, and her swung breasts
> Sway like full-blown yellow
> Gloire de Dijon roses.

'It's you, Miss Daisy,' Miss Clayton screamed her interpretation. 'It's you, Miss Daisy, swilling yourself down in a basin.' She read the whole of Lawrence's poem as the moon rode up the summer night sky. She read in her own voice and accent, shrill, with the singsong tones of the canals, her voice rising at the end of every line. Her voice came up the stairs and up into the roof.

'It's you, dear,' she screamed, sending her pleasure and excitement up through the house. 'It's you, Miss Daisy, *you having a camper's bath*.' Her voice vibrated, 'It's a lovely po-emm, Miss Daisy, it's a luv po-emm, it's ever so nice. Oh Miss Daisy, it's ever so nice, int it? *It's like a painting!*'

I listened to their love, the adoration of the rose.

Miss Clayton lived with my aunt for years. She was small and thin and sharp-tongued. She was energetic, and quick at mental arithmetic and spelling. She was very knowledgeable about things geographical, historical, political, medical and personal even though she had not had much schooling. She was a true daughter of the industrial Midlands, a daughter of the canal boats.

The relationship between my aunt and Miss Clayton moved on satisfactorily by the frequent repetitions of emotional release that followed a dreadful row. These two had rows all the time, either when they were alone or when other people were present. They simply ignored an audience. The rows were violent and at screaming pitch, in an agitation of rocking chairs, and they came unheralded and ended quickly in low-voiced soothing moans and endearments uttered from these same rocking chairs, which gradually subsided on either side of the hearth. Sometimes when they declared their love for each other they cried.

My father explained how he was brought up to love and to care for his sister. She (Aunt Daisy of the above passage) was younger than he was. His love for her was one of being his sister's keeper; it was a form of devotion that persisted for many years. He set us an example by visiting her every week in order to help her in the house or the garden, but more especially to listen, with patience, to her long list of worries and tirades of complaints. I was brought up to be my sister's keeper and to believe that all people were essentially loving and kind – for that was my early experience of people. I was also taught by my father, and later at school, that the people who seemed hard to love were the ones who needed love the most. Throughout my life I have made all kinds of mistakes about people but these mistakes were mostly because I inevitably took on more responsibility than I could manage and then had to 'let someone down'. Perhaps the ending to my novel *The Newspaper of Claremont Street* is a metaphor for this. It was only some time after I had written this book that I began to have more understanding of this perplexing situation.

On thinking over my own attitudes towards love, I can see in my writing that I have been attempting to explore relationships and the effects of love and responsibility, and the contribution of these towards survival – not simply survival from poverty and hunger, but emotional survival and the ways in which hardship in life and in relationships is endured in order to preserve what must be the most precious thing we can have and which can be so easily lost. To love someone and to be loved means complete trust, each in the other. If trust fades or is completely lost, life ceases to have any real meaning.

As in the story of Ruth, love and devotion can contain small doses of manipulation. But there is a thin line between a little devotion and its accompanying teaspoonful of manipulation, and the strangling effects of too much of these.

In my novel *The Well* I examine a love that becomes distorted by fear. The fear of losing the beloved. Hester Harper, an elderly wealthy landowner who adopts an orphan girl, Katherine, isolates herself with the girl in the unspoken and unacknowledged hope that she will be able to keep Kathy in a state of permanent teenage, thus allowing herself a continuation of the kind of companionship and experience she never had herself when she was young. Even when Katherine has outgrown puffed sleeves, hand-embroidered dresses, little socks and Peter Pan collars, and her head is full of romantic thoughts. Hester feels insulted when a neighbouring farmer's wife is outspoken about this, suggesting that Kathy should either have a career or, better still, wedding bells. All the same, she sees enough to cause her to dread Joanna's letters and Joanna's impending arrival.

Joanna is Kathy's friend from her orphanage days and is due to be free from her years in a remand home. Hester fears that Kathy will run away with Joanna or, worse, marry the first uneducated oaf who rides up from the nearest run-down farm. Apart from caring for Kathy and keeping her, Hester's poor-quality vision of love reaches only as far as what she thinks of, with extreme distaste, as cowshed activities. The loving relationship between Hester and Kathy becomes distorted to the extent that it cannot survive any kind of intrusion. In the event of an intruder, even though he is disposed of, Kathy becomes hysterical and retreats into fantasy, and Hester has to go straight to bed with a killing migraine. (Now read on – this is not the end of the story . . .)

In spite of what is gloomily described as 'the state of the economy' and 'the state of the world today', I am optimistic. I have always hoped and still do hope that human love, mother love and grand-motherly love (using these words, in a sense, to label love), fatherly love and grandfatherly love, will prevail and be uppermost in all our dealings, and so bring an end to some of the most awful suffering.

My optimism extends into my writing. My characters may have bad or even ridiculous experiences but, in their own ways, they weather these. At the end of *The Well*, for example, all the charac-ters are pointing in the direction in which their lives can and will continue – with hopefulness and with acceptance.

William Cobbett died in 1835. Perhaps Cobbett, realising the dangers and the fears that threaten love, was trying to show ways in which a loving relationship could start off with all the qualities, as he saw them, needed to make it last.

Edward Lear, writing in 1871, carries on Cobbett's idea of the continuing survival of love in the famous love story of 'The Owl and the Pussycat'.

These two, overcome with passion, elope in

a beautiful pea green boat.

They spend their time, to start with, in singing. The owl sings to the cat:

O lovely Pussy! O Pussy my love,
What a beautiful Pussy you are.

But good sense is alongside passion and praise:

They took some honey and plenty of money,
Wrapped up in a five pound note.

The lovers must think seriously of their responsibilities. They find a pig who is

willing to sell for one shilling
the ring at the end of his nose.

So, the love story includes a marriage. Cobbett would approve the moral prudence of these two lovers.

Cobbett did marry the girl who was scrubbing the washing tub out of doors, early in the morning, in the snow. Mrs Cobbett, mother of several sons, has some tried and true recipes in Cobbett's book *Cottage Economy*. Either she had no standards to put forward for the perfect husband or lover, no tests of his eating habits or ways of walking, or she was not given the chance to offer opinions on the man who chose her and was her lover.

Friends and Friendship

The only way to have a friend is to be one . . .

Ralph Waldo Emerson

'A friend is a person with whom I may be sincere. Before him I may think aloud . . .' Ralph Waldo Emerson, the American philosopher and poet, wrote in 1841 in his essay 'Friendship'. 'The only way to have a friend is to be one'.

Here I am now, towards the end of my life, discovering this wisdom when I could have made great use of it so much earlier. At times we are all friendless or we think and believe that we are without friends. If we think and believe something like that, then that's how it is.

Before coming to Australia I heard about the wonderful mateship that existed here. All men were mates. My first experience of mateship was between two taxi drivers in Sydney and it was through gritted teeth. And later, on another occasion, in a very busy intersection, two taxi drivers who did not speak much English (I thought they might be from Greece or Egypt) shouted at each other. Their voices, rising, seemed to be reaching a dangerous pitch. I crouched, hoping that the two men would, before coming to blows, be separated quickly as the traffic, unblocking, moved on.

'He my mate he my brozzer,' my cab driver explained as we resumed the journey. 'He like know how my family – and I like know how his.' He shrugged his shoulders and settled to wait in the next intersection.

People have more freedom, outwardly, in relationships at the present time. There are many different kinds of relationships, there is no need to list them here. If a friendship or a marriage comes to an end the people concerned are not looked down upon or treated as outcasts. Outwardly a 'breakup' is more simple; inwardly it is just as painful as it always was, with the same complications of guilt, resentment, shock, heartache and those bleak times of sorrow and disappointment – and, of course, concern for the wellbeing of those innocently involved.

Since the earliest times human beings have hurt themselves and each other by not knowing how to be a friend, a partner, a lover or a beloved. Being rejected is one of the most difficult realisations to accept. The pain of hurting someone and of being hurt has persisted through the ages. It is material for the novelist, the poet and the dramatist, from the ancient Greeks (for example, Euripides' *Medea* and *Electra*) to the present time.

'The only way to have a friend is to be one.' How important it is to know this! In the 1990s, more than ever, friends are necessary. Computers, mobile phones, televisions, dishwashers and automatic teller machines are very useful, but they are *not people being friends*. Each one is like an acquaintance, nice to have and very useful. An acquaintance should not be confused with a friend. Friendship, like love, has to be sincere. It requires complete trust between the people concerned and it requires the ability to give and to accept without reservation. Friends have the power to find, together, a philosophy that can make human life endurable. And, as Bertrand Russell writes in his autobiography, 'In human relations one should penetrate to the core of loneliness in each person and speak to that . . .'.

There is an excitement in the discovery that a particular person is in fact a friend.

To feel friendless is very unpleasant but to be the person who is making someone feel excluded and friendless is even more unpleasant. This fact has often to be discovered through an experience seen in retrospect. The regret following closely on the event is often inexplicable at the time but, looking back, our sense of shame is increased.

> The journey to school is always, it seems, at dusk . . . This first journey is in the autumn when the afternoons are dark before four o'clock. The melancholy railway crawls through waterlogged meadows where mourning willow trees follow the winding streams. Cattle, knee deep in damp grass, raise their heads as if in an understanding of sorrow as the slow train passes. The roads at the level crossings are deserted. No one waits to wave and curtains of drab colours are pulled across the dimly lit cottage windows . . .

This passage from my novel *My Father's Moon* is a metaphor showing the loneliness of the character, Vera, during her first uneasy journey to boarding school. It is a prelude to a scene of cruel mental and physical teasing in which Vera does not attempt to comfort the victim. She even denies knowing the victim, saying she is not her friend. She follows this by stealing the hot bath and the hot milk intended for the badly bruised and bleeding victim. Subsequently Vera suffers by being haunted by her own behaviour and by the recurring image of the victim's crouched and shaking shoulders, which are denied any caring and kindly arms.

In writing, with hindsight, from half-remembered childhood experience, it is possible to come to an understanding which was previously unthought of, unrealised.

When I am working – that is, writing – I do not feel lonely or friendless. The characters are not my friends, not at all, but the explorations I make into their lives, their thoughts, wishes and feelings keep me close, always, to human needs, to the fears, the hopes, the wishes and the actions. Close to something that resembles friendship in its intimacy.

We live in times of change. In Australia, as in other countries, we are in a time that, later, might be described as a renaissance; a time that might later be compared with the Renaissance now described as the golden age of creativity and change, a revival of art and letters influenced by the classical models of the fourteenth and fifteenth centuries. There were then many writers whose work has been preserved and is in an available form for the present-day reader. Among the many names are: Cervantes, *Don Quixote and the Gold Age* (1605); Montaigne, *The Old World and the New* (1588); Albrecht Dürer, *A Painter's Travels* (1520); and Francis Bacon, *Henry VII: A New Monarch* (1622) to name a few.

Sometimes, unexpectedly, it is possible to meet a friend where no such person exists at the present time, except within the pages of a book. As in a novel containing examples of real life made readable in imaginative and fluent prose, a friend may well be found in the personal writings of essays and autobiography. Among the many friends to be found from the golden age of literature and art there is Girolamo Cardano (1501–1576) an Italian mathematician, physician, astrologer and encyclopaedia writer. He wrote a personal essay on *Himself*. This description immediately draws the reader, with affection and sympathy, close to him. He writes about his medium height, going down at once to his feet, which are 'short and wide near the toes and rather high at the heels'. He can never find well-fitting shoes and has to have them made. His head is too small and slopes away at the back and no painter is able to make a good portrait of him. He describes his warts and a hard ball in his neck – not too conspicuous, an inheritance from his mother. He describes the foods he likes; honey, cane sugar, dried grapes, melons (after he learned of their medicinal properties). He finds olive oil delicious and garlic does him good. The lists are endless. The reader has the excitement of coming to know him. His illnesses are listed. He is afraid of high places and of mad dogs. Sometimes he is tormented by a tragic passion and plans then to suicide. It is his custom to remain in bed for ten hours – the essay includes his recipe for insomnia and his worrying over his sons. He suffers from congenital palpitations, haemorrhoids and gout. The most endearing quality, which makes him seem to be the kind of man who, having suffered, will have much sympathy for a friend, is that 'I have discovered, by experience, that I cannot be long without bodily pain, for if once that circumstance arises, a certain mental anguish overcomes me, so grievous that nothing could be more distressing.'

The best part of having a friend within the pages of a book is that when his harsh, shrill voice and his fixed gaze, his indigestion and his cough, become too much for the reader, the book can either be closed, or opened to a different experience, a different friend – Albrecht Dürer, for example. Dürer kept a travel diary in which he recorded enormous meals, fine linen, china and silver, gracious houses and beautiful paintings – Van Eyck's 'Adoration of the Mystic Lamb', to name one. He describes himself standing on a bridge 'where men are beheaded'; there are two statues (1371) on the bridge as a reminder that there a son beheaded his father . . .

To read these unselfconscious autobiographical details gives insight into the wisdom of acceptance of the self. Without examination, the wisdom of acceptance and tolerance, it is hardly possible to follow Emerson's advice: 'The only way to have a friend is to be one.'

Manchester Repair

Who knits here? Who knits here in the top of the wardrobe along with all the birthday cards, the pumpkin-seed beads, the black beads, the moonstones and the opera glasses? Who knits here? Whose knitting needles are these and whose is the pigskin box and whoever would wear a black necklace? Then there's all these patchwork pieces, squares, triangles, diamonds and circles. Who can sew a circle and keep it flat? And this unfinished knitting, the tiny soft garment, without seams, intended for the newly born child. A long time ago. There are sixty-seven stored birthday cards up here, a tin with fifty-cent bits and paper one-dollar notes, a soap shaped like a hamburger . . .

What sort of novels do you write? they ask. *Are they nice? Have you been writing long?* they want to know. *All the problems*, they say, *have been written about already. There are no new problems, are there? How do you as a writer deal with this?* . . .

Well, I suppose you could say that Birthday and Christmas wrapping can always be smoothed out and folded – I mean, it's an economy to keep it, isn't it? Of course it's often on very reasonable specials in the supermarket. I've been given this book, it's called *The Secret of How to Win Freedom from Clutter* by a man called Don Aslett. My son gave me this book just before I went into hospital to

have the Manchester Repair. This is a wonderful name for an operation and it would make a good title for something. The trouble with
titles is that you need something to put under them. When my son,
because of what he calls clutter in the house, gave me this book, I
told him that he must understand that I grew up in the Depression
and was brought up to keep all paper and string and the bits of broken parts that had been removed from mended things and clothes
that were ugly and did not fit in case I needed them in old age and
poverty. He opened the book at page twenty-three and there was
the excuse: 'I was raised during the Depression and we were taught
to save everything.' This man, Don Aslett, though I have never met
him, seems to know exactly what I am like and what my house is
like. The symptoms of junkosis fit. I seem to be on every page.

'This shelf is for hats,' my son, opening the wardrobe, said. 'Start
with this shelf.' So that's what I did. That was the last thing I did
before leaving for the hospital . . .

I did keep the knitting needles and, of course, the birthday cards
do have great meaning, and I've kept my Bronze Life-Saving Medal
(1936). Two people are on the medal, one is saving the life of the
other, a very moving scene in deep water. I doubt if medals of such
good quality are made now. A grandson might like to inherit it. I've
kept the opera glasses for the same reason.

 . . . I am washing the knees of my grandsons, not their feet, just
their little round knees. They, the children, are sitting in a row on
the garden bench. I am using the bucket and the sponge that is usually kept for the floors. I feel I should not be using these but go on
polishing their knees all the same. It is getting dark in the garden
and the damp is rising cold from the newly cut grass. White roses
like stars lean out from the glossy dark-green leaves, dark-green in
the dusk . . .

Spit here, dear. Someone is drying my face. Am I crying? I suppose this is the coming round part though I can't remember a going out or under or whatever it is called. I don't see the children. I am not finishing off their washings.

Just turn over dear, that's it. So this is what it feels like to be coming out from an anaesthetic. A GA and an epidural, they say it was.

Where are my legs?

They're here, dear. Yes dear, your legs are a bit numb. No, you're not paralysed. No, you won't be in a wheelchair for the rest of your life.

Your geese, the neighbour is telling me, *I'm sorry to have to be the one to tell you, your geese – they've disappeared or died.* He's found one, he's telling me, up against the fence and another one's in the pen. *She's dead,* he's explaining as I go down the slope between the blossoming trees in the orchard. *As for the rest,* he's saying, *there's no sign of them. I'm sorry,* he says again, *to have to be the one to tell you. Is there anything,* he asks in the darkening emptiness and quietness of the valley, *is there anything you'd like done with the hay?* He's turning off the water, he's saying, there's no point in having the water running to waste if there isn't a goose on the place. He wouldn't be a bit surprised he says if that old Foxylady wasn't around like last year and the year before. You never saw such yellow eyes.

Listen, I tell him, this is the lady, the pastel coloured lady who does the bins. She's doing the bins she comes round first (every morning I suppose). She picks everything out like the little deckle-edged cards. She picks them up and turns them over scrutinising, yes scrutinising, the messages which have accompanied the flowers. One by one she reads them and puts them back. You've a regular flower shop in here she says, a lot of work for someone. 'I've been,' she says, 'round these wards nearly twenty years.' She's tearing stamps off envelopes now for charity. When she reads the cards and the envelopes she moves her lips reading as if she is praying and saying the words under her breath. Someone's put a needle in the bin she says needles shouldn't be put in the bins. She'd just like to know who put a needle in the bin. Who, just who, she says. A needle in the bin, she's bawling down the passage.

I said to him, I said, the pastel lady who finds the needle is telling me, I said to him, my husband, that is, I told him straight out it was me paid off the house and now you're selling the boat and the trailer I'll have five thousand thank you very much. He sits home doing nothing. I bought some taps she's telling me. He's to put a sink in the laundry but what d'you bet he'll have chocked it up on a coupla bricks with a hose coming in up under the eaves. What do you think I bought the taps for I'll tell him when I get in. What have I bought the taps for, I'll yell at him, I don't want no bossted up hose dangling through a hole in the roof. Who d'you think you are anyhow.

Just taking your blood pressure dear. What is your normal blood pressure? You don't know? Well I suppose we can't know everything about ourselves. I'll be back to check shortly. Just turn over dear, that's it.

MUTTON FOR THE WORLD

To the Editor *The West Australian*
    Dear Sir,
    I am writing in support of that very good letter of a few weeks ago;

Mutton, as most cooks know, can be treated in sides or quarters cheaply, quickly and effectively. The finished product is cooked

corned mutton which will keep for a long time. It could be
shipped anywhere . . . Is Australia – a land of over supply (not
over-production!) and enormous resource and goodwill not pre-
pared on an apolitical basis to at least examine the possibilities
seriously . . .

To the Editor *The West Australian*
  Dear Sir,
  It would be wonderful if, instead of Battleships, we could have
Great Ships carrying meat and grain from countries with a surplus
to the countries where there is famine. I do think and would like
Readers to consider that a Blockade for whatever reason is the great-
est evil men can do against other men. It is always the poor and the
hungry and the homeless who have to suffer. The great food ships
would bring about the World Peace which we all long for for our
children and grandchildren . . .

  About the questions they ask;
  It seems that the writer can offer
  a meditation on human wishes and
  experience or he can follow the
  climactic curve of conflict and drama
  or he can combine both.

I feel embarrassed really I do waiting here at the edge of the under-
ground car park. Waiting for the toilet. The Ladies Toilet, what silly
words, is being cleaned by a *man*. I mean there are two men and
this big metal trolley in the doorway and the mop too and us ladies
waiting.
  Sorry to keep youse waiting, the one man says as if he *knows*.
  Really this must be an electricity cut. No matches and no candles

only the silence and the darkness. Continued silence and darkness. I can wait even if it is cold and getting colder as if some disaster is about to come. If only there could be a little gleam of light under the door as it used to be before the servants went to bed.

I think I am beginning to understand why my mother, towards the end of her life, no longer listened to music. I am finding, as I listen, that tears seem to force themselves from under my closed lids.

I am cold.

There's no need to cry dear. Here's a hot blanket and remember when you go home you're not to lift anything heavier than the kettle so it is, you'll understand, a good idea to clear out the whole house.

Where is the wardrobe? Where is the wardrobe where I left off? The whole thing is full of plastic bags I'll start on them and work through bit by bit and clear away all the confusion.

As the Maharaja said: 'On days when one feels gratitude it is as well to show it.'

DEAD TREES IN YOUR ABSENCE

You are not here
And this is what bereavement must be like.
Till I met you there were no seasons
And now again there are none.
Swooping
Magpies attacking the morning
With their voices tumbling
Above the twisted brittle vine
Ghosts with black burned buds.
Dry twigs scorched black leaves
Curled in death.
Useless
Piped water pouring on dry earth
Pitted with sharp warm fragrance
Of dust and dusty trees.
In the quiet heat of summer all life is withdrawn.

Footfalls Echo
in the Memory

Time present and time past
Are both perhaps present in time future,
And time future contained in time past.

T. S. Eliot, 'Burnt Norton' (Part I)

If forgetfulness gave us simply the pleasant things to remember memories would be a consolation and an advantage.

There is something to be said, however, for unpleasant memories as they can be a reminder to avoid certain people or places or situations found previously to have been difficult, unprofitable and unrewarding.

Over the years the same memories remain vivid and follow the same reminders. Images once created and stored do not change.

There is a green hill far away
Without a city wall . . .

The same hill comes to mind every time this hymn is sung or heard. For the child, while singing the hymn, the hill seems to be unfortunate in not having a wall round it. For the adult, the hill should be in the landscape suitably outside the city wall; but it is interesting to note that, when questioned, most adults still have in mind the lonely hill without a wall round it, instead of an image that suggests the real state of hill and wall.

In spite of an increasing forgetfulness, as if the part of the brain responsible for memory is too crowded with thoughts and information and especially daily things that must be remembered, it is amazing how much can be stored in one small head. And especially when it is realised that the adult brain is well packed, layer upon layer, with images and perceptions and attempted explanations from early childhood onwards.

And even more amazing is the way in which one small event or half-remembered scene or word can lead to a dozen others. No wonder then that elderly people forget that they have told an anecdote several times. An old lady, in a restaurant recently, complained about a telephone ringing persistently and it was then discovered she had her own phone in her handbag but had forgotten this – even while it was ringing.

Someone wise said that it is not wise to make an arrangement with the mind that the body cannot keep. That is good advice. And it could be said too that the mind should remind the mind of the arrangement. If the mind can no longer be trusted – then a note in a conspicuous place, perhaps the kitchen table.

Memories of places and people are a tremendous gift, a wealth that should not be taken for granted. Another gift arrives in the form *of memories belonging to someone else and given or lent by that other person.* My father gave me many of his memories. I have no idea how these memories, the given ones, can come rushing into my mind just when they are needed to create more depths in an imagined character. Often the rich inheritance is not expected and a certain excitement accompanies the receiving. I have never asked for or expected the particular memories to surface. I am always deeply grateful for the enrichment.

Near my kitchen door there is an enormous tree (it drops leaves and twigs into the gutters and into the swimming pool next door); its branches creak and strain even in the slightest wind. To hear this creaking is to recall vividly the idea of the timbers of a great ship crossing one immense ocean after another. Whenever I am within hearing of these creaking branches I think of the incredible progress a ship makes, her rail moving gently up and persistently down, above the horizon and below the horizon.

During the first journey we made to Australia, I remember standing on the deck one evening and being overwhelmed with admiration at the sight of the massive construction and the complication of ropes and pulleys, which were only a part of the whole plan, being in themselves necessary for the transporting of the ship across the oceans.

Because of this tree, in the garden near my door, I remember the rolling of the ship and the pulse of hidden well-cared-for engines. The ship had seemed, in spite of the rolling, steady in the ring of water. She had not risen to answer the waves, and the monsoon had not broken. Most of the passengers were, I remember, huddled out of the wind. I have used the image (because of the reminder from the tree) in some of my fiction; the story 'The Fellow Passenger' is one place and possibly there is a suggestion of it in *The Georges' Wife*.

The stairs on the ship were brass-bound, well polished, and the echoing footfalls of the passengers, hurrying down to the dining rooms, reminded me of my school and the stampede down the stairs (lead-covered to protect the worn treads) to breakfast in the mornings.

The voyage, brought back to me daily by the tree, remains as a physical and emotional experience that cannot be erased.

At some point in the long journey the migrant (the voluntary exile) is hit by the irrevocable nature of the decision that was made a whole year previously. Even if the migrant, on reaching his destination, starts back immediately, he or she will never be the same again.

In my own journey, years ago, there was suddenly the realisation that the world is enormous. During a day when the ship was waiting, as if becalmed, in the Great Bitter Lake, before entering the Suez Canal, the quiet expanse of colourless water, with its apparent lack of concern for human life, caused a sense of desolation more acute and painful than anything experienced during the first term at boarding school. The strangest thing of all was the vision of my father walking alongside the ship waving farewell as he used to walk and wave alongside the train every time I left to go back to school after the holidays. And, ridiculous as it was, I wanted to rush back to him, to hear his voice once more. But which of us can walk on water, I mean long-distance?

The creaking tree brings memories whether I want them or not. Mostly they are very useful and often, surprisingly, they emerge just at the right time to become part of a background for one of my characters. An example is the memory of the bluebell woods of my childhood, I gave the woods to Professor Edwin Page in the novel *The Sugar Mother*. In the story, Edwin Page thinks of the long sea voyage and he remembers the bluebell woods he went to as a child. At the right time of the year whole families, he remembers, would make for the woods. They would, as if by special agreement, leave the cramped dirty streets of the industrial town and spend whole days bent down in the misty blue fragrance industriously gathering . . . These flowers, Edwin remembers, have to be *pulled* and not snapped off or picked as many flowers are. He remembers the happy shoutings of children ringing through the quiet woods. He remembers, as well, the bundles of flowers, their blue heads darkening with dying, their long, slippery, unbroken stalks gleaming white, the bunches being tied on the backs of many different sorts of bicycles as the pickers pedalled homewards after a day of unaccustomed fresh air and the delight of being, for some hours, in the middle of a mass of flowers.

Remembering the bluebells, Edwin recalls the little paths, the hollows and the groups of distinguished-looking trees that remained the same from one year to the next. The woods, in a sense, were recaptured during every visit. Edwin realises later that the flowers were being greedily taken back to places where it was impossible to grow flowers. The houses, in front, opened straight on to the streets. Behind these houses were other houses opening on to narrow yards and alleys paved with blue bricks. Flowers could not grow there.

Because, at the right moment, the memory came back to me, I was able to give Professor Edwin Page my Railway Goods Yard, the whole of it. It was a wooden engine I had, not very big, with wagons which could be loaded with bits of coal, 'timber', sand – and some animals from the toy farm; but no wheat. I had no knowledge then of great paddocks full of wheat. (And, of course, Edwin Page does not think of wheat.)

Using my own remembered game, Edwin Page as a boy makes a railway yard in the sandy soil at the end of a garden. He banks up the earth into slopes and tunnels. He makes platforms and sheds and a passenger station decorated with flowers. He has lights and signals and pens for animals. He makes fences and plants bits of broken-off bushes. When it rains realistic puddles lie in the hollows and he sets about correcting the drainage problems . . .

In Euripides' play *Medea* the chorus discuss the advantages and disadvantages of having children:

> . . . childless people
> Have no means of knowing whether children are
> A blessing or a burden; but being without them
> They live exempt from many troubles
> While those who have growing up in their homes
> The sweet gift of children I see always
> Burdened and worn with incessant worry . . .

These different attitudes towards the bearing and rearing of children are presented in the play immediately before Medea, whose destiny it is to kill her own children, murders them. The audience is captured in cathartic emotional involvement. Their thoughts are compelled towards childhood and the needs of children.

Edwin Page is also thinking about children. He is anticipating his own baby being carried by Leila, a surrogate mother, as a surprise for his childless wife, Cecilia, who is away for a year on academic study leave. He becomes obsessed with thoughts about babies and young children. He likens his well-ordered present situation (Leila's mother being a good cook and housekeeper) to the well-ordered Goods Yard of his childhood game.

He thinks that it is possible that every place or person or thing, once created during childhood, persists for ever. It is possible, he thinks, that every person, walking in the street or catching a bus or sitting down to a meal, has been sketched or traced and coloured in with crayons or paints by some diligent child at some time.

Perhaps this was why some individuals had no necks or were completely bald or devoid of teeth or, if they had teeth, seemed to have a mouthful of pickets. Some people had long legs and others had legs that did not match. And some, mainly women, had legs that came out of the edges of their skirts and could not, by any stretch of the imagination, fit at the tops of their thighs to their bodies. The legs, if you took a line upwards, would pass by each side of the body unrelated and useless. It was an idea held by the Ancient Greeks, he thought; they believed that an animal or a person, an idea or a vision, a vision in particular, *if written about could be brought into existence*.

St Augustine in his *Confessions* (Book X) writes about the ways in which he can distinguish the scent of lilies from the scent of violets even when he has not recently breathed in their scent, but simply from the memory of these scents. Similarly he writes that he likes honey better than wine, judging them from memory. Smooth things he prefers rather than rough – all from memory. He writes:

> All this goes on inside me, in the vast cloisters of my memory. In it are the sky, the earth and the sea, ready at my summons, together with everything that I have ever perceived ... In it I meet myself.

In our memories we meet ourselves.

Happiness and Restoration
of the Spirit

I have often wondered whether it is possible to know whether animals are happy or not. A well-fed cat lying on the sun-warmed boards of a verandah looks happy. Sheep, when there is not enough pasture for their number, show signs of stress, i.e. unhappiness. There is a danger of confusing relief and contentment with happiness. The anticipation of happiness has been described as being the real happiness. Can cats joyfully anticipate, in the morning, their evening saucer of milk, and can sheep similarly enjoy, in anticipation, the happiness of being moved from a bald paddock to one with good feed? Perhaps this power of anticipation makes humans different from animals?

In Samuel Johnson's novel *Rasselas* the Prince Rasselas lived with his sister and companions in the Happy Valley where flocks and herds were feeding in the pastures and *all beasts of the chase frisking on the lawns: the spritely kid was bounding on the rocks, the subtle monkey frolicking in the trees and the solemn elephant reposing in the shade.* An idyllic scene of happiness for some.

Others have different visions of happiness. Herman Melville describes people of all ages, all social classes and all kinds of livelihoods making their way to the ocean in any spare time they have. Their object being simply to get as near to the sea as possible even if only for a glimpse of it from some vantage point on land. *Nothing will content them but the extremest limit of the land.* In suggesting that complete happiness and restoration of the spirit comes about from 'going to sea', Melville says that to go as a passenger on a ship is a mistake: *For to go as a passenger you must needs have a purse . . . Besides, passengers get sea sick – grow quarrelsome – don't sleep of nights* – the perfect recipe for unhappiness. He suggests that to be a simple sailor is complete happiness, having to work and leap about it is true, but being fed *and* paid and, in the forecastle deck, having all the benefits of the pure sea air before the commodore on the quarterdeck has breathed it.

Some of Jane Austen's characters seek happiness in the anticipation of finding a good and noble husband. It is suggested that happiness comes about in the absence of jealousy and fear. Family life later on can often seem to be an external power that hampers freedom and happiness – the subject of a great deal of contemporary fiction.

To go back to *Rasselas*; the Prince, questioning the happiness in the Happy Valley, sets out with his sister, the Princess, and their companions to study the realities of human life in the outside world. At one point when comparing notes during their travels, the Princess reports to her brother after visiting the houses of ordinary people: *where there was the fairest show of prosperity and peace* (could be any well-to-do suburb in Australia!), she found *not one house that is not haunted by some fury that destroys its quiet.*

Happiness being then, as now, something slender and intangible in the household. The present-day fiction writer finds happiness hard to confront directly. For humans, in fiction as in life, must need to seek it somewhere beyond existing conflict. Perhaps happiness, as well as being in anticipation, comes about in achievement and in overcoming whatever lies between us and our hoped-for ultimate success both in our work and in the finding of another person who trusts us completely and who, in turn, we can trust with complete faith. To lose trust is to lose peace of mind and happiness.

Perhaps it is a mistake to think that happiness depends upon one single ingredient. Modern advertising can make the individual believe that the possession of a certain car, certain clothes, a certain skin cream, having a certain holiday, can bring about perfect happiness. There are, as well, people who actually seem pleased that they are unhappy. These people talk and sigh and complain and burden other people with their unhappiness. Often it seems that people who suffer in this way do not want to be helped towards being happy. They resent being told by someone else that they are unhappy and that their negative attitude is a strain, draining energy from other people. Bertrand Russell in his autobiography writes: *Most human beings are possessed by a profound unhappiness venting itself in destructive rages and that only through the diffusion of instinctive joy can a good world be brought into being . . . the slow achievement of men emerging from the brute seems the ultimate thing to live for . . .* He goes on to say that he does not live for human happiness but for some kind of struggling emergence of the mind.

An emergence of clear thinking and the pursuit of real enjoyment and happiness (for most people *would* prefer to be happy rather than powerful) might be a way of preventing the terrible wars which are either threatened or in progress all over the world at the present time. The profound unhappiness and destructiveness mentioned by Russell is being twisted into acts of aggression making 'heroic' headlines thus concealing an underlying dishonesty and corruption. To me the ability to be happy seems to lie in being able to take certain moments as they come, in spite of being deeply affected and disturbed by the illnesses, the hardships and the incredible suffering experienced by a great many (too many) people. One such moment for me was when, during a time of worrying thoughts, a goose, pausing in her industrious grazing, came over to where I was and, sitting on my feet, laid an enormous egg. A goose egg will make scrambled egg for three or four people; but it was not that thought which gave me happiness. It was rather the offering itself. The apparent nonchalance with which I seemed to be chosen to be the one to receive the gift, the mysteriousness of egg-laying and the inexplicable kind behaviour of a goose.

I think an effort is needed to keep up any lasting level of optimism and happiness. Ibsen, particularly in his play *The Wild Duck*, explores the necessity for the individual to have the 'life-lie' by which to live. In a not too blatant manner some kind of reason for existence has to be provided by the self for the self, or in more 'hopeless cases' by an individual seeing the need in another. *Take the life-lie away from the average man and straight away you take away his happiness.*

In the play, Gregers Werle, a hunting dog of a man, removes what he feels to be a falsehood in the lives of his childhood friend, Hjalmar Ekdal, and his wife and daughter, with disastrous results. There is not space here for more on this subject. Certainly some people are better at maintaining, without being objectionable and with confidence, their own life-lie. Perhaps a sense of humour and a sense of the ridiculous help towards a balance between being sad and being happy.

When I was about seven there was a little girl I knew whose father had a car. One day she showed me two cellophane toffee papers that she had saved. One red and one green. She told me she was going to sit by her father in the car, in the front seat, and she was going to look first through the red one and then through the green one. For a long time I had great pleasure imagining what it must be like to sit smoothly gliding along watching a red world and then a green world slipping by. It was a tentative sidelong acquaintance with happiness that I have never forgotten. It seems incredible sixty years later to be able to recapture what seemed then to be the ultimate in something nice to do, the ultimate in happiness.

E. M. Forster wrote in his *Commonplace Book* in 1932: *I have been happy for two years. It mayn't be over yet, but I want to write it down before it gets spoiled by pain – which is the chief thing pain can do in the inside life; spoil the lovely things that had got in there first. Happiness can come in one's natural growth ... I have been happy and would like to remind others that their turn can come too. It is the only message worth giving.*

Finally to add to 'the only message worth giving', I would like to say that when I watch the tiny goslings struggling, making their haphazard way, lost in the tall grass, down to the dam, and when I see the small courageous bodies of my grandsons splashing in their shared bath, I am reminded over and over again of the miraculous and the mysterious force, something quite beyond our full comprehension, which gives a continuation of life in all forms. Perhaps there is no sweeter music than the small snorings from a bedroom full of sleeping grandchildren. I am afraid I have 'gone overboard' rather, but the small yet immense reminders of my own powerlessness and my own gratitude do make me happy.

GREAT BRANCHES FALL

And what of the dead
We shall see and more probably we shall not see
A life open to death
Annihilation
Even so the annihilated built the cottage and made
The path from the township slowly
Cleared the land and for some reason was it weakness
or reverence? left here the old trees which from
Other slopes have gone beyond imagination.
Some sat in this place feeling the winter sun fade
And staring up through pointed leaves trembling
Saw the sky
The trees the birds the quiet wild things
Indifferent yet caring perhaps serving
The wind moves the trees great branches fall
In the wind or in the stillness
A few feet nearer and I should have been crushed
Into the greater stillness.
If we love what does not yet love us
Can we not give it love
The dead, whether annihilated or surviving, the trees
The high up eagles as they look into the sun
Together can we not wait serenely for whatever
Awaits us.

ACKNOWLEDGEMENTS

The essays, extracts and poems in this book were originally published, sometimes in slightly altered form, in the places below. I would like to thank the publishers and authors who have given permission for reproduction. In a few cases my efforts to trace the provenance of an essay were unsuccessful, for which I apologise in advance. The publisher would be pleased to hear from anyone in this regard.

'A Scattered Catalogue of Consolation' in *Contemporary Authors – Autobiography Series*, edited by Joyce Nakamura, Gail Research Inc., Detroit and London, 1990

'Sisters' as 'My Sister Dancing' in the anthology *Sisters*, edited by Drusilla Modjeska, HarperCollins, Sydney, 1993

'A Summer to Remember' as 'Outlines and Shadings' in *The Age*, 6 January 1995

'The Silent Night of Snowfall' in *The Age*, 24 December 1994

'One Christmas Knitting' in *Woman in a Lampshade*, Penguin, Melbourne, 1983

'Paper Children' in *Woman in a Lampshade*, Penguin, Melbourne, 1983

'Bathroom Dance' in *My Father's Moon*, Penguin, Melbourne, 1989

'Black Country Farm' broadcast by the BBC in 1991–92. A slightly different version appeared in *The Georges' Wife*, Penguin, Melbourne, 1993

'Motherhood' in *New Woman*, October 1992

'Fairfields' as 'Frederick the Great Returns to Fairfields' in the *New Yorker*, 22 July 1985. It is almost identical to the opening of *My Father's Moon*

'A Small Fragment of the Earth' as 'Life's Colors Shimmer in Western Heat' in *The Age*, 2 May 1987

'Pear Tree Dance' in *Woman in a Lampshade*, Penguin, Melbourne, 1983

'Only Connect' in *Central Mischief*, Penguin, Melbourne, 1992

'Wheat Belt Smash' is an extract from *Foxybaby*, University of Queensland Press, Brisbane, 1985

'The Goose Path: A Meditation' in *Encounter*, London, March 1989; in *Gone Bush*, edited by Roger McDonald, Transworld, Sydney, 1990; and in *Central Mischief*, Penguin, 1992

'The Will to Write' in *The Australian*, 1993

'The Little Dance in Writing' in *Cite*, Issue 1, *Curtin University of Technology*, Perth, Summer 2002

'Quick at Meals, Quick at Work' in *The Age*, 13 July 1993

'Friends and Friendship' in *The Australian*, January 1997

'Manchester Repair' in the *Independent Monthly*, 1990

'Happiness and Restoration of the Spirit' as 'Happiness: The Lesson of the Goose' in *The Bulletin*, 25 December 1990

All the poems appeared in *Diary of a Weekend Farmer*, Fremantle Arts Centre Press, Fremantle, 1993

The quote on page 83 is from Sonnet 60 by William Shakespeare

The quote on page 130 is from 'The Wind Among the Reeds' by W. B. Yeats

The quotes on pages 135 and 138 are from 'The Scholar Gypsy' by Matthew Arnold

The poem 'Rebecca in a Mirror' on pages 150–1 is used by kind permission of the author, Judith Rodriguez

The quote on pages 264–5 is from *'Tis* by Frank McCourt and is reprinted by permission of HarperCollins Publishers Ltd © Frank McCourt

The quote on page 274 is from 'Gloire de Dijon' by D. H. Lawrence